# On-Call for Murder

*Adria Burrows*

PublishAmerica
Baltimore

Hardcover 978-1-4512-6811-9
Softcover 978-1-4512-6810-2
PUBLISHED BY PUBLISHAMERICA, LLLP
www.publishamerica.com
Baltimore

Printed in the United States of America

*This book is dedicated to my father,*
*Stanley Burrows, M.D.,*
*Who is no longer on this earth,*
*But who will forever live in my heart.*

# On-Call for Murder

# Chapter 1

When I was called to see Valentino Suma as a medical student, I remember remarking to myself what an unusual but romantic name he had. He was a patient in the hospital, scheduled to have open heart surgery the next day and I was the medical student on-call that night.

Dr. Lerner, the cardiac surgeon who called me, almost sounded apologetic on the phone.

"I'm sorry to bother you with this, Nicky, but he's having a problem with one of his eyes. It's red and burning… may be an infection, maybe nothing, but I need you to check it out. Thanks."

What made this call so unusual was that Dr. Lerner was not the pussycat that he sounded like over the phone. He was always barking orders to me and was the typical heart surgeon: he had an ego as long as a city block and hated women. I could see it in his eyes when I spoke to him about patients… it was a look that read more like, "women should be in my bed, not in my hospital." And it was almost his hospital because he was the busiest surgeon. All of his patients were upper class and were used to paying for the best they could get in anything, whether it was medical care or their diamonds.

I was one of the lucky medical students, because I didn't take Dr. Lerner seriously. I refused to allow him to make me upset and I also refused to be afraid of him. I also knew that I was not going to pick surgery as my career, so I didn't need his recommendation. Maybe that is why he was always talking more gruffly to me. He wanted to see some fear in my eyes, like the other medical students. He wanted to feel his power over me as I shifted from one foot to another as he spoke to me. Don't get me wrong: I respected R. Lerner, M.D. tremendously. He was still the best heart surgeon in the hospital and had one of the nicest homes in town. I just wasn't going to be afraid of him. He was human like the rest of us. I knew that and deep inside I think he knew it as well.

I decided that Mr. Suma must be a particularly rich or important man if R. Lerner was being so nice to me on the phone. "Treat him well, Nicky," he concluded. "This guy is a big wig."

It was late at night by the time I was able to make it to Mr. Suma's room. I had had a lot of emergencies and it wasn't until about eleven p.m. that I was walking down the hall to Mr. Suma. Most of the lights were out in the rooms I passed and the nurse's station showed like a beacon in the dimly-lit hallway.

"Where've you been?" one of the nurses asked me as I approached. "Mr. Suma has been asking for you and needs something for his eye. What time did Dr. Lerner call you?" Now I knew he was definitely a beg shot if the nurses were anxious. Nothing affects the nurses unless it's really important.

I still refused to let Dr. Lerner or Mr. Suma intimidate me. I was having a rough night as it was, with all of the admissions from the emergency room to take care of.

So, I reached for the chart, under the watchful eye of the nurse, grazed through it quickly for any history of allergies and the like, and then walked slowly to the room. I could feel the nurse's gaze latched onto my back and could hear her thinking, "why doesn't that doctor hurry up?"

I was surprised to see that room 201 had two bodyguards standing in front of the door. They were dressed respectfully in black suits, but there was no mistaking their height and muscular strength. They were both about six foot five with massive shoulders and hands that could probably tear down walls.

I felt protected in my white coat, my stethoscope wrapped around my neck, my pockets bulging with tongue blades, Q-tips and prescription pads. That is one thing about being a doctor: everyone knows you are out to help them, especially if you are a petite medical student with a smile. I was not a threat to these guys and besides, I was coming to help their boss. So, even though they looked pretty scary in that dark hallway as they looked me up and down, I knew we were on the same side. I felt comforted with that as I walked past them without a word and into the room.

Mr. Suma had the room that the doctors and medical students called the hotel suite. It had carpeting, a hand-painted mural on the walls, a fifty inch television set with DVD player and a cordless phone. Mr. Suma had added a desk, where a male secretary sat with an extra phone, and a lady who was taking shorthand in the corner. Wait till my colleagues heard about this. I didn't even know the hospital allowed this, especially at eleven p.m. It was odd to be so active and high-strung the night before your own heart surgery.

But there was Mr. Suma, a towering man, dressed in satin pajamas and a silk bathrobe. He paced back and forth by the window, talking loudly into the cordless phone in Italian. His hair was slicked back, his eyes were blazing with anger and he waved his arm in front of him as he spoke. This was an important man indeed, and even his mannerisms denoted grandeur.

However, he also looked like the typical heart patient with a large belly, fat fingers and a temper that was evident at that moment. He was human too, no matter how many secretaries or bodyguards he had. I was not afraid of him, though I'm sure he flourished on other people's fright.

When he saw me, he stopped talking immediately and smiled. His face was transformed and the anger in his eyes melted instantaneously. "Hang on," he said into the phone.

Then to me, he said, "are you the doctor here to look at my eye?" I nodded. "Ronnie, I'll call you back." And he hung up before the other person could even answer.

Mr. Suma sat down on his bed and bowed his head to me. He could certainly be charming as well as domineering."It's this right eye, Doc. Though I guess you're a medical student. Do they call you 'doctor' anyway? Well I'm going to. After all, you almost are graduated, right? One more year I hear." Dr. Lerner had apparently told Mr. Suma quite a bit about me. "I hear you're going to be an ophthalmologist. So I said, 'get her right over here to look at this eye.' It's red and burning. Son of a Gun, it had to start up on me tonight. So here I am, in your hands."

He didn't look like a man who was used to putting himself in other people's hands. He looked like he needed to be in control and enjoyed barking at people, like Dr. Lerner. Another ego-based personality too, I thought. Yet, this man was obviously successful and who was I to judge him? He knew what he was doing, judging by his air and success, and I admired him for that.

After examining his eye and telling him I would prescribe some eyedrops for an allergy, he shook my hand tightly. "You've been very kind and I never forget a kindness." He reached into his pocket and pulled out a one hundred dollar bill. "Take this as a token." No, I couldn't do that... I was just doing my job. "I wish more people who worked for me knew what was their job and what wasn't. You're a good kid and I think you'll go far. Now go take care of people who really need you. Thanks, Doc." I liked him and wished him luck with his surgery tomorrow.

"You're in good hands," I told him as I left.

I could quickly see why Mr. Suma was so successful. Yes, he was tough, but he also had a heart and could turn his charm off and on. I suppose that was the secret to being a good businessman... shrewdness, toughness and charm.

One thing about being a medical student is that you find out about death in the coldest way possible: by seeing an empty bed. There is something very impersonal about a bed whose sheets are stripped, exposing the vinyl of the mattress and metal legs. For some reason, hospital rooms that are vacant also have their closet doors deliberately left open, revealing crooked empty hangers and the inner barren walls.

Mr. Suma did not make it back to his room... in fact, he did not even reach the cardiac intensive care unit. Dr. Lerner told me the next afternoon when I bumped into him in the hallway. This was also the first time I felt Dr. Lerner was really sad about a patient. Heart patients almost always survived, so when I heard Dr. Lerner's sad description about Mr. Suma, I was taken back with surprise. I hadn't even thought twice about it after leaving Mr. Suma the night before... I had just assumed he would survive, the way I assumed all patients live to tell about their surgery.

Dr. Lerner guided me into a dictation room when I asked about Mr. Suma.

"It was a real tragedy, Dr. Steinway." It was odd that he was addressing me as "doctor," too, because he always insisted on calling me "Nicky." He called all the other medical students "doctor," and I think he used my first name to degrade me a little... all in trying to make me fear him. 'The surgery was a success, but we couldn't get Mr. Suma's heart going again. I had to leave him on the table with the heart-lung machine churning away. Do you know what it's like to stare at a patient, his chest wide open after hours of surgery and realize he's not going to make it? Such a successful businessman... he was all over the place and had offices in three countries. He has a wife and son I know well and here I had to make a decision as to what to do. The man was lying in front of me, his eyes taped closed, the heart-lung machine resounding behind me and finally I had to give up. His heart just wouldn't start up again. It wasn't meant to be. I had to pull the plug, Doctor." He looked like he was going to cry... strong, obnoxious Dr. Lerner was finally affected by something to his croe. No jokes about nurses today, no comments about a pretty pair of legs; no making fun of a student's handwriting. Dr. Lerner was affected by something and perhaps realized that he is not super-human after all.

I bowed my head and looked at the floor. "He was an impressive man," I answered. "I was going to visit him today." Dr. Lerner patted me on the back and gave me a half-smile. This show of affection was also uncharacteristic of him. We parted silently.

As I walked on, I thought of the new project I had taken up and thought that this was something Mr. Suma would have been interested in. The eye bank had called me the week before and had told me that there was a shortage of corneal donations. This was a perfect opportunity to squeeze some good out of the situation. I went to the medical records department, found Mr. Suma's chart, the death certificate on top, and found his home phone number. I might even make an impression on Dr. Lerner if this worked.

I found a lounge and dialed the number. The hardest part would be getting past the condolences. I hoped Mrs. Suma wasn't too torn apart.

"Is this Mrs. Suma?" I asked when a woman answered.

"Yes."

"My name is Dr. Steinway. I'm a medical student at the hospital and I met your husband briefly. I'm very sorry and I want to tell you he impressed me very much."

"Thank you."

"I have a delicate question to ask you. It could bring something wonderful to another person... maybe new sight..."

"You want him to donate his eyes?" She had made it easy for me. "That's actually a good idea. He would have wanted that." I sighed, made the necessary arrangements and decided that I had to get to the morgue quickly. He had died a short while ago, but there wasn't much time: eyes were only good for six hours after death.

I was quite depressed by this time. I had been hoping to get to know Mr. Suma a little better, find out what business he was in and talk to him some more, even about mundane topics. It was always sad when a patient didn't make it and there was something about Mr. Suma that intrigued me. Was it his success? He impressed me as being a man who could handle anything, from deciding where to have his pants pressed to knowing who to hire and fire. He seemed to have people jumping at his command... even Dr. Lerner. And Dr. Lerner was someone who needed people jumping for him.

One thing I was relieved about was that Mrs. Suma had been calm on the phone and hadn't become angry about my suggestion of the donation. Whenever I called about a donation, the two fears I had were that a relative would start to cry on the phone or would berate me for my crude suggestion. Not that I couldn't handle either one of these things: it just makes for an uncomfortable situation. So far, neither thing had occurred, so I guess I was lucky.

I ran to get my instruments from my locker and made my way to the morgue. So far everyone who had donated their eyes were people I had not met when they were alive, so it did not bother me to go to the morgue and see their bodies. I knew that seeing Mr. Suma would affect me, however. In our short meeting, I had come to feel something for him, whether it was admiration of him or just sadness at his death, I was not sure.

The morgue was the most depressing place in the hospital. Only the garbage area in the back of the hospital where all the homeless people congregated was second to the morgue in depressing me. Sometimes I would meet up with the funeral parlor workers in the morgue and you could spot them 3in an instant. First of all, the morgue was usually deserted, so anyone stood out. Second, there was something so stereotypical about the funeral parlor workers… they looked like people out of a morbid cartoon. They always wore black shoes that were polished till they shone. They were also dressed in black. If they wore suits, they were black. If it was a rainy day, their raincoats were black. They seemed to revel in their role and their job. If I worked for a funeral parlor, I would wear black at the parlor, but who sees you when you pick up a body from the hospital? Only the medical student – future ophthalmologist – coming for the eyes.

I must admit that I was the only medical student I knew who bothered about eye donations. There was a certain satisfaction I felt, however, each time I heard that a corneal transplant had restored vision and it was because I had obtained the donation. The other medical students thought I was a little odd for taking care of these things on a regular basis. Some of them thought I just wanted the $80.00 I received for each donation. I quelched those ideas, however, when I spent all the money I had received in donations every few months by taking all of the medical students on my rotation out to dinner.

The morgue was in the basement of the hospital, tucked at the end of a long corridor. It was very out of the way, as though it was hidden, and the walls of the hallway leading to it needed a painting badly. That just added to the morbidness of it. If one looked closely at some of the walls, one could make out five layers of past paint jobs in the chipped areas. The first paint job could have been done fifty years ago. Someone always seemed to make sure that the hallway leading to the morgue was dimly-lit. There were burned-out light bulbs hanging by wires from the ceiling every time I went down there. Never was there a day when all the bulbs were on. Maybe the mortician liked that effect.

When I reached the morgue, it was deserted as usual, but I knew where to go. The "new arrivals" were always in one spot and there was only one today, for some reason, so I knew it was Mr. Suma. Sure enough, the tag on the body cover read "Suma."

I sighed and paused. This was not going to be pleasant. Well, I was going to get it over with. I uncovered the head with one quick movement and gasped. It was not Mr. Suma.

I knew there had to be a mistake. I re-checked the tag on the body cover and the tag hanging from around the big toe, but they both read "Suma." Could there be another Suma in the hospital that had died? Perhaps, but Mr. Suma's body should have been here. It was too soon to the time of death for the funeral parlor to have taken him away.

I gazed at the refrigerator doors but knew that he couldn't be in there. Those were only for autopsies and Mr. Suma wasn't having one. Well, it was time to find the mortician and clear this up.

Ralph was an odd fellow, but did his job well and seemed to enjoy it. He helped the pathologist with autopsies, kept track of the bodies and was always cheerful. This is something you wouldn't really expect from someone who spent Monday through Friday in the bowels of the hospital, breathing in the dampness of the basement and dealing with the funeral workers everyday. But Ralph was one of the most contented people I had ever met. He came from a very poor backround and this job represented a way out of his poverty. He also felt it was a prestigious job because he dealt with doctors and professionals. Ralph took life in stride and if a problem came up, he knew how to handle it. But a case of mistaken identity like this would probably be a new situation for him. Or maybe not.

"Ralph?" I called. He was usually within earshot. No response. "Ralph! It's Dr. Steinway." Still no answer. That probably meant that he was in his office with the door shut. The walls and doors in the basement were so thick – they were built well over fifty years ago – you could barely hear a small explosion down the hall, if it occurred, if your door was closed.

I walked to his office and knocked on the door.

"Yes,come in," Ralph's voice sounded muffled. There he was, sitting at his desk. His office was always meticulously clean. He even emptied his own garbage cans twice a day because he didn't like them to be even half full. I often joked with him that if he got tired of his job, I would hire him to keep my apartment clean. Even the papers on his desk were stacked in neat piles and he knew where every card and note was located.

"Hey, Doc, how's it going? Another pair of eyes, eh?" He gave me a large smile and shook my hand.

"There's been a big mistake, Ralph." His smile disappeared and he looked concerned. He was always so conscientious that any problem became something he took to heart. "Mr. Suma's body." I paused, hoping he would say something like, "oh yeah, there was a mistake with the tags and I'm taking care of it. The real body is in refrigerator number one." But he didn't say a word: he just kept looking at me, waiting for me to say more. "Mr. Suma donated his eyes, but that body is not Mr. Suma's."

"What are you talking about?" Ralph said incredulously. "That's the body they sent down. They don't make mistakes."

"I saw Mr. Suma when he was alive, Ralph. That's not him under that cover."

"You know that sometimes those faces, they look different in death than they were when they were alive. I know you're a doctor and all, but those faces can change a lot. We're very careful with the patients, Doc. You know that."

"Ralph, that's a completely different person under that cover. You know what would make me feel better? If his chest showed that he had had heart surgery. Let's go look."

I know Ralph was just amusing me when he followed me back to the morgue. He had such faith in the system, he felt that nothing could go wrong. Any place that could keep track of all the paychecks, he once told me, and who earns how much money, could do no wrong. The hospital in his eyes was incapable of making any mistakes ever and that was that.

But good old Ralph followed me silently. We came to the body again, it's head still exposed and it was definitely not Mr. Suma. I pulled the cover down more to expose the chest, and there were staples placed over a chest incision. So, this patient had had open heart surgery, but he was not who the tag said he was.

"Ralph, you have to believe me. This is not Mr. Suma."

"There are the chest staples, Doc." Ralph was still unbelieving. The hospital was still infallible in his eyes.

"Could you at least double check on this one?" I asked. "I won't take these eyes… that's how sure I am that this is not Mr. Suma."

"Well, who else could it be? This is the only body I got today. He's the only one who died today according to the hospital's computer, so it has to be him. Even when there are ten deaths in a day – and that hasn't happened in a long time – all the bodies are right."

"Ralph, could you please check on it for me? I know –"

"All right, Doc. I'll do it for you. You'll see I'm right. I'll check it out and let you know for sure. But I got to tell you… this kind of thing never happens." I nodded and shook his hand. He was such a good person. He would do anything for the doctors… even question the practices of the hospital. And the hospital in his eyes almost had religious significance.

"Page me when you know for sure, Ralph."

"Sure thing, Doc."

I decided that I had time to go to the hospital cafeteria and get a late lunch. Maybe I would run into Dr. Lerner, but I wouldn't mention anything to him just yet. I was confident that Ralph would straighten things out and then I wouldn't have to say anything to anyone.

The cafeteria was empty because it was a time between lunch and dinner. The interns on-call at night all tried to meet at 6;30 p.m. for dinner to share stories about patients and to make predictions to each other about what the night would be like. If a full moon was scheduled to appear, if one of the interns had found a nickel or if the emergency room had had a lot of admissions earlier that day, it was going to be a busy night. Believe it or not, these superstitions usually were correct. The medical students tagged along with the interns wherever they went, so we knew all of the predictions.

I sat down with a sandwich and thought of Ralph. In his family's eyes he was like a doctor or the president of the hospital. He told me he barely had enough food when he was growing up and sometimes his older sister would feed him potatoe chips for dinner. Growing up was an eternal battle to stay in school and stay off drugs. His father beat him regularly and complained that he was a bum, staying in school and not bringing home any money.

"It wouldn't have mattered anyway," Ralph had told me. "My Dad would have drunk any money I brought home. I knew I didn't have no future without at least a high school education, so I stuck it out and worked part-time. But that was no good in the end too.'"

'When I was sixteen I got a job in a warehouse moving stuf. My boss was so good to me. He used to put fifty dollar bills in my pocket – extra, you know? – at the end of the week and sometimes even in the middle. I thought it was because I was such a hard worker. He seemed like a nice enough guy, having a big business and all. He had worked his way up from a poor home like me, but now he was rich and had a lot of workers. I thought maybe I was the son he never had 'cause he had three girls and said how he was always wanting a boy. That shows you all I didn't know.'

'One day it was a few weeks before I was gonna' graduate high school and I was real excited because this is what I had stood a lot of beatings for. I had been at this job for a year now. My Mom had rented this black gown for me, and that was a lot of money for us, and she was gonna' have a little party for me. Just my close friends and relatives.'

'Well, Mrs. Fredericks – that was his name – told me he had a special graduation gift for me and would I come pick it up after work in his home. I really thought he liked me special, so I said sure, and got his address. It was in the nice part of town and a really nice house that he had. He even had someone who answered the door for him special. This guy I thought looked at me funny-like when I came.'

'So the guy pointed upstairs and told me the first door on the left was where Mr. Fredericks was. O.K. I went up and it turned out to be his bedroom. Mr. Fredericks was sitting on a chair wearing his bathrobe and slippers. It was only six o'clock in the evening, but I thought maybe he wasn't feeling well. He was really happy to see me, though, and told me to come in and close the door. As soon as I was in, he stood up and opened his robe. He dropped it and this guy was absolutely naked in front of me. Then I knew what all those fifties were for and why he liked me so much. I just ran out of there, but he ran after me, calling my name, trying to grab me. He kept saying, you know you want it, Ralph. Give me some of that long, mean cock, boy." I never ran so fast, but he finally got me on the bottom of the stairs. I had to knock him down with my fist before I got out.'

'He owed me a week's pay, but I never went back for it. That's when he called my father and tried to make trouble for me. So, I ran away from home and got this job. I was real honest to Dr. Bernard, the pathologist here, when I came for my interview. I knew I didn't have nothing but my high school diploma, but I told him I was honest and I would be the hardest worker he ever had. I guess he trusted me or felt sorry for me, cause I've been here for twenty years now and he being ready to retire. I'll never forget what him and the hospital done for me. You can't beat that."

I thought of the smile he gave me after his story and nodded my head. He had had a tough life until he came to the hospital to work. Now he had a wife, two children, a house and a paid vacation three weeks every year. One child was even in college. No wonder he had

20

such faith in the hospital. It was like the big hand that had solved many of his major problems and had made him an independent person.

My beeper went off. It was the morgue. I had just finished eating and had some extra time, so I decided to go down and enjoy my winning. I knew I was right.

The hallway leading to the morgue was as dim as ever. As I approached, I began talking to Ralph, assuming he was within earshot. I felt good about my catching this error. After all, if I hadn't come for the eye donation, I never would have caught this. Were there any other bodies in the past that had been switched by accident? I shuddered at the thought.

"Ralph, I'm here; it's Dr. Steinway. What did you find? Refrigerator number one or two? Whose body was that anyway?" I heard my voice echo against the decaying wall, but there was no response. He must be in his office again, I thought. I hoped there weren't any other people around to hear my silly comments. Ralph was someone I felt comfortable enough to joke around with, but perhaps others wouldn't understand.

I entered the morgue again and everything was untouched. The body labeled "Mr. Suma" was still there, but it was covered up completely. I walked up to it. "Ralph, did you find the body?" I was still joking around. "Are the eyes ripe for taking?" I uncovered the body, expecting to see Mr. Suma, but it was the same person. "Ralph?" I walked to his office and knocked on the door. No answer. "Ralph? Stop fooling around. Let's get down to business." Still no answer. I opened the door.

There was Ralph, his head lying on the desk, turned away from me. I had caught him napping before at his desk in this position, though it was unusual for him to do this when he knew I'd be calling or coming down. The office was also a mess, with papers all over the floor and the trash can tipped over. Ralph was always ashamed to be caught sleeping. "Ralph?" I came closer. Then I saw the pool of dark red blood under his head, soaking a pad at the edge of the desk. Ralph... I walked around the desk to look at his face, as if expecting him to still be alive and look up at me. He looked up at me, all right, but with a glazed, unseeing stare. It was a little more than an hour since I had last seen him alive and judging from his eyes, he had been dead for at least a half hour. Who had done this? Who had beeped me? I stood in shock, staring at the single bullet hole on the side of his head which was filled with the dark blood.

What were you supposed to do when you discovered a body? After the initial moment of shock, I gazed around the room. The piles of papers on Ralph's desk were still neatly stacked and the books in his bookcase were still standing at attention. I walked over to one of the big medical books and took it out of the bookcase. It was "the special book," as Ralph had once told me, because it was where he hid some money for an emergency. I opened it up and saw the hundred dollar bills, also seemingly untouched. Ralph had shown me the secret money, ironically because he said in case anything happens to him, his wife should get the money. It was my responsibility to see that she did.

So, barely thinking, I took the bills and put them into my pocket. After all, they would be evidence after the detectives took the place apart and who knows when his poor family would get the money. It was probably illogical and dangerous on my part to do this, but perhaps I wasn't thinking straight... and who would in such a situation? Ralph was always like a special friend to me and my knees shook as I stared at him again. Right now I was the only person in the world who knew of his death.

Who would want to do such a thing to such a wonderful person? Maybe he was in the drug trade on the side. No, that was unlikely. Ralph wasn't secretive enough for that business. It didn't appear to be a robbery either. Who would come into the morgue to rob the mortician specially?

My mind was whizzing and my eyes filled with tears. How could this happen? What would we do without Ralph? What should I do next? Call the police. 911. I picked up the receiver and dialed. "Yes, I want to report a murder." I said it quietly and calmly, the way I would tell a patient he had an inoperable, malignant brain tumor.

"Who am I speaking to?" The voice on the line asked.

"The body is in the morgue of the City Hospital. Basement." I hung up the phone and stared at Ralph's head. I didn't feel like going into details and I certainly didn't feel like being in the room anymore. A wave of nausea overcame me and I knew I would throw up if I stayed a moment longer. I ran out of the room and down the corridor. My head started to spin, but I kept running. My feet pounded into the pavement and the feelings of fear and sorrow melted into anger. What right did anyone have to take Ralph away? Did the gunman know how charming he was, how caring… how he always cheered me up after a hard day? He didn't deserve such an ending and I pictured his wife, who I had met at a barbecue. She was so lovely too… who would end up telling her the news?

Where was I going? I reached the elevator. Dr. Lerner. He would have to be told about the body and Ralph. Maybe he could deal with the police. Maybe he could make everything right again, though I doubted it. I was never a big fan of Dr. Lerner and he probably knew it, but right now he seemed like the only person to go to. He had to know. Maybe I should have gone to him in the very beginning, when I had first discovered the wrong body in Mr. Suma's place. He wasn't my idol, but Dr. Lerner probably should have taken care of this instead of Ralph.

Dr. Lerner was one of the few doctors to have his private office located in the hospital itself. It was not even what you would call an office: it was more a suite of offices. The hospital definitely treated him well, due to all his operating and thus his bringing in revenues to the institution. His office began with two massive wooden doors that greeted you. They slid open to the sides electronically, into the wall, as you approached, and Dr. Lerner's name in large brass letters faced you on the wall in the front hall. You would make a right to see his receptionist and waiting room. A fifty inch television set bellowed in the corner, playing and re-playing tapes of Dr. Lerner welcoming you to his practice. He would repeat over and over again what good hands you were in and that if you let him take care of you, you would never have to worry about chest pain again or at least for a long time. It was so corny, we medical students used to make fun of it. I think the surgical residents did too but they would never do so in front of us. They respected Dr. Lerner too much, for his excellent technique and the huge reputation he had built up. Each one of them also had a secret wish that Dr. Lerner would choose one of them to join him and eventually take over the practice. I could tell them in one second that Dr. Lerner would only take in someone to be his partner if he was breathing his last breath. He loved the surgery, the prestige and his reputation too much to give it up even partially. I always noted how he sucked up the applause he received at medical meetings where he was lecturing.

It was true, even though he was too much of an egoist for my taste, he was a learned, fabulous surgeon. As much as I hated to admit it, I would send a relative to him for care. After all, when judging a doctor, it was his skill, not his personality that really mattered.

I told the receptionist I was there to see Dr. Lerner and that it was an emergency.

"Well, he has a few patients scheduled," she answered sweetly. I looked at the people in the waiting room.

"Tell him this is a real emergency."

"Someone in the emergency room?" she asked with sugar again. But I was losing my patience.

"No, but there is a real crisis in the hospital concerning one of his patients and if he isn't made aware of it now, he's going to be real angry." That seemed to affect her and she buzzed him.

"I'm so sorry to disturb you, Doctor." Now I could see why this receptionist had lasted longer thatn the others. She treated him like the king he thought that he was. "Again, my apologies. But Dr. Steinway is here and she says it's urgent. O.K." She looked up, told me to sit down and that he'd be right with me.

I fell into a comfortable chair and stared at the five men in the waiting room, all looking at magazines, all a little overweight, some coughing their smoker's cough. Typical Lerner patients, as we called them.

I was feeling cynical about everything at the moment. If a good man's life could be blown away so quickly, what was there to live for anyway? These people could have their cardiac surgery tomorrow and die of something else the next week.

I thought of Ralph's wife, Millie, with her shining smile and affectionate eyes. No matter what she was talking about, whether food or a movie, her eyes had a warm glow to them. She was a large woman who loved to cook and watch peple eat her food. I could tell that she adored her husband from the brief time I spent with her at a barbecue where I had met her. She asked his opinion about everything. "Ralph, do you think they like the roast? Is there enough ketchup?" I heard her voice so clearly.

Ralph always had a snack in his desk and there were plenty of occasions when I was offered home-made cookies and cakes from a drawer. He loved to brag about her and how much he loved her: "And there's nothing like coming home to a house at the end of the day that smells of roast or chicken. Boy, that lady takes care of me." Ralph would chuckle just thinking about Millie. Who would she cook for now?

Dr. Lerner appeared in the waiting room and stared at me, obviously puzzled about why I was there. We medical students and interns never entered the private sanctum of his office unless there was a real emergency. Actually, in an emergency we would call his office, not come by in person, even if we were just a few doors away. I'm not sure why... there was a general feeling that anyone who was not a patient contemplating heart surgery would only be in the way in the office.

Dr. Lerner had an unlit pipe dangling from his lips, which I disliked, and he probably knew that too. Once he said to me on his own, "in case you are wondering why I keep this pipe while seeing patients, it's because I enjoy it. Physicians like me, Dr. Steinway, can and do get away with anything. My patients accept it or they accept another surgeon." That was a typical statement from Dr. Lerner, but he was right... he was well-respected in the operating room. He was a knowledgeable and fabulous surgeon, often playing with stress.

He was a tall, thin man, with a full head of salt-and-pepper hair and deep green eyes. He looked older than his fifty hears, with wrinkles growing from the corners of his eyes and a deep crease in his chin. He must have polished his teeth, because they seemed almost too white and I don't think they were capped.

Dr. Lerner took deep pride in his appearance, shaving twice a day and keeping a clean shirt in his receptionist's desk. I knew this only from hearsay, but the source was reliable, being his receptionist. She was lunching in the hospital cafeteria one day, talking loudly to a nurse about Dr. Lerner's habits in the office. I promptly stopped talking and listened to her every word. "Nothing is worse," the receptionist imitated him to the nurse, "than a surgeon with whiskers." And yet, I often thought, he didn't seem to think twice about that pipe he held in his mouth.

I followed him behind the reception area and into his office. It looked more like a den than part of a doctor's office. There was a large wooden desk in front of a wall of bookcases. A sofa with a coffee table lined another wall and another large television set faced the sofa from the other wall. Green curtains covered the large picture window. It was well done, considering that Dr. Lerner had been divorced a long time ago. I always pictured doctors' wives decorating their husbands' offices. It was almost a given under most circumstances.

Dr. Lerner sat down behind his desk and I sat across from him, starting to shake, not sure just where to start. He looked at me sternly, as if to say, "this had better be good, to take me away from my patients." Suddenly, everything overwhelmed me and I felt tears flood into my eyes. I felt deeply ashamed to be losing control in front of this man, probably the biggest male-chauvinist I had ever met, but I couldn't help it. His face softened immediately and he got up to get me a tissue.

"I'm sorry, Dr. Lerner. I have to tell you what's been happening."

"It couldn't be that bad, Dr. Steinway. What's wrong?" He sat on the chair next to me, put his pipe down and crossed his legs, obviously ready to listen.

"It's Mr. Suma and Ralph." Dr. Lerner stiffened. He only seemed to hear the first name, because he repeated, "Mr. Suma?"

I told Dr. Lerner the whole story, from going for the eys, to finding Ralph, to calling the police.

"You what?" He seemed very angry when I mentioned the police. "You called the police to the hospital? First of all, who gave you the right to call my private patient's family and ask for the eyes? And how could you call the police? There will be a scandal for sure in this hospital. And my name connected. Just who do you think you ae, Dr. Steinway? I thought you had a god head on you! A switched body? The most idiotic thing I've ever heard!" He stood up and his face was red with heat. I began to cry again, not being able to hold in the tears any longer. What a mess everything was at this moment. Had I really been an imbecile/ Could it have been Mr. Suma's body after all? But what about Ralph?

Dr. Lerner turned away from me and faced his window. We sat in silence for what felt like an eternity but what was probably more like thirty seconds. When he faced me, he was composed.

"All right, Dr. Steinway. This is what we're going to do. First of all, the hospital doesn't make mistakes and switch bodies. You should have come to me if you thought anything was wrong. I would have been able to prove to you that that was Mr. Suma's body. There was only one death in the hospital and it was his."

"Second, Dr. Steinway, Ralph was probably robbed or involved with people we don't want to meet. Who knows what was going on in that bastard's life?" I felt my stomach sink at the word "bastard." How could he call Ralph that word? Well, he obviously didn't know him well.

"Third, Dr. Steinway, is that your career and reputation are at stake this very minute. If the police think that you murdered Ralph-" I gasped. "Wait, let me finish. If they think that and you are even accused of it and just arrested, you'll be thrown out of medical school. You will have no hope of ever becoming a doctor."

"But why would they accuse me of—"

"Why? Why?" His anger was returning. "Because your fingerprints are probably all over his office. Because you were the last one to deal with him before his death, as far as we know. You don't want your pretty ass anywhere near this, Dr. Steinway, or you'll jeopardize everything you've worked for till now. You may have to go on trial for murder too!"

"But I didn't—"

"I know you didn't touch him. You think I don't know about you? You're a first class medical student with the brain of a top-notch physician and the heart of the soppiest woman. You're not capable of anything like this… even of thinking of something like this. You've been programmed to help people, not hurt them and you've been programmed like the best of them." He patted me on the back.

"All right, this is what we're going to do." He began to pace around the room as he spoke. "The only smart thing you did was not tell the police who you were when you called. I'm going to take care of this for you, Dr. Steinway. I want you to get back to work. Go find you intern. Don't say anything about this to anyone. Your fingerprints could have been down there in his office from other times you were there. I don't even think the police will bother you. They won't be able to make any connection between you and Ralph unless they take prints of everyone in the hospital. And even if they do… so what? You've been down there plenty of times harvesting eyes. No problem." I felt better and also was amazed at how well he could take charge of a situation. Just like in the operating room, if an artery burst or a blood pressure dropped suddenly, he could handle it and pull out of it. I was ashamed of every bad thought I had every had about him.

"Now, go Nicky. And promise me one more thing. From now on, no more donations from private patients unless you ask the attending first. Second, if you ever see a problem, come to me before anyone. Understood?" I nodded. I was afraid if I spoke, I would begin to cry again. "All right. This whole thing will just be between you and me. Don't worry about it. Now get out of here." I nodded again and said a meek, "Thank you" before I left.

When Jane, my intern, saw me, she did a double-take. I must have looked pretty awful, with my swollen, red eyes and slight sniffles. Perhaps there was still a tinge of fear on my face too. She asked me what happened and all I said was that I got in trouble with Dr. Lerner.

Jane smiled. "Oh, don't worry about him, Nicky. You don't have to be in his good graces unless you're going into cardiothoracic surgery. Change your mind about ophthalmology?" I nodded no and smiled back. "He probably yelled at you, right? Poor Nicky. Listen… it's a light day and we have the hospital party tonight. Why don't you go home early and I'll see you later at the party?" She was going to be a nephrologist, or kidney specialist, and she certainly had the brains for it. Jane was Chinese, with beautiful, long hair to her waist and an ability to keep track of patients in her mind. She could be caring for twenty patients in the hospital and she would be able to recite each one's most recent blood count. She also had a soft heart, which was certainly showing now. I thanked her and decided to take her up on her offer. I needed time to calm down and sort everything out. I had to think about Dr. Lerner's reaction more and whether I had done the right thing in handling the whole situation. Ordinarily, I would never take an afternoon off for any reason other than extreme illness because medical students had their reputations ruined too easily. The program was competitive and if any rumors could be spread about anyone, medical student, intern or resident, they were spread with pleasure by the other doctors. Oh, Nicky went home? She got screamed at by Dr. Lerner. What did she do? Must be something terrible if she had to go home. Well, I didn't care at this moment. I had to get out of the hospital and think. I would come up with a story later.

I walked out of the hospital and saw four police cars and a police truck outside by the curb. The truck must be for Ralph. They were probably downstairs now. I pictured men in uniform and the private detectives – wearing raincoats no doubt, as they did in the movies – combing the office and the morgue. The body was still there, waiting for the funeral parlor workers to come. Well, there was nothing more I could do. I had tried what I thought was right and it had failed. Medical students had no pull in the hospital and if it was my word against someone like Dr. Lerner's, your cry would certainly not be heard by anyone.

I sighed and turned a corner. I needed to walk. Yes, I would walk by the water…the river was only a few blocks away and it was a nice day. It felt so good to be out of the hospital with its stale air and dim rooms.

Dr. Lerner's reaction to everything had been very strange. I had expected him to praise me on my catching the mistake with the body – if it had really not been Mr. Suma – and my trying to save Ralph's reputation by not going to Dr. Lerner first. Maybe the body was Mr. Suma's. Maybe he had changed a lot since the operation and death. The body did have chest staples and there was only one heart operation a day at the hospital… that's all Dr. Lerner could handle.

What happened to Ralph I would never know. It wasn't a robbery. However, maybe Ralph had something that someone wanted. Like Dr. Lerner said… who knows what sorts of people he associated with?

But why was Dr. Lerner so upset that I had called the police? What else was there to do? I suppose he felt that he – or at least someone more senior than a meager medical student – should have made the call. Well, they didn't know who telephoned "911" right now and they never would. I guessed everything was actually all right now. Except for a questionable body, which I decided to stop thinking about for my own good, and a murder, everything was under control. What a mess.

I reached the river and sat down on a bench facing the water. I had to repeat over and over to myself that there was nothing more I could do and that I should just get on with my work and career. There was no way I could voice my concerns to the police because I might become a murder suspect. Between my fingerprints being all over Ralph's office and my claim at a switched body, I would seem like a lunatic besides a murderer. Thank goodness Dr. Lerner was handling it. I had to stay out of it now.

All right, I would go back to my role as an unassuming medical student following the intern around the hospital. I had to stay out of trouble and just complete this rotation quietly. And I would avoid Dr. Lerner. I felt so ashamed about crying in his office. He would probably hold that display of emotion against me. He hated tears and he always said so.

"Doctors." I heard his voice saying in one of his lectures to the medicals students and residents. "You will find yourselves in many situations as physicians. You will come across patients who will try to manipulate you and tell you how to treat them. Women have the ultimate weapon: their tears. Just remember: if a woman tells you she doesn't want to take medication, for example, and then bursts into tears, she is trying to soften you. Men can stamp their feet if they want you to do or not do something and women will cry. You must handle patients firmly and make it clear what is best for them, whether they like it or not." And here I had performed the ultimate transgression by not only crying, but doing it in his office. Well, like Jane said, thank goodness I wasn't planning on going into surgery. I would never need a reference from him. I just had to get through the rotation and stand seeing him in the halls or lecturing.

From now on, I would always turn to the attending any time something seemed odd, from a switched body to an abnormal blood test result. Let them worry about it all. And I wasn't going to get any more eyes. It was time for a rest from that. Even the thought of going back to the morgue made me nauseous.

Yes, I was going to be a speck on the wallpaper of the hospital. No more taking anything into my own hands. I would just follow at the heels of my intern quietly, do what I was told to do and be quiet about everything.

I pictured Ralph at his desk again, his head resting on his blotter, police surrounding him and probably taking pictures. Maybe they were calling the hospital administrator now, asking him who had dialed "911" and whether Ralph had any enemies.

A cool breeze rippled across the water and I watched a sailboat go by. Those people must be pretty well-to-do to be able to take a weekday off to go boating. Ah yes, there were people who had normal lives right now. Well, my life would get back to normal too… the best thing was not to think about any of this. No one could bring back Ralph. No one could explain Dr. Lerner's temperament.

I felt the bills in my pocket from Ralph's book. Tomorrow was Saturday. I would visit Millie then and offer my condolences. Maybe she knew who would do such a thing. Meanwhile, it was time to go home and change for the party. Maybe I could force myself into a nap and into actually enjoying the evening.

I turned around abruptly to find a man in a black coat staring at me intensely on the other side of the walkway. He was leaning against a tree and had a hat pulled down over his forehead. I looked away and began to walk home. I was almost afraid that he would follow me, so I didn't look back until I reached the street again. Then I turned around quickly, as if to catch him with my eyes, but there was no one behind me. The street was deserted.

# Chapter 2

The party was supposed to be a fundraiser for the hospital, though medical students and interns went free of charge. These were the best parties to go to because the food was the finest, there was some sort of band for dancing and it was the only time that the attending doctors on staff treated us underlings politely. Usually in the hospital, we were made to feel like the ignorant doctors we were. At least at the party we were introduced to husbands and wives as fellow physicians. We were made to feel more human than we felt at the hospital.

This party was in a glamorous hotel on Fifth Avenue. True, it was in the basement, but I didn't think that that mattered so much. If it was a classy hotel, it was classy in the basement too.

I stared at the dress hanging on the door of my closet. Tonight I was going to look my best and perhaps even meet someone. It had been a few months since my last boyfriend and I just hadn't met anyone since. It was partly because I was so involved with my career and partly because I wasn't impressed with any of the men I had met lately. They were either too stuffy or too egotistical. After all, most of the men I met were doctors in the hospital.

I had originally gone through the stage of looking up to all the residents and attendings in the hospital, thinking it was a status symbol to be asked out by one of them. I remember being so proud when a resident asked me out for dinner for the first time. The only thing was, he decided to take me on a tour of the hospital he was doing a rotation in at the time. The dinner consisted of a table in the cafeteria. I was still happy with my date, until I described the evening to my roommate, who made a face and remarked at what a cheapskate he was. She was the all-knowing, experienced roomey, who knew everything about me. Now she was on a rotation in Boston and would return at the end of the month.

I took the dress off the hanger and spread it across my bed. Today had been quite a day. Maybe I should skip the party and just soak in a hot bathtub tonight. Well, I needed something to get my mind off of what had happened. A party would be perfect. I pulled the dress over my head and stared at myself in the mirror. The dress was a deep red and with some jewelry and matching red lipstick, I would look more than presentable. I was known to be one of the more attractive medical students on the rotation and had quite a few of the interns pursuing me. I was sure I would be kept busy dancing tonight and would feel better after the evening was over. It was a sure bet that someone would walk me home too. I was always being escorted home, though I frequently didn't want an escort to the parties, in case I met someone. I was quite fickle.

It was such a nice night, I decided to walk to the hotel. It was only ten blocks or so and the memory of the man at the water had withered. I was probably imagining things earlier due to my bad day.

The lobby of the hotel was full of people coming and going and even all the chairs were taken. I found the staircase leading to the basement and liked the feel of the soft carpeting as I walked downstairs. The music was getting louder and louder as I approached the bottom of the stairs. Where was everybody? There were double doors, which I opened to find a room full of people, music and food. What a night this would be. Thanks goodness I had something to take my mind off of the events of the day.

I looked for some familiar faces and saw Jane in a corner of the room, sipping from a glass and talking to one of the attendings. Would I see Dr. Lerner tonight? Oh, who cared. I needed to stop thinking about him and Ralph.

Jane caught my gaze and motioned for me to come over to her. I felt the stares of some people on me, but then that was common at a party. I was always popular and could dance every dance if I wanted to.

"Hi, Nicky," Jane called out to me over the music. "Fashionably late as usual."

"Hey, I'm never late in the hospital."

"Yeah, that's true. Nicky, do you know Dr. O'Brien?" I knew of him. He was one of the most eligible doctors on staff. Hugh O'Brien was a new plastic surgery attending, just out of training, but already very busy doing face-lifts and tummy-tucks. No one knew how he got so busy so quickly, but we attributed it to advertising and being in the right place at the right time. He had opened his office in a very posh section of town.

Dr. O'Brien smiled at me, and we shook hands. I was probably the only medical student who wasn't after this man. Why? There was something about a large ego that turned me off completely. I had once seen him in the operating room, flirting with the nurses, bragging about his surgical results. Any time a physician boasted about himself, it made me feel sick. There were other ways to point out to people that you were a good surgeon. The best way to build up a reputation was by word of mouth. If you were a good surgeon, the nurses knew it and they would spread it around the hospital soon enough.

"You look great, Nicky." Dr. O'Brien commented with a smile. "Want to dance?" I shook my head no, returning his smile.

"Thanks, but Jane is a much better dancer than I am." I knew she wouldn't mind dancing with him, so with that I turned around, gave Jane a nod and a wink and walked away. I knew he was staring at me... I guess he wasn't used to anyone saying no to him.

I walked to the buffet table and got on line. The food was amazing, as it always was at the fund-raisers for the hospital. So, I filled a plate and sat alone at a table. I was in a bad mood and began to think that it hadn't been a good idea after all to come. I didn't feel like being with people.

I looked up from my plate and saw him staring at me from across the room. Oh no... it was Martin, my old boyfriend. Our eyes locked for a moment and I looked down. What was he doing here? I played with my food and pretended to be very absorbed with it, in order to avoid Martin's stare. I hadn't seen him in a year and had heard that he had actually gotten married. I always thought that I was the only one who could ever put up with Martin's eccentricity, but I guess there was another woman in the world who could too.

"Nicky." It was his voice behind me. "Mind if I sit down with you for a minute?" He was being extremely formal. In the "old days" he would have just sat down next to me and said, "here I am, the old goat meeting the young hare." He always called me his young hare because I had so much energy and a quick wit, as he referred to it.

I had met Martin in the hospital when I called him in to consult on a patient with a brain tumor. He was a neurologist and known to be the most brilliant doctor in the hospital. That's probably what had attracted me to him at first. After all, he wasn't particularly good-looking. He was five foot eight, which meant I couldn't wear high heels when we went out, because I always liked to be shorter than the guy I was with

– call it old-fashioned, but I felt more comfortable looking up to a man, literally. He had brown eyes, black hair and was thirty-six years old. Yes, he was a little old for my twenty-three years, but I always liked older men and also thought it was a status symbol to be seen with Martin. Sure enough, once we started to go out, we went out to eat with all sorts of academicians. I could look in one of my medical journals and count five authors I had had dinner with that month, thanks to my relationship with Martin.

But Martin was not easy to be with. He was, indeed, eccentric and had a bit of coldness to him. He had twenty pairs of the same navy blue pants and twenty- three white shirts, so he always looked the same, though his clothes were clean and fresh. And he always changed his ties, for some reason. He was abrasive to people - both physicians and patients – who he felt had "the intelligence of Snodgrass," as he put it, and he never hesitated to intimidate these people when he could. He cried out to their cars on the road, when we went out driving, calling them "idiots" and "donkeys with wheels." He often said that the average person in the world shouldn't even be allowed to drive.

With me, however, he was more sedate and respectful. Not only because I was one of the few people who would stand up to him, but also because I treated him like a human being, instead of a god. Martin could figure out difficult diagnoses over the phone that five consultants couldn't handle in person, so everyone in the hospital was in awe of him and his brain.

We met when I saw a difficult patient with my intern and no one knew what to do. We wanted to be present when Martin examined the patient, so he beeped my intern when he was ready to do the consult. We ran up to the patient's room immediately because we knew he wouldn't wait for us.

As soon as we entered, Martin looked me up and down and during the entire examination, he spoke very gently to us (which was very unlike him. Usually he was quite gruff to the average intern or medical student). Of course, he ended with a list of possible diagnoses, recommended some tests for the patient, and then motioned for us to walk into the hallway.

"I hope this was all helpful to you both." He said to us in the corridor. We nodded. This was the first time I had met Martin, though I had heard of his brilliance and intimidation, and was surprised he was being so nice to us. "Well, in the future, I think Dr. Steinway should be here each time I examine this patient. This is a very educational case." My intern nodded without making a sound, so I did too. "I will beep you when I need you, Doctor." I smiled and thanked him.

So, each time the famous Dr. Martin Orion examined this patient, he would page me, I would watch his examination, marvel at him as he wrote notes on the chart and then be dismissed.

The interns and residents had a bet going as to whether he would ask me out but I didn't anticipate it. Attendings often took a liking to me, whether it was my sense of humor or my pretty face, and I thought Martin was just trying to educate me. Thus, I was not expecting his page on my beeper one afternoon, especially since it was after we had examined that patient.

"Hello, Dr. Steinway," he said on the phone when I called the number on my beeper. "I'm going to Florida this weekend to check on my condo." I didn't answer because I still didn't know what he was getting at. "I also have tickets to the museum exhibit at the Met and you're welcome to join me when I get back. I'll be back this Sunday morning, so how about Sunday afternoon?" I was shocked, but couldn't wait to share the news with the residents and interns. This was going to put me up higher in the ranks.

"Sure," I said, suppressing my excitement. "That would be nice."

Thus started a tumultuous relationship which lasted a year. Being seen on Martin's arm was quite a status-promoting event and that's the main reason I started going with him. However, I did know that I cared for him and liked his company. I also learned more and more medicine on our dates. It was an up and down ride with him because Martin was very jealous of every phone call I received, whether it was from a man or a woman. He resented my independence. If I made plans to go to Philadelphia for a weekend to see my parents, he resented that I didn't ask him to go with me.

I never pictured Martin as my husband and felt we were going out knowing that this would not lead to a permanent situation, but would just make us good friends in the end. Well, that was not Martin's intention because one night at dinner he dropped a diamond ring in my glass of water and asked me to marry him.

He wouldn't even come out with a formal proposal. When I saw the ring in the water and retrieved what looked to be a three carat round stone, I stared at him in shock.

"Well, you know what that means, Nicky," was all he said. He smiled and anticipated my answer by adding, "congratulations. We're engaged."

"I don't think we are until I say 'yes," Martin. I didn't know you were thinking about this." I liked Martin tremendously, but I don't think I ever loved him. We had never made love… when he slept over, it was just to hold each other and nothing more. He claimed he wanted it that way so we didn't have to worry about diseases, but I interpreted it as meaning that "we're also not as serious as people might think." I didn't see other people, but mainly because I was too busy to do so. He didn't see other women because he didn't want to.

So, this all lead to a tragedy because Martin had fallen in love with me. But, after I said no to his marriage proposal, he looked at me with venom in his eyes from that day onwards. It was so bad, he publicly showed his feelings for me at a lecture he was giving. The room was full with approximately two hundred doctors in an auditorium of the hospital. I came in late as he was showing a slide of a patient. He saw me and stopped his lecture. The room was dark and silent. Everyone was anticipating his next comment, but he stared at the back of the room where I was standing by the door because no seats were to be found.

"Being late to a lecture is just unconscionable," he said to the audience. "Dr. Steinway, this lecture is not for medical students and you should leave now." I was surprised at his open display of hostility towards me. He would never do this to another doctor, but I just vanished as quickly as I could through the double doors and decided to avoid him in the future.

I missed him, but I knew that I didn't love him enough to marry him, so if we passed in the hallway, we both looked away from each other and I was thankful he didn't mutter a nasty comment under his breath.

Yet now here I was at this party, sitting next to him and he was not being hostile at all. In fact, he had come up to me to talk.

Martin looked good, in his usual navy pants and white shirt and a plate of food in his hands. He was well-rested, which was unusual for him, but he was staring at me in silence as he sat down and put his plate on the table. He turned to me, making it clear that he was not going to eat.

"That's a pretty necklace," he started with. Something was on his mind and I knew he wasn't feeling comfortable. Well, after all, we hadn't spoken in a year. I thanked him and gazed at his ring finger. Sure enough, there was a wedding band.

"It's been a long time, Martin." He nodded and continued to study me. "How have you been?" I asked. It was good to see him and I was glad he was being friendly.

"I got married." I nodded. "Soon after I broke up with you, I decided to tie the knot with an old girlfriend… the woman I went out with before you." Why was he telling me this? He must know that I knew. News in the hospital spread like wildfire, and he was aware of that. "Why didn't you get married?"

I shrugged. "Because I never met the right guy and because I'm not ready to anyway." The music was loud and we were screaming at each other. "Where's your wife?"

"Home sick with the flu." Now he was looking at me sadly, but he perked up and suggested we walk outside where it wasn't so noisy. I got up and was happy at this turn of events. Ever since we broke up I had always wanted Martin as a friend and I hoped he had changed his mind about this.

The night air felt good against my face and I took a deep breath as we began to walk down Fifth Avenue. The store windows were lit and we stopped occasionally to look into one; Martin kept staring at me and I suspected that he was still in love with me. He was always so easy to read. Maybe walking out together wasn't a good idea after all. Maybe I was being too naïve about everything, as I usually was. What trouble was I getting into? Was I encouraging anything I shouldn't be? I decided to get right to the point.

"Martin, why did you ask me out here?"

"I felt like having your company. I never met anyone like you, Nicky, and I never will." This was a generous statement from him because in the year we went out he gave me a total of maybe two compliments. He took my arm and wrapped it around his as we walked.

It was a beautiful night and the street was almost deserted at this hour. It would ordinarily be very romantic.

"Why can't we be friends, Martin? I miss you. I miss talking about patients. I miss joking around with you. Maybe we could go out with your wife." His face hardened and he stopped walking to face me.

"I married Abby because I was rebounding off of you. I was really in love with you, Nicky, and I knew I would never meet anyone like you again. Abby was a second best, so to speak. I still think about you a lot. I still take Abby to the same places we used to go to and I stare at the tables we sat at and try to picture you there. I wanted to be your husband: that's the greatest compliment I could give you." I sighed and looked down at the pavement. With Martin it would be all or nothing, I supposed… either husband and wife or nothing.

"So, what are you getting at, Martin?" I tried to start walking again so I wouldn't have to look at him, but he stood still as I took a few steps. I turned to face him. His eyes were piercing.

"I want you back." I knew Martin never touched alcohol, so he was not in a stupor now.

"It's too late for that. You have a wife."

"Nothing is irreversible."

"You're crazy." We stared at each other. What were my feelings for Martin? I knew I still missed him, but was I in love with him? Did absence make the heart grow fonder, as the saying said? Well, one thing I did know was that I wasn't going to have him divorce his wife for me until I knew and I would never know. After all, it wasn't as though we could date while he was married. Every fiber in my being prohibited that. I would not have an affair with a married man. Why was everything so complicated all the time? "Why can't we be friends?"

"Because I'm in love with you." At that he grabbed me and hugged me. I reflexively put my arms around his shoulders and we parted a little to look at each other. His eyes were wet. That's something I had never seen in Martin... any display of emotion (besides hostility) was never visible. He kissed me hard and then pulled back to look at me, as if to gauge my reaction. I only felt sadness because we could not give each other what we wanted. I couldn't give him love and he couldn't give me friendship. He could see it in my eyes, because he stiffened. "You are a cold human being, Nicky. No, I take that back. You are not even human. Just stay away from me. I don't want to see you in the hospital and I hope you leave this city after you graduate. I never want to see you again. I wish I had never met you." He began to walk away and I called after him. He stopped, but didn't turn around, as if he were giving me one last chance to make up my mind.

"Martin, isn't there any other way?" He began to walk again and I watched him disappear around a corner. My heart felt heavy because I knew I had hurt him deeply again. But I wasn't in love with him and I wasn't ready to settle down now.

What a way to end this harrowing week. I felt lousy, inside and out, and knew that I needed to get home and get some rest. Maybe I would feel better tomorrow. I hated to hurt people and was sorry I had gone to the party in the first place. Why didn't I have better judgement about things? Why was I so stupid?

I turned around to walk in the opposite direction that Martin had taken and my eyes landed on an old sedan parked by the curb. The engine was running but its lights were off. In the driver's seat was the man in the raincoat I had seen by the water earlier that day. When he saw me looking at him, he pulled down his hat, turned on his lights and zoomed off, going through the traffic light.

Now I was being followed to boot… probably by the police. On the other hand, could he be the person who had killed Ralph, wondering how much I knew? Something told me to get a cab and hurry home. I didn't want to be on the street anymore. Had he been watching the whole scene with Martin? Had he been creeping forward in his car, following us as we walked?

I hailed a taxi, jumped in and looked around. There were no cars or people. I sank into the seat and closed my eyes as I stated my street and felt the car move on.

# Chapter 3

Ralph lived in the Bronx. I would have had some reservations about going into that neighborhood at any other time in my life. However, I felt I had been through so much recently, that if nothing had happened to me thus far, nothing was going to happen to me now. Was I invincible? No, but resilient, yes.

Nevertheless, walking out of my apartment building, I looked right and left for any familiar faces. I gazed at the parked cars on the block to see if the man in the raincoat was hanging around. No sign of anyone. It was a warm, brilliant spring morning… and it was Saturday, which meant no hospital obligations. Well, this was obligation enough. I had the nine hundred dollars in cash which I was going to return to Ralph's family today. With a bright early start, I would be home in plenty of time to walk in the park… something that always cheered me up. The last two days had been a nightmare. Maybe I could clear it all from my mind and get on with my life. But who was following me? I would have to keep my eyes open.

It had occurred to me that maybe I should mail the cash to the family, but I felt a responsibility not only to make sure that they received it, but to express my condolences as well. His wife, Millie, was such a lovely person. Maybe she had an idea who could have done such a terrible thing. Although, the police had probably been to the house by now.

The subway ride was uneventful. I kept changing cars at every stop and checked if anyone was following me. No one came into the car I chose to sit in each time I changed.

This was the subway ride that Ralph had taken each day on his way to work. He had seen these stations, these seats… everyday for twenty years. His gaze would never again be a part of this ride.

Ralph's apartment building was in the heart of a poor neighborhood. There were people sitting on the stoops and the sidewalk and they all stared at me. Yes, I was an outsider, dressed in my pants suit, high heels and adorned with my diamond heart necklace. Maybe I should have left the necklace at home. Maybe I had been stupid to walk with so much cash in my pocket.

Even the sidewalks were cracked and uneven, as if they had not been repaired since being laid down, and I had to watch where I walked. All of the buildings were in questionable shape, some even abandoned. Those that were occupied had their windows open, with and without heads peeking from them, and tattered curtains that blew in and out.

Children screamed in the streets and one boy was trying to figure out how to gain enough strength to open a fire hydrant.

Ralph's building was a battered brick one with its main doorway painted with graffiti. The "lobby" consisted of a hallway with rows of mailboxes lining one of the walls. The floor was made of tiny tiles of different colors, making swirls of designs, many of the tiles chipped or missing. The staircase had the original ornate brass railing, but the brass needed a polishing badly.

Ralph's apartment was on the fifth floor and I walked up slowly, kicking empty beer bottles and soda cans out of my way as I went. I knew I had reached the correct floor when I heard the voices of people and saw that one of the front doors was open.

I knocked on the open door and peeked into the living room. There were folding chairs everywhere and people standing around holding paper cups and nibbling from food on the coffee table. No one was crying… in fact, everyone seemed to be pretty animated.

Then I heard a cry from a corner and saw a few children sitting on the floor. Sitting on one of the childrens' laps was a small girl, maybe four years old, crying and asking why her daddy wasn't coming home. Oh, that must be the youngest, I thought, and my heart sank.

One of the ladies picked up the crying girl and tried to soothe her. No sign of Millie.

"You know Ralph?" a voice said near my ear. I turned around and faced an elderly man with a cane.

"Yeah, I worked with him: at the hospital."

"You a doctor?" I nodded yes.

"Medical student."

"You the one who used to come for the eyeballs?" I nodded and he held out his hand to shake mine.

"My names' Sal Seymour. Ralph's father."

I shook his hand and told him how sorry I was and what a wonderful person Ralph was. It was more tragic to bury a child than to bury a parent. "Ralph spoke about you, you know. He liked you. Thought you would make a good doctor. It was nice of you to come today. The family's a mess. I'm the only strong one in this whole god-damned family. And I'm seventy-two years old. I don't know who took Ralph's life, but I'm going to offer a reward or figure out some way to get that demon. Ralph was too young to be joining the Lord so soon… and with – oh well, I don't want to burden you with all this. You're very nice for coming. Sorry if it's a scene here. He did speak of you kindly. In fact, he told me recently… didn't you just get into an eye doctor program?"

"Yes, I will be studying ophthalmology."

"Well, good for you. Ralph brought that news to the dinner table one time. You see, I live with the family. Seems I'm going to have to find a job now and I won't be home much. Ain't much an old man like me can do. That demon took my golden years away from me." He looked down at his cane. "You want something to eat, you help yourself."

"Where's Millie?" He pointed to a room in silence. "Mr. Seymour, if there's anything I can ever do for you, let me know." He nodded and walked away. I could see that he was a little dazed.

I walked over to the doorway that Mr. Seymour had pointed to and found Millie sitting on a bed staring down at a handkerchief she was wringing in her hands. A young girl was sitting on the floor nearby, leaning her head against Millie's knees.

"What're we goin' to do now, Momma?" The girl kept repeating over and over, but Millie sat in silence. "Well, I'll take are of you, Momma. I'll get a job or something."

"What're you crazy?" Millie seemed to come out her trance. "You'll finish school first. Now stop for awhile, Sandra. Just stop babbling… it's making me a headache."

"Millie." I spoke quietly to match the mood of the room. Millie turned around and put a hand on the pile of coats on the bed.

"Why, Dr. Nicky," she said with a half smile. "What a nice surprise." I walked in and was prepared to shake her hand, but she opened her arms wide for a hug. She pulled me into a tight hug and kissed me on the forehead, the way she would kiss one of her children. She was a very large woman with warm eyes but three chins. "Sandra, this is a doctor that your Daddy knew. Why, Dr. Nicky, I didn't expect you at all. Really nice of you to come."

"I'm sorry about Ralph. I really will miss him. He was a great person." Her smile faded and she looked down at the handkerchief again.

"Sandra, can you leave me alone with the doctor?" Sandra nodded, gave me a bit of a smile and closed the door behind her. Millie motioned to the bed next to her and I sat down. Her eyes closed halfway as she spoke. "Ralph was a good man, Doctor Nicky. You knew him. He wouldn't harm anyone and he didn't hang out with any gun-toting bigshots. Why, we once found a mouse in our apartment and Ralph found a way to trap it alive, so he could take it to a local pet shop. I don't know what that pet shop did with it, 'cause I don't know a living soul around here who would want a mouse for a pet. We're trying to kill the mice in this neighborhood, not keep them in silly aquariums so we can gawk at them. But Ralph wanted it to have a life, as he put it, so he took time off from his schedule, and he caught that good for nothing mouse."

"He minded his own business, too. There are a lot of thugs in this neighborhood, and a lot of gambling and drug trading goes on, but Ralph was not a part of that scene. He was a hard worker... he left early in the morning and came back as soon as he was done from work. Then he just stayed home and relaxed with a beer by the T.V. Who would want to kill him? He didn't even have any enemies that I know of. I would know, too, 'cause he told me everything. What happened, Dr. Nicky?" So, she didn't have any answers after all.

"I thought you'd be able to tell me." I answered.

"And Ralph loved his job so much. He was so proud working in the hospital and all. What kind of murderers hang out at a hospital?" She smiled. "I remember the day he came home when he got that job. So proud, he was. You would think he was going to be a doctor like you. And each time he brought home that paycheck, he waved it around like he was a real important person too."

I cleared my throat, putting my next words together in my head. "Ralph always kept this in one of his books." I put the envelope of money in her hand. "He said that if anything ever happened to him, I should give you this. We were sort of close, you know, and we trusted each other." Millie opened the envelope and sighed.

"Looks like a lot of money," she whispered and dabbed her eyes with the handkerchief. I wasn't going to let her know that I had counted it, so I just nodded, instead of saying something like, "Yeah, nine hundred dollars."

"Isn't that just like Ralph," she whispered again. Then she looked up. "How'd you know Ralph was killed?"

"I heard it through word of mouth... you know, the grapevine."

She nodded. "Dr. Nicky, who would do this to him? What happened to my Ralph?" She started to cry and grabbed me with her massive arms to put her head on my shoulder. I stared at the bedpost behind her, as I felt her tears soak my shirt.

"I don't know, Millie. I'm here to help you, though, in any way I can."

So Millie didn't have a clue as to what had happened. It seemed to be as big a mystery to her as to me. Ralph wasn't getting death threats from an old enemy… he was just a homebody who kept to himself, loved his family and spent his free time with his five children.

There was a knock on the door. Millie pulled back, wiped her eyes and said, "come in."

I turned to face the doorway and gasped when I saw the man in the raincoat open the door. However, he was not wearing a raincoat today, but a dark suit. In his hand was the hat he had on yesterday.

I stood up immediately and watched silently as he approached Millie and held out his hand. I leaned against the wall, wishing that I could disappear into it. Who was this man? Why was he following me? To come face to face with him in this room was frightening.

"Mrs. Seymour, I want to express my sympathy. I'm Detective Jeffries." I leaned more heavily against the wall and almost needed its support to stand. This was the end. I was a suspect for murder… or was I? I wouldn't say anything. Maybe he would just leave the room.

Detective Jeffries turned to me and extended his hand again. His expression was friendly and soft… not one you would flash to a suspected murderer. "And you are one of the doctors I would guess." He had to know who I was… after all, he was following me. Why was he playing dumb?

"Nicky Steinway." He might as well know my name if he didn't already. I felt as though I was in more trouble now than I had ever been in my life. I had never had any exposure to policemen, except to have them as patients or pass them in the street. Then I was the doctor above them, giving them orders, deciding what medications to give them… not a lowly suspect. Now I was under their power. If he wanted to take me to the station, I had to go. The whole hospital would be buzzing about this one. Even Dr. Lerner couldn't protect me now.

But I hadn't done anything... I was innocent. Only strange circumstances had brought me into contact with Ralph that night. Maybe I should have gone to the police and volunteered what had happened in the very beginning. Well, I wouldn't say anything to him unless he said something more to me.

As my mind was racing, he took Millie's hand again and said slowly, "would you mind if I take Dr. Steinway into the next room for a moment? I have some questions to ask her." My heart sank, but I followed him silently into the living room after nodding to Millie. I left Millie looking down into her handkerchief again.

Detective Jeffries poured himself a soda and put a cup in my hand. "What can I pour you?" The coffee table had soda and juice, but I felt so numb and my head was spinning at the same time: I knew I couldn't down a thing. I put the cup down and almost mechanically told him I didn't want anything. I was afraid of what he was thinking and worried about what would happen next. Handcuffs maybe?

I looked around the room. All the people –and there must have been thirty – were in their own worlds, talking to each other or sitting solemnly in silence. I heard Ralph's name over and over again in different corners of the room. Why had Detective Jeffries singled me out? What was he thinking?

He downed his drink quickly and flashed a smile at me.

"Dr. Steinway, do you think we could go for a walk so I can ask you a few questions?" I felt a little dizzy. Was this the time people usually called lawyers? I nodded quietly but thought of Millie.

"Well, I should say good-bye to Millie," I said. Who knows if he was going to take me to the station or even arrest me?

But he laughed. "You won't be gone that long, Doctor." Well, that was a relief. I felt a little better as I followed him out of the apartment.

As we walked down the stairway, I wanted to ask him why he had been following me. Why was he scaring me and why did he want to talk to me now? I was too afraid. Maybe I had seen too many movies, but I kept hearing the phrase, "anything you say may be held against you" rolling in my head. Yet I hadn't done anything. There was nothing to pin on me. Well, I was certainly feeling paranoid.

When we reached the street, he turned to face me, still with a kind expression on his face. We paused long enough for me to realize that he was good-looking. He had sandy brown hair which was combed to the side and blue eyes. His lips were thin, but they formed a charming smile.

He was tall, too, and muscular, which I liked in men. I looked down at the ground. This was not a social event, I reprimanded myself: this man was talking to me because he thought I could be involved in Ralph's demise. I had to keep alert and watch what I said.

"There's a coffee shop around the corner, Doc. Wanna' go there for a quick cup of coffee? My treat" I smiled. What choice did I have? Of course. I nodded and he led the way. "I used to spend a lot of time in this neighborhood. We did a drug bust here. So, I know all the coffee shops that have good coffee." I followed silently. I wasn't going to say anything unless I was specifically asked something. The less I said the better.

The coffee shop was run-down and all the chairs had holes with stuffing protruding from them… yellow foam, aching to get out from under the fake leather. The front window was painted with graffiti and a mirror on the back wall was cracked from ceiling to floor. There weren't many people there and we sat in a booth by the window in the front.

Detective Jeffries looked relaxed as he sat back in the booth and began to play with the creamer on the table. All he was missing was a toothpick hanging from his front teeth... somehow I had always pictured detectives with toothpicks in their mouths. I guess that was the result of too many old movies.

"That was really too bad about Ralph Seymour," he began. "Did you know him well, Dr. Steinway?"

"Nicky... call me Nicky." Why keep things formal? If he was going to hang me on something, we might as well be on a first name basis. This was also a trick question, I was sure. This guy was a professional.

"O.K., then call me Jack." Jack Jeffries... it even sounded like a typical detective's name.

"I often saw Ralph and spoke to him because I went down to the morgue to get eye donations." Why were we playing cat and mouse? This was ridiculous already. He was following me and there must be a reason. "Jack, why have you been following me?" I had to know... had to get right to the meat of the situation. If I was suspect, I wanted to know now.

Jack sat back and laughed to himself.

"You really get right to the point, don't you?"

"I couldn't help noticing you twice yesterday and I'm wondering why. I didn't kill Ralph." This time he laughed heartily.

"Yeah? I think I know that, but you know, your fingerprints are all over his office."

"I told you I used to go down there a lot for eye donations. Actually, if you get right down to it, my fingerprints are all over the hospital." We smiled at each other, but mine was not a true smile. It was more a polite look with a slight turning up of the lips for manners only. I was starting to wish that this detective would stop playing games and would ask what he wanted to. Suddenly I was feeling strong instead of scared, for some reason, and very innocent as well.

Sure enough, his expression became serious and his eyes narrowed. "I know you're in medical school. I know you've had a lot more schooling than me, but you need to know something, Doctor. I'm a hell of a good detective. I know my business and I think Ralph was murdered for a reason. I don't know why exactly, right now, but I will. And until I find out why, I'll be on everyone's back and under everyone's feet. I'll be in the mirror when you look at yourself in the morning... I'll be in your morning coffee and all over the hospital. When you walk down the hallway in the hospital, you'll hear a second set of footsteps besides you own behind you and they'll be mine." He was trying to scare me and he was doing a good job, but I wasn't going to let him see my feelings. So, I stared at him quietly with a serious face.

"So, you're saying I'm a suspect?" I asked softly.

"Well, where were you when Ralph was killed?"

"When was he killed?"

"We have the time of death as being between two and three on Friday."

"I was running around the floors doing what medical students do."

"And what is that, Doctor?" His face had a playful yet sarcastic look to it.

"Write notes in the charts, follow my intern, eat dinner." He nodded.

Our coffees came and I carefully added milk to mine, happy that my hands weren't shaking. The way I was feeling, they should have been. I was very close to standing up and telling him I couldn't talk to him anymore until I called my attorney. But so far, the conversation was not incriminating, so I would first see where it lead. If it got too close, I would have to get a lawyer.

Jack stared at me as I stirred my coffee and took a sip. I did not feel like drinking coffee: it was all a charade to look calm.

"You play this game very well, Nicky." I shrugged.

"I'm not playing games, and I think you're trying to bully me. You don't really think I killed Ralph, do You?"

"Did I ever say that? Look. You know more about this than You're telling me and I want to know what's going on: that's all."

"I don't know what's making you feel that way, Detective. I'm a medical student. I'm not a thug, a gambler or a robber. I take pride in minding my own business and there's nothing more to it than that." Martin had always told me I had a quick mind and I didn't quite know what he had meant until now. Being a quick thinker with fast responses like this was what he had meant.

Jack took a long drink of his coffee and didn't take his eyes off of me.

"Nicky, you're a smart woman with a quick wit. You also have beautiful eyes. I know that was inappropriate and I'm sorry, but you do have a way about you."

"Is flattery in your repertoire too, Detective?"

"All right, forget it. Let's just enjoy our coffee. But Nicky, don't you worry about your own safety?" Boy, he was trying all the angles.

"Why should I?"

"You tell me." I smiled. I had never verbally sparred with a detective before and I think I was faring fairly well.

"All I want to know," I said, "is why you're following me and when you're going to stop."

"Maybe I have a crush on you. Maybe I think you're hiding something. Maybe you even killed Ralph, or you know who did. You know, I could take you right to the station for questioning, if I wanted to. Do you know that?" I nodded. "I could keep you there all night." I was quiet. I didn't want to upset him because he could only make life very hard for me. I really was at his mercy.

"So what do you want, Jack?"

"I want answers. I want to know why Ralph was killed."

"I don't know. I really don't know. I loved Ralph. He was a great guy. Maybe he had connections I didn't know about... that's the only thing I can think of. I really don't know." I felt like crying. I was upset about Ralph and I was afraid of this detective. I think he sensed it because he apologized.

"I don't mean to be hard on you. I am frustrated because I'm not getting answers and no one seems to know much about Ralph. He was just a hard-working guy who kept to himself. No enemies known of in the hospital. No bad connections that we know of. I know you had a good relationship with him. I also don't think you're capable of murder, but I've been wrong about people before."

"Is that why you've been following me? You think I might have done it?"

"I'll follow whoever I want whenever I want for reasons only I will know. I've got a few leads and a few ideas as to what happened. Meanwhile, Nicky, I would watch my back if I were you. I'm not telling you this because I'm trying to impress you or because I'm planning on following you some more. I'm worried about you. You don't have family in this city and you live on your own. You should be careful." I didn't answer and wondered if he was right. Maybe I was in danger because I knew too much.

Though how much did I really know? That Mr. Suma's body was not in the right place right now? That someone had killed Ralph? The whole hospital knew about Ralph and maybe I was really wrong about Mr. Suma's body. I was confused. Why would the person who killed Ralph be after me too? That's what Detective Jeffries was implying.

He looked into my empty cup and asked if I was finished. When I said yes, he left money on the table and got up. "I'll walk you to the subway or back to Millie's. Where're you going?"

"I think I'll go home."

He walked me to the subway station and we talked about general things like food and restaurants. He was actually very nice during this part of the walk and I could see how someone could like him. But he was also a tough detective and I hoped he didn't have to question me again. I didn't like sparring with him.

When we got to the station, he shook my hand.

"You going to be all right?" he asked sweetly, as though we were finishing a date.

"Yes, I'll be fine. And if I can do anything else for you, let me know." The words came automatically, the same way they came out to patients who were leaving the clinic after a consultation.

"Oh, you'll be seeing me again, Nicky." He squeezed my hand again and paused before he let go. I turned around and walked down the stairway to the station, feeling his stare on my back. I almost felt like he did have a crush on me.

Sitting on the subway, I felt very much alone. How did Jack Jeffries know that I didn't have family in town? He obviously had done some research on me. Typical detective.

# Chapter 4

Well, I was alone, not only in this city, but in any city. I didn't have anyone to turn to because my parents lived two-hundred miles away and we certainly weren't close. They were always traveling, my father was always giving lectures somewhere as a guest professor. It was as if as soon as I got into medical school and my future was assured, my parents decided to live the life they had always wanted to live.

Growing up, I was a sheltered only child, living in a large stone house, given any toy I wanted, as long as I received good grades at school. It meant everything to my parents, even when I was six, that I bring home straight "A's" on my report card. My father once told me that as soon as I was born and handed to my mother, she said quietly, "this baby is going to be a doctor." She meant it, too. She very carefully groomed me to be a doctor and a lady at the same time.

And I was only allowed to socialize with doctors' children. I could only sleep over at physicians' houses when there were sleepovers and the other children thought that I was a snob.

I was told that when I grew up and got married, it should only be to another physician. And I should live in a stone house… not a house with stone on one side, but on all the sides of the building. Why? It was never quite clear to me, but I did know that these homes were made with the most solid construction. How my mother knew so much about construction was also a mystery to me.

Everything had to be the best for my parents' little girl. They knew for some reason that they weren't going to have any more children, so everything had to be just right this one and only time. Thus, I went to the finest private schools, was given tutors when I had trouble with a certain subject (which meant getting a "B"), and could only socialize with doctor's children. I was given speech, piano, voice and art lessons in high school.

At the early age of ten, I could be introduced to someone, shake their hand and say almost mechanically, "hello, it's a pleasure to meet you. I'm fine, thank you, how are you?" Always dressed in lace and patent leather shoes, I was out to make an impression on the world… or so my parents thought. And even though my mother had a habit of raising her voice at me or not talking to me for a week over miniscule things, I ended up being a very mellow and easy-going person. If my mother blew up at me because she didn't like my tone of voice when I answered her about something, I would quietly retreat to my bedroom and just stay out of her way for a day or two.

I always compared her in my mind to a temperamental race horse which had to be groomed and handled just right, or it became very upset and wouldn't be good for anything… especially running a race.

My father, however, was much different than my mother. He was a professor at the medical school, always teaching in the labs or the lecture halls, doing consulting work on the side. He left raising me to my mother, as he was very involved in his career, and he made it clear that whatever she said or did was the law of the house.

Even though I resented his attitude many times, he was truly my hero. I knew I wanted to be just like him and I was forever trying to get him to approve of me. Now and then he would admit that I had done a good job at something and I would be beaming for days.

All in all, my whole upbringing was based on pleasing my parents, though I did actually want to become a doctor since I was seven years old. Medicine seemed like a career for the elite, the intelligent and the one who wanted eternal security. There were no unemployed doctors, as my mother always said. I had always loved people and enjoyed science, and loved the idea of helping people, so I knew medicine was for me.

We were a close threesome until I entered medical school. It was then that my parents decided to sever the major ties. I was only to call home once a week, so our conversations would not interfere with my studying. They would come to visit me at school once a month. They made it clear that I was to devote my entire self to studying and getting through school. I could do that and still see them more often, I pointed out, but my opinion was not considered.

Medical school was the first time I lived away from home, so I was able to socialize with whomever I pleased and this was a brand new experience for me. I found that there were all types of people in the world, not just doctors' children, and that they liked me for me, not because I came from a good home. Finding out that not everything my parents said was always right, I became more independent. This meant realizing that I could survive without seeing them so often, without leaning on their opinions so much. So, I became strong from within and relied on my own judgement in tough situations. Maybe this is what my parents were aiming for all along... I wasn't sure, but it turned out that way.

But now I wished that my parents had been different so that I could ask them about the situation I was in now. How should I act? Should I consult an attorney? Should I get a bodyguard? Had I misjudged everything over the last few days?

I sighed as the subway lurched forward from a stop. They were in the Phillipines now, my father a guest lecturer at the university there, so it was not even possible to talk to them. My mother would be aghast that I had had coffee with a detective, not only because I might be a suspect, but worse: he might ask me out at this point. She took everything over-seriously and perhaps speaking to them would make things even worse.

No, I was in this situation by myself and I alone would have to decide what to do. Of course, at the moment there was nothing to do anyway. I would sit back and see if Detective Jeffries got in touch with me again – which would mean more trouble – or if anyone else was going to be following me. I would definitely have to keep my eyes open.

I stepped off the train at the next stop and looked around the platform. Everyone was rushing to their destination without noticing me.

I climbed the stairway to the street and took a deep breath. Today was Saturday, my day off. I should be enjoying myself... days off were few and far between. Maybe no one was even noticing me now and the situation was finished. Perhaps today was the start of a new beginning and what had transpired over the last few days was history and over with.

I walked down the street towards my apartment smiling to myself, feeling a surge of hope. I had survived and maybe this was the end of the bad, the beginning of the new... Onwards to happier, more settling times.

That's when I heard the racing engine and at once I saw the black Cadillac racing down the street towards me. It lurched onto the sidewalk and began zooming in my direction. In one second, it seemed, I was face to face with the car and in a split moment I jumped into a doorway and heard the car roar away. The sidewalk trembled. People were screaming and two women were sprawled on the sidewalk, apparently run-over. I peeked out of the doorway and watched the car speed off the sidewalk and screech around the corner to disappear in no time.

A man screamed as he knelt over one of the women who was lying on the sidewalk. She was dead. The other was bleeding badly. "Stupid drunk!" someone yelled. "Call the police!" another voice pleaded.

I was numb. I crossed the street and walked another block, wondering if that car had been out to get me. Was I being paranoid due to my conversation with Detective Jeffries, or was I being realistic?

I entered my apartment building, got into the elevator and was happy to reach my living room. I needed rest and I needed to think. This was too coincidental...or was it? Did someone just try to kill me, or was it just a drunk driver who flew onto the sidewalk for one block?

I collapsed onto the sofa and closed my eyes. I was definitely staying inside for the rest of the weekend. Thank goodness I felt safe at home, behind my front door with the five locks. I wished I could look at the situation more objectively. Too many things were happening all at once. Should I call Detective Jeffries? No... I would probably seem like a nut. So what if a car lost control and drove up on the sidewalk? It happened all the time in this city. I was taking everything too personally...or at least I hoped so.

# Chapter 5

The hospital was always a bit of a haven for me. If I had problems that I wanted to forget, they somehow became secondary to my patients, my intern and the meetings I went to. Then, if they came to mind again later in the day, they didn't seem so bad.

Doctors can lose themselves in the hospital and become so engrossed in their work, that it consumes their minds, squeezing out thoughts, troubles or even hunger.

So, Monday morning, going back to the hospital, I felt better as I entered the main lobby and even more important, I felt safe. The hospital was full of people and I never felt alone. I also thought that if I could lose myself in my work, I could forget the recent events and maybe look at them more realistically too.

On my way upstairs I met Dr. Lerner's intern, Steve. He was rotating through cardiac surgery now and hated it. Steve wanted to be a plastic surgeon and had to do the necessary rotations in order to achieve the supremacy of a plastic surgery resident. He not only lacked any interest in cardiothoracic surgery, but he also saw Dr. Lerner as a pompous show-off (though he did admit to Dr. Lerner's vast knowledge of the heart). Dr. Lerner seemed to sense Steve's opinion of him and tried to make life hard for him as a result. He was always quizzing Steve in the operating room and giving him extra work to do. Dr. Lerner once even said blatantly to him that he was going into plastic surgery for the money. At this point, and I was a witness to this scene, Steve calmly said, "Dr. Lerner, if I was going into a field purely for the monetary reward, I would have chosen cardiac surgery, like you did." That was the first time I heard Dr. Lerner raise his voice and curse uncontrollably at someone, though it happens often, I later learned. Steve took this episode well which made Steve and I the only people in the hospital, I believe, who aren't afraid of Dr. Lerner. We do what he orders to be done... we're not afraid of him, but we're not foolish either.

So there was Steve in the elevator, looking as unhappy as ever, probably mentally counting the days when his rotation with Dr. Lerner was over. He was a handsome fellow, even when he looked unhappy. His hair was straight and brushed to the side, his eyes were green and he was thin and tall. I guess I actually had a small crush on Steve, but I knew he had a girlfriend, so it was only going to be a silent, small crush.

He smiled at me as I entered the elevator.

"Hi, Steve, where're you going?"

"Operating room. Where else? Dr. Lerner has another bypass. Anyway, I'm glad I bumped into you. Do you have a minute? Get out on this floor." We both left the elevator and he pulled me aside. "You remember Mr. Suma, that patient who died?" Chills went down my neck and I nodded yes silently. "Well, his funeral is tomorrow. Dr. Lerner wants everyone who cared for him there, even the night nurse who gave him his sleeping pill."

"But I'm just the medical student."

"Nicky, I saw Dr. Lerner on rounds this morning and he specifically said, 'and make sure that medical student, what's-her-name… Steinway is there.'"

"Why does it matter if I'm there?" I wanted to put all of this behind me.

"I don't know, Nicky, but I do know that he's going to page everyone he can think of later and remind them to come tomorrow. Why argue? It's only a funeral."

"Listen Steve." My voice became a whisper. "Do you remember Mr. Suma?"

"Only a little. All I did was write some orders on his chart the night before. I stopped in to say hello. That's all."

"Were you in the operating room during the operation?"

"No. Dr. Lerner had all this paperwork he needed done and asked me to do it for him. I must have gone through a hundred charts that morning. Why do you ask?"

"No reason. I was just wondering what happened."

"Well, I heard his heart stopped during the operation and they couldn't get it going again. But I wasn't there. So they gave up. Really bad news. Well, the funeral's at the St. James Church on 52$^{nd}$ Street. See you tomorrow." He ducked into another elevator before I could say anything more.

My heart was in my stomach. If someone were trying to kill me, the funeral would be a perfect place to do so. I shook my head. I must be crazy. Why would someone try to get rid of me? I didn't know a thing. I wasn't worth a thing to anyone in the underworld, if the underworld was even involved. Besides, there would be too many people at the funeral to bump someone off.

I sat down in the nurses's lounge at the end of the hall. I had to see the whole situation as it really was and not place so much importance on myself. So, Ralph was killed. It had nothing to do with me. Yes, I mistook Mr. Suma's body. He did have the staples in his chest, fresh from surgery. So, a detective was on the case, as in any murder case, and he asked me a few questions. And the car the other day on the sidewalk was a freak accident… probably a drunk. That was the whole story.

So, I would go to the funeral tomorrow and everything would be behind me. This would be a memory and the end of it all. I would get back on track.

My beeper rang and I wasn't surprised to see Dr. Lerner's extension on the display.

He answered the phone after one ring. "Nicky? Thanks for calling back so fast. Nothing like an efficient medical student. Anyway, I want you to go to Mr. Suma's funeral tomorrow. It would be good for the family to see the whole medical team there. Can you come?"

"Of course, Dr. Lerner." You never said no to Dr. Lerner.

"Good. And Nicky, how are you holding up? I know you've been through a lot recently."

"I'll be all right." He was being too sweet. This was not normal for Dr. Lerner.

"Well, don't let it affect your work. I'll see you tomorrow." He hung up as my beeper rang again. It was the floor and probably my intern. That was good. I was ready to dive into the day and start thinking about other things besides dead bodies and funerals.

# Chapter 6

The St. James Church was a small building, sandwiched between two townhouses and across the street from a dry cleaner. The street was narrow, so all the limousines parked outside choked what space there was. Car after car inched through a narrow space between the limo's and let off one person after the other before driving off. I sat outside alone, watching the people leave their cars, cabs and limousines. One looked more important than the other. The ladies tended to wear black dresses with black veils and pearls and the men all wore dark suits. Faces were hard to discern because one either had sunglasses on or a veil covering the face. The women inched in on their high heels and the men walked heavily beside them. Everyone looked like a somebody and it was almost like a fashion show.

Mrs. Suma must have been inside already and I was looking forward to seeing what she looked like. So far, I hadn't seen any familiar faces or anyone I knew; maybe they were all inside already. I didn't care, however, because I felt secure sitting on the stoop of a neighboring townhouse, enjoying the fresh air and the sight of the people arriving.

A cab stopped in front of the church and R. Lerner got out. He saw me immediately and walked up to me. Why couldn't he just go inside and leave me alone? He stood before me with half of a smile… that was the most of a smile I had ever seen on his face.

"Nicky, what are you doing here? You should be inside. They're going to start soon."

"I'm not part of the family. I can wait awhile." He shook his head.

"I know you'd rather not be here. I don't blame you. You're a trouper for coming and I consider it a favor to me." He held his hand out and helped me up. "Come, let's go inside together." This show of sympathy was not the real Dr. Lerner… or was it? He was always so hard and gruff in the hospital. Which was the real Dr. Lerner? I never thought of him as being nice or thoughtful.

He held onto my elbow as we walked in, and I didn't like it, but if I pulled away, it would be rude. I wasn't an invalid who needed help walking and we weren't a couple, with the man caressing the lady's elbow in affection. I slowly straightened my elbow and pretended to have an itch on my shoulder so I could gently pull away completely.

The chapel was very old and everywhere I looked I saw either stained glass or wooden paneling. The casket was in the front but I couldn't see if it was opened because some people were standing in front of it. If I could get another look at the face, I was sure I could determine if it was the Mr. Suma I had known in life. I must get another look.

Without turning to say anything to Dr. Lerner, I walked quickly down the isle towards the coffin. I inched around people as I went and even knocked into a man in my excitement. I must get to the front immediately.

Suddenly a strong arm grabbed me and turned me around. A man I had never seen before confronted me. He must have been six foot five inches tall with puffy cheeks, narrow eyes and a big belly. His sports coat didn't look as though it would button and it hung open. He looked mean, but he smiled and the meanness vanished from his lips, but not from his eyes.

"You Dr. Steinway." It sounded more like a statement than a question.

"Yes." I responded, wondering if my annoyance could be heard in my voice.

"I'm a good friend of the Suma family and I know you went to see Mr. Suma on the night before he died. You're the medical student, right?" I nodded, wondering where he was leading, wishing he would finish already. "I heard about you and I know Mrs. Suma would like to meet you." I had really wanted to see if the coffin was open before I did anything, but I had also wanted to meet the wife. I gazed towards the casket, but still couldn't see whether it was open or not because of a small crowd of people nearby.

Without another word, the man took hold of my upper arm and led me down the aisle, away from the coffin, pushing me forward. Where were his manners? We reached the last row of seats and he looked towards the front row. If she was sitting in the front row, what were we doing in the back row? And what was I doing with this man?

I pulled my arm away from him. "If you'll excuse me, I would like to take a look at the casket," I said firmly. He grabbed hold of my arm again.

"There isn't anything to see. It's closed."

"Then I think I'll sit down."

"But I wanted you to meet Mrs. Suma. Come with me." He pulled me gently, but firmly, now in the other direction, to the front of the church. We looked at the rows of people as we walked. I think I spotted her before he did.

She was sitting in the front row, wearing a large-brimmed black hat and a plain black dress. She did not have any jewelry on except for a large diamond ring on her left hand. She was beautiful, with straight black hair to her shoulders, high cheekbones and green eyes. Mrs. Suma only had on some lipstick for make-up, but she didn't need anything else. And even though her eyes were swollen from crying and she clutched a handkerchief forlornly, she was a stunning lady.

She was staring at the ground when I walked up to her, or rather, was pushed up to her by the man, whose name I didn't even know.

"Mrs. Suma, Dr. Steinway is here to say hello." She looked up and wiped her nose. Her voice was calm.

"I'm glad to meet you," she said quietly. "It's thanks to you that my husband's eyes will do someone some good. I appreciate what you did and I'm sure my husband would too." She held out her hand to hold mine for a moment. "Thank you." I nodded silently, not knowing quite what to say. I was glad, however, that Dr. Lerner's concerns about my asking for the eye donation were not founded after all.

The man by my side gave my arm a squeeze and I realized he had been holding it all this time.

"You can go sit down now," He said.

"And what did you say your name was?" I asked. His eyes narrowed.

"It's not important, but you can call me Jim." I nodded, gave Mrs. Suma a smile and walked away. I was now in front of the coffin and sure enough it was closed. Oh well, I would sit down, leave the service early and get back to the hospital. After all, I was only here to make an appearance and there was no stronger appearance than meeting the wife. She really was striking… quite a lady as well.

A large man in a gray suit stood by the podium and announced that he wanted to say a few words. He began to praise Mr. Suma, saying what a good person and shrewd businessman he was. He would be missed. I was sorry I had ever met him, though again I reprimanded myself for connecting Mr. Suma's death with Ralph's. I really had to forget this whole experience.

The man finished his speech and the priest took his place, talking about the next world and the fact that Mr. Suma was looking down at us all now. I had had enough. The whole thing was getting depressing and I was ready to get back to work.

I got up and began to walk towards the doors of the church in the back. As I walked, a few people looked up at me, but I didn't know any of them. I didn't even notice any of my fellow interns. So, I looked down at the ground, avoiding any stares, and made my way outside. The cool city air blew through my hair and felt good. The sunlight also felt good as it warmed me. Well, it was probably rude to get up and leave in the middle of the priest's speech, but I wasn't family – I was barely an acquaintance – and they were all lucky I had made an appearance in the first place. If it hadn't been for Dr. Lerner's special request, I never would have come.

The hospital was only eight blocks away, so I decided to walk. The fresh air would do me good and I had time to spare. My intern thought I was going to be at the funeral for at least an hour.

It felt good to be on the street, walking anonymously among other people, just another face in the crowd. Now, I thought, the whole thing is over. Mr. Suma would be buried today and with him everything associated with him. Dr. Lerner would never mention him again, I would try not to think about the recent events and Ralph, and life would go on.

I decided to stop into a tiny muffin shop and buy a muffin for breakfast. The smell of baking dough seeped into the street, and I walked in. The shop consisted only of a counter, behind which were shelves of muffins. The whole store could only fit about five people at a time, but it was empty when I came in.

A large lady was behind the counter and she smiled at me.

"I'll take one apple muffin and a cup of coffee." She nodded and promptly pulled out a paper cup and some tissue paper to wrap the muffin in. I leaned on the counter and gazed out the window of the shop. People were scurrying to work, their faces full of thoughts as they looked at the ground.

I saw the Lincoln pull up in front of the shop and double park as I paid the lady. The muffin was still hot and I left the shop, taking a sip of coffee. The Lincoln's motor started up again. I held the muffin in one hand and the coffee in the other as I walked, knowing I would be able to finish by the time I reached the hospital.

I noticed that the Lincoln didn't pass me. Had it stoped and parked? I turned around and saw that it was moving very slowly. Was it following me? I shook my head. I was becoming so paranoid lately. It probably was lost and trying to read the numbers on the buildings.

I stared into the car. There were two men in the front seat and they were both staring at me. I stopped walking. The car stopped moving and it was approximately ten feet away. Those men were definitely looking at me. I no longer felt that this was a coincidence.

Well, they couldn't do anything right now because the street was full of people. Driving up on the sidewalk was impossible because the curb was lined with parked cars. Shooting at me was unlikely because of all the pedestrians.

I turned around and began to walk again, seeing the car begin to move from the corner of my eye. Were these policemen? Jack Jeffries was definitely not in that car. I wished he were with me at that moment. Well, I wasn't alone. I would just keep walking until I reached the hospital and then I would duck into the main lobby.

I crossed the street in a hurry and gazed back at the car again. Now the passenger's window was rolled down and a man's head was sticking out. I turned around to face him, feeling bold on the crowded street. The car stopped. Why, it was Jim, that idiot in the church who wouldn't let go of my arm.

"Jim!" I cried out to him. "What're you doing?" He didn't answer and the car inched up to me. He just kept staring at me through is narrowed eyes.

Then I saw his hand come up and it held a gun, which he pointed at me. He was going to kill me. I gasped and couldn't move from fear. No, it wasn't happening.

I heard the loud explosion as it fired and felt someone push me to the ground. The concrete grazed my cheek and I couldn't move because of a heavy body on top of me. There were more explosions and then silence.

"What's happening?" I cried out to the person on top of me. I looked up and saw Jack Jeffries' face. He rolled off of me and I heard people screaming. The Lincoln sped off and I saw Jim's window going up.

Jack told me to stay down as he got up. He looked around and I saw a gun in his hand too.

"O.K., Nicky, you can get up." He held a hand to me and helped me up. Pedestrians had scattered, so the block was deserted but two men came running up to Jack.

"We missed him," one said. Jack nodded.

"Did you get the license number?"

"No."

"Go back to the funeral. I'll escort Dr. Steinway."

The two men nodded to me and Jack and walked away. I was still numb and in shock.

"I – Jack, you saved my life I think." He smiled.

"I think I did, though I also stained your dress pretty badly." Then I noticed and felt the hot coffee stains. He tilted my chin up and touched my cheek gently. "You've got some bad scratches here too. Sorry."

"What happened? Where did you come from?"

"Well you knew I was tailing you, didn't you? Those thugs were trying to get rid of you, Nicky, and I knew it was only a matter of time before they tried."

"Why? I'm just a medical student."

"I'm not sure why. Let me get you another cup of coffee."

"Why didn't you tell me you thought there would be an attempt on my life? What if they come back?" I felt like crying and I felt helpless and scared. He must have seen it on my face because before I knew it, his arms were around me and I was shaking uncontrollably.

"I'm sorry." I said, as my tears began. "I don't mean to do this." He held me more tightly and guided me into a small market. I felt safe for the moment, burying my face into the folds of his coat, his hold on me tight and secure.

Everything was overwhelming now. Ralph, Millie, Mr. Suma, the funeral, … their faces flashed through my mind all at once.

"Don't worry, Nicky… we won't let anything happen to you." I felt his chin on the top of my head and then I felt him kiss my forehead. He handed me a handkerchief and I wiped my eyes.

We were standing inside a fruit market, near the cash register and, of course, being stared at. I apologized to the cashier but didn't feel like leaving. I felt safe here and I didn't know what awaited me outside.

"Maybe I should take you home," Jack said quietly. "Why don't you take the day off?"

"I don't know."

"Call in sick. For heaven's sake, tell them there was an attempt on your life. No, that's not such a hot idea… you don't want to draw attention to yourself too much." Jack's eyes were vibrant as he spoke and I liked looking into them. I guessed it was because he was the only person I could turn to right now for reassurance and protection.

How could I go back to work? I wouldn't feel safe in the hospital, in the street, even at home. There was only one more week to my rotation in medicine and then summer vacation. I had to figure out what to do, where to go.

Jack kept his arm around me as he led me outside and hailed down a cab. I couldn't think straight and followed him numbly into the car. He was staring at me as we rode and I had no thoughts except that I had grazed death. He knew my address as he directed the cab driver, and seemed so strong and sure.

We reached my apartment building and he followed me into the elevator. I automatically took out my keys. He still looked at me and I felt like putting my heavy head on his shoulder and feeling his arms around me again. I didn't move, however, and knew it wasn't appropriate.

When we got out of the elevator, he took my keys from my hand and told me to wait by the elevator.

"I want to check out your apartment first. You stay here."

"No, I don't want to. Don't leave me here in the hall by myself."

"You're safe here, Nicky, and I need to go into your apartment first. Stay here." I stood still and watched him walk down the hall and open the door to my apartment. The minute or so that he was gone felt like an eternity and each time I heard the elevator whirring to another floor, I shivered.

Would there be more shots? Was there someone waiting in my apartment for me?

Jack reappeared and motioned for me to come inside.

My little apartment seemed so heavenly now and as he closed the door, I felt safe for the first time since the shooting. I sat down heavily on the sofa. My apartment was a small one bedroom apartment with a dining table to the side of the living room. The kitchen was practically a closet. Right now, this apartment seemed like a haven and I couldn't picture leaving it for a long time.

Jack sat down on the sofa next to me and studied my face.

"You got a bad scratch on your cheek, Nicky. Let me wipe it for you." He got up, went into the kitchen and came back with a wet paper towel. His touch was gentle as he wiped off some dried blood from my cheek.

"I don't know what to do now, Jack." My voice was shaky. "I'm really scared." I felt tears welling up in my eyes again. Before I knew it, his arms were around me again and I was crying. I had to pull myself together and figure out what to do next. This was not the real me... I was always strong in tough situations. But then again, I had never been shot at before.

As if sensing my thoughts, he pulled away and looked at me. "Let's call your intern and tell her you won't be in today. You have a bad flu." He picked up the phone and dialed the hospital to page Jane. She would understand. I had never called in sick before, so she'd think it was true.

I was right. "No problem, Nicky," she said, "let me know how you are tomorrow and feel better." I hung up and Jack smiled.

"See, that wasn't so bad, was it? I used to do that all the time when I was in school. I was a professional hooky player." I laughed nervously and sat down in a chair across from him. Now I felt more calm and was thinking more clearly.

"What do I do now, Jack?" He sat back and crossed his legs.

"Well, I've got a bit of a plan, but first I want to ask you some questions. Are you up to it?" I nodded yes.

We spent the whole morning going over everything that had happened since Ralph's murder, trying to put our heads together as to why someone would want to kill me. Neither of us could figure out why, but at least I felt a sense of relief: not only was I not a suspect for Murder (not that I should have been), but I had someone on my side.

"Well," Jack finally concluded, "sooner or later we'll find out who's after you and why. Meanwhile, we have to make sure you are safe." I nodded gingerly in agreement. "You have to be able to walk down the street and not worry about your life. After all, you're going to be a doctor and we have to make sure you can keep on saving lives." He walked to the sofa to retrieve his coat.

"You're leaving?!" I asked incredulously. My whole sense of well-being was dissolving quickly. I was only safe if Jack was my bodyguard. He chuckled.

"Nicky, this is what we're going to do. I'm going back to the station and we'll get you two things. Number one, a police tail, so you'll be watched. Number two, you'll wear a radio transmitter so we'll know your whereabouts and what people are saying to you. It's very high-tech. O.K.?"

"How fast is all this going to take place?"

"As soon as I get back to the station. In fact, why don't you come with me and we'll take care of it immediately. You'll just have to go home by yourself... but then again, you won't be by yourself because you'll have a police tail. Have you ever heard about a tail? You don't even know they're following you. You'll walk down the street, turnaround and see no one... absolutely no one. But they're there, around the corner, or above you on the second floor balcony, or wherever. You'll be safe." I felt better.

"Let's go, Jack."

The radio transmitter was a contraption that I wore under my clothes, pinned to my bra strap. Yet wearing it there, everything I said (or that was said to me) was transmitted back to the police station and recorded on tape. Sometimes as I walked, I felt like saying something like, "hey, it's awfully sunny ouside, guys. You should come out and take a walk with me." I finally felt secure. Now and then I would turn around to see if I could spot the police tail, but I never could. They were such professionals. No wonder the FBI had such a wonderful reputation… look at what the city's police force was capable of!

So, I went about my daily activities, running around the hospital, treating patients, sewing up lacerations, not thinking about the recent events. For some reason, I felt very safe in the hospital once again. It was still my haven from the outside world, despite what had happened to Ralph. I had the best of both worlds, being able to continue with my work and having the police nearby at the same time. I was a little self-conscious about what I said and I did turn the transmitter off when I did personal things like go to the bathroom, but I would always talk into it with a warning that I was about to turn it off. That way, I felt, I wouldn't turn on any alarms by just turning it off.

Thus, I completed my medicine rotation without any adventure. With each day that went by normally, I felt more and more at ease and more self-confident. I felt so good about it all, I began to wonder if I had been too paranoid. If someone really wanted me dead, wouldn't they try another attempt on my life? Maybe that gunman in the car, Jim, was actually trying to kill someone else who was walking on the street near me. Or perhaps I was being too naïve. Well, denial can go a long way and putting things out of my mind was something I was getting good at. If I started to feel disturbed about the past, I would stop thinking about it and remind myself that I had my transmitter and police tail. Besides, being away from the hospital for the summer would do me good in many ways.

For the summer, I had made plans to work in a nursing home... I was to do anything from organizing Bingo to reading an electrocardiogram. I didn't mind doing a little of everything: the pay was good and there was no call at night. The work in the home would be lighter than the hospital's responsibilities and the change of surroundings would probably put the finishing touch on my confidence and sense of security.

The nursing home, called "Living Well Community," (it was not a community, but an old hotel turned into a senior residence), was in the suburbs, but only a half hour bus ride away. It would be nice to get out of the city during the day and walk on grass outside instead of hard pavement. There was a swimming pool maintained that I could use during my lunch break and free meals. It seemed like a good deal for me and I felt lucky to have gotten this position. As is usual with good jobs, it was who I knew, not what I knew that had assured me my spot. A good friend who had graduated medical school the year before had recommended me to the management before she had left.

I was told the transmitter would reach within a one hundred mile radius of the city, so my cares were still minimized. I was only mildly uneasy that Jack hadn't called me to see how I was. Well perhaps he was listening on the transmitter all day. Yet I had felt as though he had had at least a mild crush on me and I was anticipating his asking me out to dinner. As soon as I had the transmitter, however, he dropped out of the picture completely. Not that it would have been good anyway for us to start seeing each other. I liked the way his arms felt around me and there was something so reassuring and attractive about him. Yes, I wouldn't have minded kissing him at all. But we were like a fish and a bird. Me, the hard-working medical student with sights on doing surgery all day. He, the courageous detective, risking his life everyday, drinking coffee in his car as he worked. My parents definitely would not have approved of him and it didn't seem like a match to me.

On my last day of the medicine rotation, I decided to call him at the police precinct. I had a good excuse to: I could tell him I was finishing my last rotation for the year, was off for the summer and that everything was all right. I knew he knew all this already from my transmitter, but it would be a chance to talk to him. I actually missed him and was tired of waiting to see if he would call. He wasn't in and I left a message, but he never called back. I took that as a sign from him that he wasn't interested. So, another man down the drain… I had apparently misread him and our relationship was purely professional. I would see him again only if another attempt was made on my life. Well, maybe there would be someone to meet and go out with at the nursing home.

# Chapter 7

Living Well Community was built on a hill and overlooked a highway. The lobby still looked like a hotel lobby with the front desk manned by three people and the sofas were left over from days past. I went up to the desk and asked that the coordinator be paged. Those had been my instructions in the letter I had received a week ago. Grace Sutton was probably a social worker and she organized keeping the seniors occupied by things like movies and Mahjong. I was to be working under her except when someone had a medical problem: I was the first to see them and determine if the attending doctor (a full-fledged internist) should see them. Believe me, I was planning on sending everything from an earache to a headache to him… I wasn't planning on taking any chances or on being heroic. I hadn't seen that much illness to feel comfortable with diagnoses. My screening was just a formality.

Grace came into the lobby minutes after I paged her and I spotted her immediately. Somehow I had pictured her with a large clipboard and sure enough she had one. She was quite pretty, with long brown hair that was so thick it frequently fell into her face. Her eyes were light green and her body was very muscular. She must work out regularly, I thought. And why not? There must be a gym in this home too.

Grace recognized me and gave me a warm smile as she introduced herself. She gave me a strong handshake and ushered me into her office: a small room behind the front desk.

"It's not much," she commented with a wink. "Just large enough for my desk and two chairs, but I don't spend much time here anyway. When I get promoted, you can have this office to hang your coat up in." We giggled and I liked her immediately.

"Now, did anyone tell you about your responsibilities?" She became businesslike in a flash. I nodded.

"Bingo to check-ups." I answered.

"Well, I have to tell you this: Most people in this home have a lot of money and they also have their own private doctors. Some of them, even if they're having chest pain, will wait for their private doctors to come before doing anything else. A lot of the doctors make house calls here too because the residents are prepared to pay handsomely for doing so…off the record… cash. So you'll be much more busy with things like arranging a game of horseshoes than with listening to people's lungs with your stethoscope. Bring your stethoscope and equipment here anyway for safekeeping, just in case."

"We really do need you here, Nicky, and I think you'll manage great. You seem like someone who can take things as they come and who can handle a temperamental personality. A lot of the residents here are a bit moody. See, they're paying gallons of money to be here, so they think they have things coming to them. But don't worry. If you don't feel comfortable with something, just call me. I practically live here."

Well, her speech did scare me a little, though my friend who had this position before me had said it was a fun job. So, how bad could it be? How obnoxious could these people be? They lived through a lifetime, obviously knew a lot about life, if they were all so rich, so they would know something about handling other people. I always found that doctors were treated better by others than average, so maybe the residents would be more respectful of me. Grace was a social director, so maybe she received more poking than I ever would. Well, hopefully so.

"Now, are you ready to start your first day?" I nodded yes. "Any questions?" My nod said no. "O.K. Our first event today is a race in the pool. It's not a swimming race, but a walking race. We do this every morning and the winner gets a mug with our logo on it. Some of our residents have so many mugs, when they win one, they don't accept it. They'll probably give it to you. You'll have a whole set by the end of the summer." We laughed together. I wanted to find out more about Grace and maybe even be real friends if possible. She was such a warm person... I could see why the nursing home and the residents liked her so much (something my friend had told me).

The pool was located behind the building and looked like any other large pool. There were tables with umbrellas, lounge chairs and scattered towels. The only difference was the occasional walker or wheelchair, empty or occupied. There were about ten people waiting for us, all sitting by the edge of the pool with their feet dangling into the water. You could tell it was going to be warm day because it already felt hot at ten in the morning.

"Good morning everyone," Grace said sweetly. "I want you to meet our new doctor. Dr. Steinway, this is our wonderful swimming group." I smiled to silent faces that just stared at me without expression. "Now, now, let's all welcome Dr. Steinway." Silence.

"What happened to the other doctor?" A voice cried out.

"He moved to Oregon."

"Why?" Someone else asked. "We liked him."

"Well, you never used him," another voice piped in, "so why does it matter?"

"Now everyone," Grace chimed in, "let's make Dr. Steinway feel welcome. The last doctor got a very good job in Oregon, so she will be here for the summer. Now, what do we say to new people who join us?"

"Welcome, Dr. Steinway. We are happy to have you here," they droned like robots. I didn't feel very welcome at all, but Grace changed the mood by telling everyone to form a line in the shallow end of the pool for the walking race. The goal was to see who could walk in the waist-deep water to the other side of the pool. "Don't worry," she said to me on the side, "you'll be fine. It takes time, but they'll accept you."

The race was performed over and over again and the person who won the race more than five times received a mug. Thus, we were by the pool for the whole morning. All the events were geared to last a long time and to keep everyone busy.

Over the course of the day we concentrated on all sorts of activities, from Bingo to crocheting class to typing exercises. Practically the same people came to each activity, so I soon knew everyone by name and they became much more friendly to me. I was now called "Doc," and each doctor, according to Grace, was afforded a different affectionate name. One had even been called "handsome," just plain "handsome," because he was so good-looking. Well, "Doc" was fine with me and it had an endearing quality when someone cried out something like, "hey, Doc, can't you call out any of my Bingo numbers?" The things poor medical students will do for money... but I had a good first day. I went home on the bus humming a tune from the 1940's. Tomorrow was dance class and the home was very lucky to have Grace on the staff: she was really adept at all sorts of things, from crocheting to music and dance lessons.

The next day went well and I was beginning to feel at home in my new position. Eating in the lunchroom, different residents joined me at each meal and I began to learn how each one philosophized and how each viewed life.

As I sat eating lunch, Grace came up from behind me and patted me on the back.

"How's our new doc doing, everyone?" she said to the table. The three sitting with me all nodded in approval. "Well, Nicky, we have the horse races after lunch, so when you finish eating, come into the conference room and help me set up, O.K.?" I was on my last bite anyway, so I got up with my mouth full and a nod. Lunch was always the meal I was starving for, so I appreciated free food as part of my salary.

I followed Grace down the hall and she gave me a smile. "I think you're working out great, Nicky, and I think everyone really likes you. It was a wonderful idea having lunch in the dining room with them." I shrugged.

"What did the other doctors do in the past, take their meals outside so they could be alone?"

"No, but didn't you know that there's a staff dining room? Oh someone was supposed to tell you. You're more than welcome to eat with us too." I nodded. I didn't mind eating with the residents at all, finding out what kind of work they did and how they felt about the best way to get ahead in life. I could always use pointers. However, now and then I decided I should eat with the staff and get friendly with some of the higher-ups in the home to assure myself a position here next summer. I decided I wanted to come back again next year.

We entered the conference room, which was like a small, carpeted auditorium with rows of chairs and a movie screen at the front. It was used for all of the activities that involved a lot of people, like Bingo and movies and slide shows. It was used for meetings when the building was a hotel.

"This is how the horse races work, Nicky," Grace explained as she took an old movie projector out of a closet. The projector must have been about twenty years old... it was the kind of thing that was new when I was in elementary school. "I show various shorts from horse races, the residents bet on a particular horse and the ones that win receive – guess what? – a mug. Sometimes we play for money, when people request it. There's always someone who wants to play for money and it's always the same person. You see, we have horse races twice a week and most residents don't like to spend or lose money during our activities. It's not popular to play for money. You're going to meet a very lively resident today, Nicky, because she comes to all of our horse races and she always wants to play for money. She's a bit of a character, but a nice character. She actually should be here any minute. She's always early for the horse races and sits in the front row center. This is the only activity you'll see her at. And there she is now... Mrs. Suma." I nearly choked on my saliva. Sure enough, a small lady with a cane came walking in confidently. She waved her cane at Grace and smiled.

"Hey Grace, who's that with you?" she asked. As she walked towards us, it was clear that she didn't depend on the cane for support. She kept waving it at things as she passed and finally pointed it at us as she came up to us. Her hair was dyed bright red and she wore a dress that was expensive but fashionable about twenty years ago. Her make-up was carefully applied – only lipstick and a little rouge – and her nails were manicured. She stopped in front of us and looked me up and down. "This our new doctor?" Grace nodded yes. "Well, I've heard a lot about you, honey. Come see me in my room when you get a chance and we'll talk." I wanted to ask her right then and there if she was related Valentino Suma, but I almost didn't want to hear the answer. She walked away before I could respond with anything. Mrs. Suma sat in the front row and stared at the blank movie screen in front of her as more people came in and sat down.

Grace handed out cards to place bets on and the races began. The projector turned on and Mrs. Suma stood up and began to scream at the moving horses. The film was obviously very old, because there were lines and cracks in the picture, but no one seemed to be bothered by it… certainly not Mrs. Suma. Her shrieks intensified as the race ended and she jumped up and down, clearly having won. Then she turned to Grace and cried, "next race is for money, right Grace?" A chorus of "No's" sang out and Mrs. Suma sat down with a frown. "Bunch of old fogies." She said. "You all don't know how to live."

There were five races and no one got as excited as Mrs. Suma did. The rest of the crowd, about twenty people in all, were actually pretty quiet. Finally, Grace turned on the lights and gave all the winners their mugs. Mrs. Suma received four.

"You think I don't have enough of these?" she asked Grace and then turned to me. "Well, I've got plenty and I want to give one to the Doc. Is that O.K.?" Grace smiled and nodded yes, so she handed me a white mug with the name of the nursing home on it. Mrs. Suma winked at me. "Something to cheer you up after what you've been through recently." She turned abruptly and walked out of the room. "Don't forget to visit me soon, doc!" I stared at her and wondered if her words had more meaning than they seemed. A shiver ran down my spine.

Grace looked at me as she rewound the movie tape. "Quite a lady, huh, Nicky?"

"Where'd she come from?" Is she always that peppy and lively?"

"Always. She comes from a wealthy family who takes good care of her. On Sunday she must have thirty people come to see her. All family. They seem very close to her. She must have ten grandchildren and some great grandchildren. Go and visit her sometime. She'll tell you some great stories." I would do that soon... very soon.

The rest of the day was unremarkable. We had some more activities and I did some paperwork with Grace. I didn't see Mrs. Suma again, but I couldn't get her out of my mind. What did she mean by saying, "after what you've been through recently?" Was it innocent, or did she know more than I thought? There was only one way to find out.

I was sitting with Grace when I reached for the directory. Grace grabbed my hand and her face took a serious turn.

"What?" I asked. "I just want to look up a resident."

"Its' late, Nicky. Why don't you go home?" It was five o'clock... not so late. "Who do you want to see?"

"Mrs. Suma. She would be fun to talk to I think."

"You really aren't supposed to socialize with the residents. Rule number one around here. You'll see her at the races again on Wednesday." Well, this was bizarre... Grace was the one who originally told me to visit her. I wasn't going to argue with my boss, however. I nodded and got up.

"O.K. I'll see you tomorrow then." Grace's smile returned and she released my hand.

"See you tomorrow, Nicky. I just want you to know that I think you're working out really well." I smiled and thanked her as I left. But I was intrigued. Now I knew I had to meet with Mrs. Suma... something was going on and maybe Grace was in on it. Perhaps I was just being paranoid, but I would find out only one way: by talking to Mrs. Suma. Jack would agree.

So, I walked down the driveway as though I was going to the bus, but I made a sharp left into the pool area and walked behind the building. I needed to get back inside and get a hold of a directory.

The back door to the kichen was open, and there it was hanging by a string on the wall. Clementina Suma, Room 309. That was easy.

I found the back staircase and began to climb the stairs. She should be in her room now… it was after dinner and everyone was in for the evening.

I found her room without any trouble and heard opera music inside. I knocked on the opened door, but no one answered. I paused and then walked in.

The room was filled with antique furniture, with a dining table in the center, a bed on the side and a huge bureau and mirror standing against a wall. The curtains were very ornate, with tassels and lace… obviously she had taken many things from her house with her here. And there was Clementina Suma, sitting in front of a television set in the corner. She looked very small in a recliner, fingering the remote control, her eyes closed, her head nodding to the opera music. Should I disturb her? I touched the transmitter which lay against my chest. They would find this extremely interesting.

Mrs. Suma opened her eyes, looked up and smiled at me.

"Ah, you came for a visit. I'm so happy. Sit, sit down." She pointed to one of the chairs by the dining table. I drew it up next to her as she shut off the television with a flick of her finger. "Modern times, no? I sit with all my old furniture and push buttons. Come closer and we'll talk. I know more about you than you think. But maybe you know more about me than I think too." What a complicated woman... what was she getting at?

"Tell me, Dr. Steinway, how is it that you came here?"

"I got this job through a friend who was graduating."

"Destiny then? Maybe. Maybe not."

"What do you mean?"

"My family, we have a lot of influence in this area."

"What does your family have to do with me?"

"Maybe nothing, maybe something."

"You always talk in riddles, Mrs. Suma." I smiled to hide my frustration, but I really wanted to shake her.

"No, I won't anymore. I want to tell you about myself so you'll know everything and then no more riddles. You have some time?" I nodded yes. I would hear anything she had to say... for me, for the police department. Maybe she was indeed the key to the whole string of my recent adventures. Maybe I was really here because of her. I felt as though I was coming under her spell as she spoke.

"I am a good person, Dr. Steinway. What is your first name, my dear?"

"Nicky."

"Ah, yes, Nicky. You and I , we are good people... good blood in us. Not so with everyone. I don't have to tell you." She sighed.

"I've been in this country for sixty-five years... an eternity. I came over from Italy when I was sixteen: a new bride. My husband, he came to get me."

"Me, I was beautiful. The most beautiful girl in my town. But beauty didn't put bread on the table. We were starving. My father was a farmer and somehow he couldn't make enough to feed all of us – all twelve of us. You don't see such families anymore. Imagine having so many children that you can't sit all of them at the table at once! I ate on the floor with my brothers. The oldest ones sat at the table... the younger ones on the floor. And only one meal a day. That's all we could afford.'

"So what did I do when I got hungry? I would go down to the market and smile at the shopkeepers. They'd give me food and hope for a kiss, but they never got it. I was a good girl, though always hungry. That's what I remember most about my childhood...walking around hungry.'

'One day I heard one of the shopkeepers talking about his cousin in America: A powerful rich man who had many people working for him. He sent money to this shopkeeper and wrote him many stories about cars – that to me sounded like a miracle. To move without a horse was unthinkable! – and alligator shoes and big cigars that took hours to smoke. What a life he seemed to have. And he wasn't married. He was old to me at the time. Thirty could be sixty to a sixteen year old girl. But what did I do, I set my sight on him. I asked the shopkeeper to see his picture and sure enough he was quite handsome. I remember he had a gold watch chain on his jacket and that in those times was a sure sign of being rich. He had a thick mustache and such a nice figure. He looked so confident in that picture, standing with one foot up on a chair, as though he owned the world. I knew if I could catch him, I would have the world at my feet and all the food I could eat.'

'Well, this shopkeeper had quite a crush on me and I told him I would trade a kiss for this man's picture and one of his letters. He found it amusing that I should want these things, but he didn't care. It was an easy exchange and I ran off with my new dream.'

'The forest was the most quiet place to sit down and write a letter. I took an old piece of paper, sat under a tree and wrote to this distant cousin of the shopkeeper, enclosing a picture of myself. It was no easy feat getting a picture of myself either... it cost a lot of money in those days to get a photo. I told him that I was sixteen years old, knew his cousin a little and would make a good wife for him. Can you imagine anything so courageous? In those days, to write a letter to a man was unthinkable, especially if he hadn't written to you first. But I was desperate and didn't want to live like a peasant anymore. To marry one of the men in the village was a sentence of poverty for life. I wanted better and would do whatever I had to to get it. My parents were already keeping their eyes open for a husband for me. The only men around were poor and had no future.'

'Even to get the postage for the letter was a trial for me... it was a lot of money for me then. Imagine not having enough money to mail a letter! That shows you how poor I was.'

'Well, I waited and waited. After a month, I finally approached the shopkeeper and asked him if he had heard from his cousin at all. No, he said. He hadn't heard from him for awhile and was in need of the money he usually sent him, so he was watching the mail too.'

'Another month went by and I was giving up. Maybe I was foolish to think that one letter could bring a prince to rescue me from my village. How could I think that one look at a picture would make someone decide to marry me and bring me to America? I began to look at the men in my village and to even go out with one or two. But they all had no dreams and no ambition. One of the biggest dreams I heard was of owning a mule. I laughed in his face when he told me this. What? I said. Don't you want to leave here and open a store or go to America? How can you raise a family on mule droppings and dirt?'

'So, no one wanted to go out with me. I was a snob to everyone and no men came to visit. I didn't care, but my parents cared very much. My mother was always wringing her handkerchief, saying over and over again, Clementina, how will you get a husband like this? You are living in a dream world. You are waiting for the impossible. You must marry someone and if you get a good man like your father, what more could you want? He'll treat you well, help you raise the children well enough and you'll be happy. You're so foolish, you don't even know what will make you happy.'

'But I knew, all right, that I wanted more for myself. The problem was, I couldn't figure out how to get it. If I were a man, I could go off on my own and seek my fortune in the big city. But not as a woman. I would be raped or killed or who-knows-what on my own.'

'I would often go to the forest to take a walk or sit by the lake near the town trying to figure out how to advance myself and how even to get a worthwhile husband. I just couldn't see why I should tie myself down to a life of poverty and hunger like my mother did. And only because she thought she got a good man. I developed the reputation in the town of being a dreamer, always dreaming by the lake. I didn't care.'

'One day, I was walking home from the lake when I saw a great commotion in front of our little house. There was actually a motor car parked in front and maybe a dozen people walking around it touching it and marveling at it. Who was visiting? We didn't know anyone with a car. Then my heart jumped and I wondered if it was him… the man I had written to…Valentino Suma. I looked down at my worn dress and faded shoes. Well, maybe I was still beautiful enough for him. I ran down the hill and stared at the shiny motor car.'

'What is happening here?' I asked. Someone answered that a visitor from America had come… a very handsome man. It had to be him. I smoothed out my skirt, took a deep breath and walked through the front door into the kitchen.'

'My mother and father were sitting at the table with a man whose back was to me. My mother looked up at me and smiled. She hadn't smiled at me in three months, ever since we were arguing over who I should marry.'

'The man turned around slowly, as though anticipating the moment, and sure enough it was him, the one in the picture. Only in person he was so good-looking, he could take your breath away. His eyes were dark, his moustache neatly trimmed and his smile was devastating. He wore a very fine suit and shiny shoes. A real gentleman.'

'He stood up to greet me, took my hand and kissed it on both sides. "'I am Valentino Suma, Clementina," he said in Italian. "'I came a long way to meet you."' He turned to my mother. "'May I take Clementina for a walk around your farm/? One of my men will escort us."' My mother nodded yes without a word, he bowed to her and then led me outside. I had never seen a man with such manners. I don't think anyone had ever bowed to my mother… not even my father.'

'He walked tall and proud, a man with real confidence, and his "man" walked several feet behind us. I didn't know who the "man" was, or what he was for, or why Valentino came with four such men, but I could barely breathe, I was so excited.'

"'You are even more beautiful than your picture, Clementina.'" Why I was thinking the same thing about him. "'You have had a tough life, haven't you, for a girl who is only sixteen? Well, I had to fight and scratch my way up to the top too.'" He stopped walking and turned to me. "'So you want to show me your farm?'" Why would such a gentleman want to see our cows and horses? I was too breathless to speak, so just turned to the farmhouse without a word and he followed.'

'As we stood in the farmhouse, however, and I started to tell him about the animals, including my favorite goat, my tongue loosened up and I felt more comfortable with him. I even told him about the rabbit I had caught last year which I kept in a cage. He seemed to enjoy my stories, so I kept telling him about each animal we had, its name, and how we had come to own it.'

'Well these stories must seem strange to someone like you. But I'm glad you came so I could tell them to you,' I said with a smile.'

Well, the whole town was talking about the stranger from America who had come to meet me. He only stayed for a week, but we saw each other everyday and every evening. He would take me to the fancy restaurants around the town and send me a new dress the day before to wear.'

'Of course, my mother was overwhelmed and my father didn't know what to think, even after I told them about the letter I had written. My mother let me keep the dresses that were sent to me only when I promised to give them back after I wore them. I really wasn't planning on returning them, even if Valentino went back to America without me. They were too beautiful and made of silk and lace.'

'But Valentino had to take me back with him to America. He spoke of a big house he owned in a place called Long Island and a townhouse in the city. He had many people who ran his businesses and respected him tremendously. All he had to do was walk into a restaurant and he was given the best table immediately. See what money does, Clementina? He said to me. All this. And we both had the same dreams... to be on top and never be hungry.'

'Valentino was always the perfect gentleman and barely kissed me on the cheek at the end of each evening out. I wondered if I was doing something wrong. I wanted to kiss him on the lips and see what it was like to kiss a man. Then I thought he may go back to his home and just write me a letter once a month, the way he did with his shopkeeper cousin. Eventually the letters would stop coming and the whole meeting would be a dream.'

'I couldn't sleep at night because I was so worried. He never mentioned anything to me about a future together or his feelings towards me. And I couldn't say anything because it wasn't proper. So there was my torture.'

'When the last day of his visit came, I got up in the morning and found my mother in the kitchen. What will I do when he goes away without me? I asked. Her. She shook her head and put the pot down that she was washing.'

"'Clementina, I have given this whole thing a lot of thought. Nothing here is natural. A rich stranger from America comes here just to meet you, takes you to fine places you will never see again and you are expecting him to take you back with him? He should just hand you a life of luxury? Clementina, let me enlighten you. He had business in this country, took a week off to escort a beautiful girl to fancy places, and he will go home and forget you. He hasn't mentioned marrying you, he hasn't spoken to your father about you. It's as simple as that. Now maybe you won't have so many dreams and you'll settle for a man from town.'"

'I sat down and put my head in my hands. Maybe I was wishing for too much. Well, Valentino was coming over later this afternoon and I wasn't going to let him go so easily. Maybe things would change. Maybe I could make them change.'

'As always, a beautiful dress in my size came by messenger later in the morning. I had to look extra beautiful this day, my last day. Valentino came as usual at 4 o'clock. I was ready and my father came home early to greet him and say good-bye. I think my father was also hoping that Valentino might want to ask his permission to marry me. So, on a very unusual weekday afternoon, my father was sitting at the kitchen table drinking some hot water, instead of working.

'Valentino walked in with a bouquet roses and handed them to my mother. Then he bowed to my father with a big grin on his face.'

'"I have just received some great news, my friends. I have made quite a bit of money on a business deal. But I will still be humble when I ask if I can take your daughter back to America with me as my wife."'

'My father's eyebrows climbed up his forehead and my mother stood dumb-founded, fingering her apron.'

'"I will take good care of her. She will have the best of everything and will live like a queen. I am a very wealthy man and have fallen hopelessly in love with her."'

'Valentino didn't even look at me or my parents as he spoke: he gazed out the window, as though in a trance. My heart was dancing. He was saying all of the right things to win over my parents.'

'My father stood up, shook Valentino's hand and said happily, "she is yours, my friend – I mean, my son. I hope you weren't expecting any dowry."'

'I walked up to him shamelessly and tilted my headup to him to be kissed. With surprising force, he wrapped his arms around me, squeezed me hard and pressed his lips to mine for what seemed like an hour. I don't know if my head was spinning from the kiss, or because he was holding me so tight. I was breathless as he let me go.'

'"Well, let's empty out the car and celebrate,'" Valentino said happily. He went back outside and motioned to two men waiting by the car.Soon the whole kitchen was filled with food: whole cooked chickens, potatoes, cakes, steaks. It was more food than my family had seen in a year!

'We celebrated all day, but Valentino suddenly didn't seem to notice me. He was drinking and celebrating with our neighbors and friends and toasting my name, but didn't come over to me once to talk to me or see how I was. I assumed it was because he was so happy, but it seemed strange, even for a young girl like myself. Usually new couples couldn't be separated from each other.'

'We were to leave the next morning, get married quickly and board the boat to America by eleven. As Valentino got up to leave that evening, after everyone had left, he asked me to walk him to his car.'

"'Clementina,I will make you a good husband. I will give you everything and will keep you satisfied in every way. In return, I want you to be a devoted wife and give me sons.'" It sounded like a business arrangement the way he put it. But I was so happy to be leaving my life of poverty and to go to America. I was also entranced with this handsome man, who was actually still a stranger to me, though I didn't know it."

"You will pack whatever you have and say good-bye to this place forever. I will not be back and neither will you."

"'But what if I want to see my parents?"

"'They will come to America. You don't belong here anymore.'"

'Well, I thought, that would be argued at a later time. My mother always said that if you disagree with a man, do it tomorrow when you and he are more calm.'

'That night, when everyone was asleep, my father came to my bed and motioned me to come outside. We walked quietly and sat down on the front porch.'

"'Clementina, I want to make sure that you think you are doing the right thing. Valentino seems like an honorable man and will certainly take care of you with his money, but I am not sure that you are in love with each other. He doesn't look at you like a man so much in love. You will also have to leave us and we probably won't see each other for a long time, if ever again. I only say these things because I love you so much.'"

'I nodded and felt tears come to my eyes. I had wanted to leave so much, but now that the reality had really come, I was pulled both ways. I loved my parents and I was confused by Valentino's behavior. On one side he had really asked to marry me, but on the other he had been so cold to me today.'

"'I have always tried for the family," my father went on. "I know we are poor, I know you've always had higher dreams. I could never give you what Valentino can give you. But I can give you all the love you need. I'm not sure he can.'" He sighed. So he had noticed Valentino's behavior too. "'Well, I can see that you've made your decision and I hope to God it's the right one. I have only one more thing to go over with you. Your mother really should be doing this, but she refused. She felt that you and I were always closer, so it should come from me.'"

"'You will be a wife and your first duty is always to your husband. Stand by him, even if everyone seems to be against him. Open yourself to him mentally and physically whenever he needs you. If you do all this, he will treat you like a queen and never abandon you. You have a strong will, I know. You can have your way as a daughter, but not as a wife. A wife must be obedient and passive. You will see. Just remember my words."' I nodded quietly and had nothing to reply. I supposed he was right and that this was the way to handle Valentino.'

'His car came for me early in the morning and I had all my things packed in a small sack. All of my brothers and sisters cried and hugged me good-bye. My father held me close the longest and kissed me on the ears.'

'"Write to us, Clementina. And if you are unhappy, come back to us."'

'That's when I realized all the doubt that my father had. He may have been poor, but he was very wise.'

'I was told by the driver of the car that Valentino had business that morning and would meet me on the boat. So we traveled for two hours before I saw the pier and a giant boat which astounded me. I had never seen such a boat with so many windows!'

'The driver handed me my ticket without a word and escorted me to the ramp that led to the boat. So many fancy-looking people were boarding and here I was a little girl with a sack of old clothes under her arm. But I boarded with my chin high and was guided to a beautiful cabin with a bouquet of fresh flowers. I remember the flowers in particular because they were the most beautiful flowers I had ever seen. All I had seen on the farm were daisies. I don't think I knew what a rose was till that moment.'

'I waited and waited for Valentino to arrive, like a scared bird in a cage. I kept looking out of the porthole, listening to the commotion outside on the pier and the sounds of boat horns. I didn't even know what time the boat was to set sail.'

'Finally a key turned in the lock and he came in. He looked so calm and genteel and gave me half a smile. No big hug, no "I love you," or even a "how are you." He just told me we had to go right to the captain's quarters. He had asked the captain to marry us quickly before the ship set sail, and we had four of those men who followed Valentino around as the witnesses. It wasn't the way I thought I would get married. No parents, no singing and dancing… it didn't feel like a happy occasion.'

'As soon as we were married, Valentino whisked me back to the cabin and sat me down on the edge of the bed.'

'"Did your parents give you a lesson on what it is to be a good wife, Clementina?"'

'"I think I know. I will be true to you and devoted."' He laughed.

'"Yes, yes, of course, Now I will show you what else a good wife does."'

'He sat down next to me, grabbed me by my shoulders and began to kiss my neck roughly. Sometimes he would bite me and I would cry out to him to stop when he did that. But my cries seemed to entice him more and make him bite me harder on the neck. Was this what all husbands did to their wives on their wedding nights?'

'Suddenly his hand grabbed the front of my dress and tore it open, spraying buttons all over the floor. He tore my petticoat too and handled my breasts roughly as he leaned on top of me and pinned me to the bed. His hands kept pinching my breasts till they hurt and he leaned down to bite me hard on the stomach. He was like an animal and I stifled my cries for fear he would become even more gruff.'

'I tried to help him take off the rest of my dress, which my mother had so carefully sewn, but he got angry and said, "let me do it," with a fierceness I had never heard from a man. He tore it off at the seams and kept coming at me with his lips and his teeth. Finally, his mouth closed over mine – I could barely breath – and his hands pushed my legs open. There was no tenderness, no love, just an animal's lust.'

"He thrust himself inside of me and I screamed in pain. I was scared and so confused. I thought love-making was supposed to be wonderful. He liked my screaming and snarled in my ear as he pumped in and out, hurting me with every movement. I wanted to throw him off, and scratched his back in desperation. I had had enough at this point. That made him more angry and he pumped harder and harder... I felt like my insides were being crushed.'

'Finally he gasped and collapsed on top of me, his sweat dripping down my sides. I didn't know what to do, so I lay as still as he, listening to his heavy breathing, seeing his blood under my fingernails. What had I done? I asked myself. What kind of a man had I married?'

'Well, from that moment on, I had plenty to eat, plenty to wear – all of which Valentino took care of – but no love in my life. During the whole boat ride I was confined to the cabin most of the time, except for some brief walks on the deck with Valentino. Food was brought to my room and he would leave me alone in the cabin most of the time, forbidding me to go anywhere. So, I would sleep during the day or listen to the sound of laughing on deck. I don't know where he went most of the day, but he would come to the cabin at the same time each evening and make love to me in the same rough way. I dreaded hearing his key in the lock.'

'When we walked on the deck, I would be wearing something he picked out for me. His arm would be tied around mine and he would smile and try to act witty and kind.'

"'Why are you so different out here than you are in the cabin?'" I asked one time.'

'His smile vanished and he stiffened. '"Clementina, let's get one thing straight. You are my wife and as my wife you have only one purpose: to give me a son. After that, you may do what you like and be free of me if you like. I need a son to carry on my businesses.'"

'"You don't love me?'"

'"No, I don't. You are very beautiful, so my son will be very handsome. That is good. I wanted you because you are young and fresh and were desperate to leave your home. You will bear healthy children. That is all you are to me. I have many beautiful women who are happy to have me in their beds. You will learn that and you will learn not to expect me home at night once we have a son. Besides all the businesses I run, I have many women to keep happy and spoiled.'"

'I sat down on a lounge chair and felt tears well up in my eyes. All of my ideas of marriage had been dashed to the ground.'

'" I know all of this sounds cruel to you, but you have married a man with many responsibilities. In return for the simple things I have just asked of you, you will have everything you want… jewels, clothes and plenty of food. You can have your own man on the side too, if you want.'" He found this very funny and laughed out aloud.

'"The only thing I want right now is to go back to my family. I don't want to be your wife.'" He laughed again.

'"You are so naïve, Clementina. You can't go back… you can only go forward. You will never see your parents again. I am the only one you have in this world now. You made your choice. You had the option of saying no to me when I offered to take you away from that dirty shack you lived in. So, you got what you wanted and now you are stuck with it. Come… back to the cabin.'" I knew what that meant and I resisted him. With great force he lifted me off my feet and dragged me off the deck to our cabin below.'

'When we reached America, Valentino took me to a very big house in the country. It was as big as the town hall of my village back home. The entryway was two floors high with a curved staircase and beautiful rugs. Our bedroom was like a sanctuary with thick rugs and soft curtains. I thought if was so heavenly, and if I didn't have such a cruel husband, I would have really been in heaven.'

'He would be gone all day and even some nights. When he was home, though, it meant more terrible lovemaking. He became rougher with me, especially when I was not becoming pregnant. He would slap me across the face as he jumped on top of me, or bite my cheek so hard he left tooth marks for a few days which I tried to cover up with make-up. I cursed myself over and over for choosing this life. Though I wasn't hungry for food or clothing, I hungered for company, someone to confide in and trust. I was left to myself all day: the servants were forbidden to talk to me, and all I could do was walk around the grounds and take naps in the afternoon. You would think that that is a wonderful life, but to have a closet full of clothes, a house full of expensive furniture and a Frigidaire full of food isn't everything. Without love, you have nothing.'

'I started to pray that I would become pregnant. Maybe then Valentino would treat me more like a human being. Maybe he would worship me and my body if I carried his son.'

'Sure enough, I finally became pregnant after seven months of marriage to that monster. When I told him, he was sitting in a large easy chair, sipping some wine. His face softened in a way I had never seen and he patted his knee.'

'"Come sit in my lap, my Clementina."' Those were tender words I had never heard. I sat in his lap and wondered if he was going to slap me again across the face. He began to play with my hair and kissed me gently on the cheek. '"I am so happy, my dear. We will be happy again."' When were we ever happy? I thought. But I sat quietly, as he stroked my hair.'

'So, life got a little better for me as a pregnant wife. Valentino made sure to be home every night. We had dinner like a proper husband and wife in the dining room together and he always wanted to hear about my day.'

'Every Friday he would bring home a present for me… a piece of jewelry, a jacket, a pair of shoes. He knew just what would fit me.'

'My son was my jewel sent from God. We named him Valentino, after his father, of course, and he became my whole world. As soon as my son entered the world, my husband left me alone completely. He took a separate bedroom and rarely even came home. When he did come home, it was only to see his son and to note how he was progressing. He wasn't around when little Valentino said mommy or doggie for the first time, and when he came for a visit, he brought plenty of toys and gifts for us. My husband was almost kind when he came, but he never stayed long. He was always packing his bag in no time and then gone for another month or two. I wondered if he had another house somewhere and another woman. I didn't care… as long as he left me alone, kept sending money and watching over us from afar.'

'One day Valentino came home and looked at our three year old son. '"Clementina, Valentino should get out more, now that he is getting older. You may have free use of the limousine to take rides and go out on your own. But each time you go out, you must take Valentino and the nanny with you."'

'I felt so happy. Up till now, I was forbidden to leave the grounds. So, we went to the stores and the restaurants, just little Valentino, the nanny and me. I noticed that everywhere we went in the area, the shopkeepers knew who I was and treated me like royalty. I decided it was because my husband was rich, but it was more than that.'

'One day we were having lunch in a restaurant and little Valentino threw up all over a fancy tablecloth. The waiters came over to change the table and the owner bowed to me. '"Please tell your husband how nice we were to you and that we gave you our best service,"' he said clasping his hands together. '"You may not want to tell him that your son threw up here. He may think I did not serve you good food."'

'"Why are you so scared of my husband?"' I asked.'

'"I am not scared. He is a great and powerful man."' He bowed and retreated. A man who was staring at me came over and sat down at my table. He was young and handsome and smoked a cigarette.'

'"Excuse me, Madame,"' he said quietly. '"Don't you know who your husband is?"'

'"Of course I do. He's Valentino Suma."'

'"I mean don't you know what he does?"'

'"He is a successful businessman. What do you want? Maybe you should leave me alone."'

'"Your husband is a mobster, Mrs. Suma. He will get into big trouble someday and you won't be able to help him. Here is my card if I can ever be of service to you—"' At that a large man in a black suit came to the table and tapped him on the shoulder.'

"'You should be going now, Mister,'" the large man said. The other got up immediately and walked out of the restaurant without a word.'

"I recognized the big man. He was one of the men who was always with Valentino.'

"'Are you following me?'" I asked him. He nodded and said, "I am protecting you from people like him" He sat down at a nearby table and I looked down at the business card... the big man obviously hadn't noticed that I was given this card. It read, "Brian Schuman, Investigator." And then a phone number.'

'Walking out of the restaurant, I noticed the big man not far behind and realized he must have always been following us. His car was behind ours on the way home and I felt safe yet betrayed at the same time. Was he there to protect us, or to watch what we did and report back to my husband? Why didn't he want me to talk to the investigator?'

'My curiosity was peaked. Why did Mr. Schuman say that Valentino was a mobster? Was it because he was jealous of his business dealings, or because Valentino was really crooked? I knew that I couldn't visit this investigator freely. I would be followed and maybe someone would be listening on the phone if I called this Brian Schuman. I couldn't figure out a way to call him or get to him, so I put his card under my underwear.'

'As little Valentino grew, he became so handsome and smart. His father started to take him out for an afternoon or a day, to the office or on an outing. I felt very lonely without my little boy, walking around the house or the grounds idly, waiting for my precious son to come back home. It was never an option to let me come along either. Little Valentino loved his father so much and looked up to him, saying he wanted to be just like him when he grew up. Of course, my husband ate this up and took him out more and more. Soon the two of them were so close that when little Valentino – I call him this to this day – got into trouble, he would go to his father before coming to me. He once crashed his sportscar to bits – he was completely unharmed – and I didn't even know about it until my husband told me a month later. And my husband took great pride in pointing out to me how close he had become to little Valentino. He knew it hurt me, so he would smile when he said something like, "'Clementina, did you know that little Valentino has his first crush on a girl? He told me the other day.'" I would just nod in silence, feeling so sad that my son was being taken from me slowly.'

'And my son would often talk down to me as though I were dumb and barely worth talking to. He definitely developed an attitude, which became worse, the more time he spent with his father. It's true I was from a small town and had no schooling, but I was always a good person and loved my son dearly.'

'Sometimes, when I sensed that little Valentino was in a good mood – and he was about eighteen at this time – I would ask him about his father's businesses. What did he do exactly all day? Why did he leave town so often?'

'I stopped asking soon enough because my son would start to make fun of me. "How long have you been married to Dad and you don't even know what he does? No wonder he is so disgusted with you. How can you be close to a wife and mother who doesn't know anything about you and just starts to ask questions after twenty years?'

'Felling that I was truly losing my son, I decided to visit this Brian Schuman. I managed to arrange an appointment with him during a week when my husband and son were on a business trip. I don't think I was followed. Somehow, when little Valentino didn't accompany me on my outings I was not followed. I went into a ladies clothing store and went out the back entrance. From there I went into the back entrance of the police station. I had pre-arranged this with Mr. Schuman. I think it worked well.'

'Brian Schuman had a small office in the police department and told me all sorts of things about my husband. He proved it all by showing me newspaper clippings. Yes, Valentino was a powerful and ruthless man and it looks like he had even killed a few people, though the police did not have enough evidence to bring him in. I was shocked by the whole thing and wondered where my husband and son were going when they went on "business trips." What was my husband teaching little Valentino? How to kill? How to be tough?'

'The detective ended our session by handling me another card and saying that if I was ever being mistreated or was scared, I should call him and he would help me. He was very nice, but I knew what he was really after: Valentino. And even though I was isolated and not feeling very loved, Valentino did see that I had everything. There was always a car at my disposal, as much cash in the house as I could spend , plenty of food. It was still enough to make me feel grateful for what I had. And, though he had taken over my son, he was doing what he felt was right for his future. He needed someone to fill his shoes. But if they were such dirty shoes, I didn't feel good about it. I would have to speak to Valentino. He would have to hear me.'

'Talking to my husband did nothing. He sneered at me and told me again that my only purpose in life had been to provide him with a strong and healthy son, which I had done, so now I could do whatever I wanted. I could spend all the money he gave me, relax at home. He would make no demands of me except to be his wife in public, for the few affairs we went to, and run the house, as I was doing.'

'I felt very empty during those days. I had no one to confide in, no one to be with, no one to care for. And that was my life. I wrote to my family and invited them to come, but my father was too proud. If he came to America, it would be with his money, not mine. Such a stubborn man. Valentino absolutely forbade me to visit them.'

'I painted a bright picture to my parents. I told them about the tutors that Valentino had hired to teach me English and how to write. My parents themselves didn't know how to read or write, so when a letter came, they took it to the shopkeeper they knew. He would read it to them and then write me back with my father dictating.'

'I told them about the big house we lived in, all the traveling that Valentino did and how he was "training" little Valentino. I didn't write about the scorn that I put up with privately or the suffering I felt.'

'So you see, Dr. Nicky, I grew old without my husband or son being close to me. I always had plenty of money, but I barely knew the family I created. My husband died young in an accident and my little Valentino died during heart surgery. Sounds sad, doesn't it?'

Mrs. Suma looked down into her lap in silence. "Even though I was not close to my son, it is a great loss to lose him. A mother should never outlive her son. He left me well off, though. I got all the things I had wanted as a young girl, but I had never thought about the other things that mattered."

I put my hand over hers and then looked at my watch. It was 11 p.m. I had completely lost track of the time while listening to her.

"So take a lesson from me, Dr. Steinway. Money and being in America are important, but so is family. A husband has to give love. I was blessed with one thing, though... my beautiful grandson."

I jolted my head up to stare at her. There was more family down the line?

"My grandson Nathan was closer to me than any child I had ever known. You see, Little Valentino married a girl from another rich family... an arranged marriage. He didn't love her and used her like I was used... just to produce a son. One son they had and she would not name him Valentino if she died for it. Nathan was the name she wanted and I don't know why, but My Valentino allowed him to have that name. I think Roberta – that was my daughter-in-law – resented my little Valentino in the same way I resented my husband. She knew she had just been some sort of a vessel for him... a method to continue the chain for the sake of the business. My husband had taught my son well, not only in running the business, but in how to treat his wife. So, Roberta and I became very close and we raised Nathan together practically. She was over the house everyday. You'll meet Nathan soon. He comes to visit me often. He works in The Golden Apple Club. Maybe he even owns it now... I'm not sure."

Clementina Suma yawned slowly and patted me on the hand. "I am tired now, and you must be too. You go home or do what you have to. You come and visit me again soon. After dinner like tonight is good. I'll tell you more stories."

I got up slowly and told her I'd be back soon. I fingered the wire around my neck and hoped the police had gotten the whole story. But I was very tired suddenly and knew that I had to go home. We said good-night and I walked into the dim hallway. After nine o'clock the lights in the halls were turned down automatically by a timer. It gave me an eery feeling and I walked quickly to the main lobby. Now I would have to wait for the bus in the dark. It was a good neighborhood,and I was feeling safe because of the wire around my neck and my supposed police tail.

# Chapter 8

A cool breeze blew as I looked around at the street. The suburbs seemed to close down at 9 p.m… the city would still be bustling. A chill ran up my spine as some bushes rustled behind me in the wind. I wished the bus would come already. Then I heard the heavy sound of the engine and in no time the bus chugged up to me. I got on, feeling safe again, but sat down near the driver. There were only two other people on the bus, one way in the back and an elderly man sleeping toward the center.

Now I had to think. Should I go to the police station and get further instructions? Should I check in with Jack? He would surely get in touch with me now. This was a good session and provided another link to the chain. I closed my eyes and rested my head back against the window. I would think more clearly after a good night's rest. Yes, things would pull together tomorrow and then I would know what to do. What a life that lady had had.

The next day I didn't see Mrs. Suma, even at the horse races and I asked Grace where she was. Wasn't it unusual for her not even to come to the races?

"She's probably having visitors today, Nicky. That's the only thing that would keep her away from the horses." We chuckled.

I received the phone call after lunch.

"Nicky? Jack Jeffries." I sighed in relief. "Can you come down to my office after work today, say 6 o'clock? Need to talk to you."

"Sure. Have you-"

"Don't say anything else. You're on a phone, Nicky. We'll go over everything in person." Of course… how could I be so naïve? Someone could be listening."

# Chapter 9

Jack's office was in the police station and smelled like old papers. The big wooden desk was cluttered and a file cabinet in the corner had all its drawers open. The stiff chair creaked as I sat down across from him. He stood up from behind the desk to shake my hand and then dropped into his chair.

"You're looking as beautiful as ever. That nursing home must be agreeing with you." I looked at him quietly. I was a little angry with him for dropping out of the picture for so long before contacting me again.

"Where've you been?" I asked plainly.

"Working on a drug bust. We got the suckers, so now I can focus more on you. First, how've you been? Are you O.K.?" He sure could be charming and I softened at his concern for me.

"I've been O.K. Life's been quiet lately."

"Good. Now let's get down to business. That conversation you had with Mrs. Suma the other night was very interesting. We knew she was Mr. Suma's mother and it's so fortunate that you were able to talk to her like that. Not that we got anything much, but at least we got the info about her grandson. I want you to go and talk to him."

"Don't you have detectives to do that? You don't need me anymore. I want to keep wearing this transmitter, though. It makes me feel safe. Who's listening on the other end? Do you ever listen?"

"Sometimes. This is the deal. If I send a detective to speak to Nathan Suma, it'll crack open a can of worms. He'll get suspicious, start to watch his movements, maybe tell someone that a detective came to see him."

"Why, you suspect him of killing Ralph?"

"No, not al all. But he may know who did and he may tell that person that a detective visited him and was asking a lot of questions. Then we lose any advantage that we had. Enter Nicky Steinway, innocent, naïve medical student. Wants to meet the grandson of her favorite patient, Mrs. Suma. Heard a lot about you, Nathan, you say. Maybe you'll make friends, have a few close conversations and he can give us some clues."

"I won't be a whore…"

"No, no, nothing like that. Look: just have a drink with him and talk to him a little. That's all. We'll do the rest. This whole picture just doesn't fit together, Nicky. Ralph's murder doesn't make sense and I'll bet you apples for oranges that the grandson knows something about it. And what you said about Mr. Suma's body not being Mr. Suma doesn't fit together either. If it really wasn't Mr. Suma that you saw on that morgue table, we've got a real situation. So, let's see what happens. We may even have to get the DNA lab involved here." I nodded.

Jack stood up and handed me a piece of paper with the name and address of The Golden Apple Club. "Let me walk you home. Or can I take you out to dinner? Did you eat yet?" I wanted to have dinner with him and he smiled boyishly when I told him so.

We ate at a Chinese restaurant down the street and he told me about the drug bust he had just made. He was so proud of himself, though his work sounded so dangerous.

"I could never be a police officer or a detective," I said. "I don't have the courage or the gump"

"Oh, that's not true. You've been handling this case very well."

"That's because you're guiding me. You know, when the fall starts again and I start my rotations, I don't want to be on this case at all. I need to get back into my career."

"Don't worry. We're almost done here anyway. You'll be a doctor. I think I'll come to you when you open an office. I'll be your first patient. How does that sound? You can practice on my eyeballs." We laughed and the whole dinner was really quite pleasant. Jack was charming and I was already hoping that he would ask me out again. I knew we were no match for each other, coming from different backrounds and doing such different types of work. But he was fun to be with and made me feel safe.

He held my hand as he walked me home, saying, "for a detective, I need a lot of affection. You don't mind if I hold your hand, do you?" No, not at all. I loved it.

The walk home was used to tell me about his childhood, where he and his three brothers shared a room with bunk beds. It was probably the size of my bedroom when I was growing up, though I had a dollhouse and a wall covered with shelves of stuffed animals instead of bunk beds.

His father was a police officer too, and Jack emulated him till he was killed trying to stop a robbery. So, he was trying to fill his father's shoes since he was fourteen, when his father was murdered by the robber.

We stopped by my building and we turned to each other to say good-night. His eyes softened as he held me around the waist and drew me to him. His lips were gentle on mine and I closed my eyes as he held me tightly. He kissed me on the cheek and then the neck and then pulled away.

"Nicky, you're wonderful," he said in a whisper. He let me go all at once and stepped away.

"Want to come up a minute?" I asked breathlessly.

"No, better not. Early day tomorrow. Good-night." With that he turned around and began to walk away. "See you soon." He began to whistle as he turned the corner and disappeared.

That was it? Didn't he want to see me again? We had had such a nice time. Could he turn on and off so quickly and easily? My heart was still pounding from his kiss. I felt happy after such a nice evening, yet disappointed at the same time. What kind of a man could be so charming and passionate one minute and then turn it off so suddenly and walk away? Maybe he didn't want to get involved… well obviously not.

I walked into my building feeling anger building up inside of me. He wasn't worth thinking about. I'd have to find someone on my own level. Maybe he was just being nice to me because I was trying to help him on this case. Well, if he called, I might not even go out with him again. But it would be nice if he called.

The bus ride to the nursing home was a slow one the next morning. I was looking forward to another day and felt a happy mood taking over. Maybe Jack would call me tonight. Maybe he was just playing hard to get. I could probably talk into the transmitter and say something like, "Jack, call me tonight." No, that would be too uncouth… who knows who was listening.

I walked into the lobby and smiled at a few familiar faces, as I made my way to Grace's office. Later today I would visit Mrs. Suma and talk to her some more too… another thing to look forward to. I was growing to really like her.

Grace was sitting at her desk and looked up when I walked in, but didn't smile at my hello.

"What's the matter?" I asked her.

"Two things. First, I asked you not to see Mrs. Suma the other day and I heard that you spent a few hours with her after work."

"I don't understand…"

"Well, you need to understand that I am your boss and I take responsibility for everything you do. Yes, you're a doctor and I'm not, but in this nursing home you are under my supervision. If I ask you not to do something, don't you think I have a reason? The employees are not supposed to socialize with the patients after hours." Maybe she was right, but I had seen no harm in getting closer to Mrs. Suma. "Second, your good friend Mrs. Suma passed away last night." I sat down in a chair across from her desk.

"What?! She was so healthy."

"Sudden heart attack. That's the other reason you can't get close to the residents here… if one passes away, you don't want to be devastated by a loss."

How could that be? So suddenly? Well, she was an elderly woman and anything could happen at any time at that age. I could still barely believe it.

I got up suddenly and walked out of the office, hearing Grace's voice vaguely behind me. "Nicky, where are you going?" I had to see for myself.

I climbed the stairs to the third floor and made my way to her room. It was empty. Only the bare linoleum floor and a bed frame were left. All of the antique furniture and paintings were gone. The closet door was open and only empty hangers hung on the bars. They certainly didn't waste time in this place. The smell of antiseptic was very strong.

I walked slowly, in a bit of a daze, to the nursing station.

"Hi, Dr. Steinway," one of the nurses greeted me.

"What happened to Mrs. Suma?"

"Oh, she passed in her sleep last night. Good way to go, in your sleep."

"Where is all the furniture?"

"Downstairs in the basement till her family picks it up. Rooms are in such demand here, Doctor, that as soon as someone goes, the next day we have a new resident. A new tenant is coming later today." I walked away quietly, still in a bit of shock.

She seemed so healthy and alert the other night. Could it possibly have been foul play? Did someone want her dead so she wouldn't talk to me? I shook my head. No, I was becoming too paranoid. The world did not revolve around me and the Suma family. I had to dismiss these feelings and get on with my life. Maybe I should even throw out the transistor which was in my underwear. Perhaps that was making me ADRIA BURROWS paranoid instead of making me feel more at ease.

I made my way back to the lobby, found Grace and apologized to her. I was feeling bad that I had gone against her wishes, yet it was still a good thing that I had met Mrs. Suma. She was another link in the chain that might tell me what happened to her son.

Later that night my phone rang.

"Nicky? Jack." My heart jumped. "How'd you like to go out for a drink tomorrow night?" I smiled and said yes. "Great. I'll meet you there. The Golden Apple. See you tomorrow at eight."

"Wait: did you hear about Mrs. Suma?"

"Yeah."

"Well, what do you think? Was it a coincidence that it happened right after I spoke to her? Do you think-"

"Nicky, let's not get melodramatic. Whoever was after you is not after you anymore, or we would have had more 'incidents.' My concern now is – well, I'll tell you more in person. I don't want to talk on the phone. See you tomorrow."

Ws this date business or pleasure for him? Why was I so confused about how he felt? Usually I could figure out a man and his intentions immediately, by his behavior and even his kiss. Jack was warm one minute and cold the next. Well, at least he didn't waste any time calling me again. It looked like we were about to meet Nathan Suma whether I liked it or not.

# Chapter 10

The Golden Apple had quite a reputation. I had read articles on it and the celebrities who went there for dinner and drinks. It was styled after the 1940's with plush sofas and tables, crystal chandeliers and a ten-piece band. The dance music was old-fashioned too, adding to the atmosphere, which brought its customers back in time.

Even though I had heard about the place, it wasn't anything like what I was expecting. I took a cab there in my basic black dress and high heels and decided to take a look inside when I realized Jack hadn't arrived yet. The club's band could be heard even before I entered through the two heavy wooden doors. Two doormen tipped their hats to me and I found myself in the bar area first. Even though it was a Wednesday night, the place was packed.

The vinyl bar was sprawling and curving and covered with people leaning against it. Behind the bar was the dance floor surrounded by tables and all the way to the left was the band, playing a 1940's tune. It was like another world, set back in time. The walls were covered in red velvet and the carpeting was thick. What a nice place to take a date.

I stopped a passing waiter.

"Excuse me, can you tell me the name of the owner of the club?"
I asked.

"Nathan Suma, Miss. Someone will be over to seat you in a sec."

Well, Nathan Suma couldn't be doing too badly for himself. I went
back outside and waited for Jack.

I watched as, one by one, well-dressed people got out of limousines
and walked into the club. What a place. One lady was better-dressed
than the next. Didn't these people have to go to work the next morning?
They all seemed so carefree and had all the time in the world.

"Hey, beautiful" It was Jack. He slipped his arm around my waist
and gave me a quick peck on the lips. His breath smelled like fresh
mouthwash. "Want to spend some time with a lonely cop?" I smiled
and nodded yes as he ushered me inside.

We were seated immediately – he had made reservations – and
ordered some drinks.

"Jack, how are we going to meet –"

"Just leave everything to me. Tonight you're going to see the boss
and it'll be a night you'll never forget." Why all the build-up? What
was his plan?

"Jack if you don't tell me what's going to happen, I'll get up and
leave. I've had enough suspense for one summer." He smiled.

"Trust me, sweetheart. Want to dance?"

I didn't know how to slow-dance very well, but he held me tightly
and we just swayed to the music. I suppose detectives didn't know

much about dancing either. Jack pressed his cheek against mine and whispered how good it felt to hold me. This was a good start to the evening. It did feel wonderful to be held by him again. Even though we weren't quite dancing, but more like standing in the middle of the dance floor, I didn't want to do anything else. I guess he really did like me after all.

Jack kissed me lightly on the lips and motioned to our table. Once we sat down, we held hands and he kissed my fingers.

"I didn't know you could be this way, Jack," I said softly. He leaned forward, took my chin in his hand and kissed me on the lips.

"You're delicious. I can't stop kissing you, Nicky."

We really were an odd couple with such different backrounds and careers, but at the moment I couldn't care less and could only wonder how the evening would end. Would we spend the night together?

Suddenly, as if reading my thoughts, he sat back and stared at me.

"Nicky, I brought you here tonight for two reasons. First, I wanted you to meet Nathan Suma. Second, I have to tell you something that's been on my mind." He cleared his throat. "I can't go out with you again."

"Why?" My heart sank.

"We're too different. I'm used to going out with secretaries and other cops, not doctors with your kind of pizzazz."

"What's that supposed to mean? I thought we were having a good time."

"Nicky, suppose you and I got married someday. What would we talk about at the dinner table? I'd only be able to tell you about drug busts and Mafia crimes. You'd want to tell me about some eye operation you did that day. You couldn't care about my work and I could never understand yours."

"I would love to hear about your work. Why are you so warm one minute and so cold the next? I don't see why two people from different backrounds can't get along and build a relationship."

"I'm warm and cold because I could really fall in love with you easily, but I know I really shouldn't. It's like my head and my heart are having this bad argument over you."

"I think you should listen to your heart, not your head." I took his hand and put it on my lap, but his fingers stiffened. I sat back. "You can turn yourself on and off so fast, Jack." He got up in a quick movement and stood by the table. "Where are you going?"

"Home."

"What about our evening together? What about meeting Nathan Suma?"

"That'll all have to wait. I'm getting another detective on this case."

"What if I don't want another detective? What if I'll only cooperate if you work with me?"

"You're not the entire key to this case, Nicky. I won't fall for you and I won't let you fall for me. It wouldn't be good for us in the long run."

"You take life too seriously."

"Maybe. The department will be in touch with you."

"You're really leaving just like that, when the evening was just beginning?"

"Yeah. Want a lift home?"

"Not with you. A cabby would be better company right now."

"You'll understand all of this someday."

"Don't talk to me like I'm a child. You're a jerk, Jack, if you'll pardon my expression… and if the transistor will pardon my expression. Someone is listening right now to this whole thing and also thinks you're a jerk."

"Maybe, maybe not." He turned around abruptly and left the room without looking back at me once.

So, I was deserted. He really was an idiot. I never had had much luck with men, but this was ridiculous. Just because I was a doctor and on what he thought was a higher plane than he was, he felt we couldn't get along. As my mother would have referred to it: a bird and a fish could fall in love, but where would they build a home? Ah, he and my mother should have married each other.

I fingered my glass of champagne and felt the tears come to my eyes. It could have been such a nice evening. He could have at least finished his drink. I think I would throw out the transistor when I got home. I didn't want anything more to do with the police, him or the Sumas. That was it. I'd have to find myself a doctor to go out with. I wiped my eyes with a napkin.

"Are you all right?" I looked up and saw a very handsome man standing by the table. He was tall, with olive skin, dark eyes and a boyish face. I nodded yes. "Did that guy just desert you?" I motioned yes again. If I tried to say anything, I knew I would start to cry again. "Well, men can be real horses' asses. Can I sit down?" I kept looking down at the table so he wouldn't see my moist eyes and nodded. He sat down next to me and held out his hand. "Nathan Suma. I am the owner of this place and I don't like to see a customer mistreated by anyone." We shook hands and I smiled... I couldn't have orchestrated a meeting better if I had tried. Why did everything happen so easily?

"You're very nice, Mr. Suma. Nicky Steinway."

"What a pretty name." What a line. "Did you know that guy long?"

'No, just a few weeks. He decided just as we were starting to warm u to each other that he didn't want to have anything more to do with me. I don't know why."

"You'll never figure it out. I've been in your shoes lots of times. Some people are just afraid of relationships."

"I think it's because I'm a medical student. He felt beneath me."

"Ah, that was an excuse. It's an honor to go out with someone like you and he should have felt lucky, not intimidated." I looked up at him. He was leaning on his elbow, really looking concerned about me. He was dressed nicely too, with a blue suit, an expensive tie and a gold watch. His hair was slicked into place and his eyes pierced into mine.

"You're really being so nice, Mr. Suma."

"Nathan. Did you order dinner?"

130

"No, I'm going to leave anyway."

"Oh no, don't leave yet. Let's have dinner together. My treat." Even if I hadn't met this man's father and grandmother and hadn't been asked to find out more about him, I wanted to get to know him better. What a gentleman... and so good-looking. I was developing a fast rush on him.

Of course, the waiters couldn't do enough for us. The plates came in no time and everything was delicious.

"I hope you like my chef's coking. If I told you where I got her from, you'd laugh. But she's a good person and a great chef."

"Where did you find her?"

"She was homeless when I met her. She had left her husband because he beat her up one too many times. Her money didn't last her long – she didn't have much to begin with – and she got evicted. One night, late, I was in the kitchen here helping to clean up after a slow evening, when she knocked on the door. She told me her name was Renata and that she was wondering if we had any leftovers from dinner. My heart went out to her. She was so beautiful – like you- and her eyes were so sad. I ushered her in immediately and sat her down at a table, put some duck before her and watched her devour it. I don't think she had eaten all day, or maybe for two days. I didn't take her in and feed her because I had ulterior motives either. I just felt sorry for her. That's the way I am. I have a big heart. People tend to walk all over me because of it, but what can you do? It saved me a few times, like with Renata."

"Anyway, she started to tell me that she was a cook and could make a better duck dish than what I had given her. She didn't say it maliciously: she was actually trying to get herself a job, I think. So, I let her have free access to the kitchen and told her at twelve midnight to cook me a duck. Well, what a dish she made! Then she told me about all the other dishes she could prepare and I hired her that night. Not as my main chef, but as an assistant. I also instructed my cook to keep an eye on her and make sure she was on the level. Well, she was. She worked so hard and was so conscientious, I made her head of the kitchen when my cook left for another job. She's been with me for five years, has been so devoted to me and has turned business here around completely. It's been booming since she's come. I'm sure you've read in the paper about our famous duck and pastas. That's all thanks to Renata. She's a wonderful person too. Honest, sweet... but I don't have a thing for her. I'm just happy that I was able to help her and she helped me in return. You see, Nicky – it's all right if I call you Nicky, isn't it? – if you're good to other people, it all comes back to you."

"I wish there were more people like you, Nathan. But how did Renata know how to cook so well?"

"Get ready for this. I have a gourmet cook in my kitchen who gets written up in all the magazines and papers and makes my place famous... and she learned to cook from her mother. No fancy schools, no attitude problems like, 'I'm the greatest chef and you would be nowhere without me.' She'll be with me as long as I'm in business because I saved her and now she's saving me." He smiled, proud of himself. "Want to meet her after you eat?"

"Sure."

"First, I would love to dance with you. Let's try out my new orchestra. Just hired these guys." We got up and I slipped into his arms. They felt good around me. I leaned my head against his shoulder and felt safe and comfortable as we danced. What a nice guy. So, I went from having a crush on a detective to adoring a club owner.

He seemed so different from the way his father was. Nathan was so soft and gentle and his father, even in the hospital room, had been so hard and wheeling-dealing. He had his grandmother's soft eyes, but his father's high cheeks. He held me tighter and tighter as we danced and kissed my earlobe gently.

"Nice music , isn't it, Nicky?"

"Nathan, this whole evening is so nice, thanks to you. You rescued me." He blushed and patted me on the back. "You know, I met your grandmother the other day. I'm sorry about her passing." He pulled away and stared at me in surprise.

"You knew her? How?"

"I have a summer job in the home she was in. She was a wonderful lady. And I met your father too." Nathan let go of me completely and he blinked at me silently, waiting for more. "I hope I'm not talking out of line. I met your father in the hospital. He had an eye infection the night before his surgery." Nathan walked back to the table and sat down. I followed him. I knew I had made a mistake mentioning all of this. I guess the liquor, the soft music and the caresses had loosened my tongue.

"O.K., so what gives, Nicky? Did you come here to meet me or something? Who are you working for?" I had obviously hit a cord.

"No one. I'm sorry. I thought you would like to know that I admired your grandmother and your father."

"Lots of people do and lots of people hate my family. Who are you really?"

"I promise. I'm a medical student. You can come to the home on any day and see for yourself. Check the roster at my school."

"And who was that guy you were with?"

"Oh, just a man I met recently who I thought I had a crush on. A jerk, it turns out." Nathan's expression softened.

"I guess it's possible you met my grandmother and father coincidentally. I'll trust you for now."

"I don't' understand. What are you suspicious of?"

"I don't know. My family has a lot of enemies. That's all. I have two bodyguards because of those enemies, even though I have nothing to do with my father's business." He took my hand. "I guess you'll be a friend."

We sat quietly for a few minutes, listening to the music, watching the other people dance. I was afraid to say anything, wondering if I would rub Nathan the wrong way. What was he being so cautious about?

"I really enjoyed talking to your grandmother one night. She told me all about you and your family. She seemed like such a wonderful person and a strong person." Nathan nodded. "Her stories about how she met and married your grandfather were amazing. What a woman."

"She built herself up from nothing. My father never treated her very well. Nor my grandfather. But she survived nicely. She taught me a lot."

"Me too. I'm sorry about her passing." Nathan nodded.

"Well, let's focus on happier things. I don't want to think about my grandmother or my father. Let's go back to the kitchen and see how Renata's doing." He took me by the hand and led me to the back of the club.

If I thought that Nathan was an amazing person for running a famous, successful club, I was also very impressed with Renata. Not only was she beautiful, but so organized.

When we walked into the kitchen, the salads were arranged on one shelf, ready for the waiters to grab them, and the entrees were on another shelf near the stove. The orders were coming in one after the other and Renata, who I picked out among the chefs immediately, looked busy but calm.

Her blonde hair was piled on top of her head in a big hairclip, with strands coming loose on the sides and one large strand bouncing in front of her face. She was tall and thin, with high cheekbones and green eyes. She repeatedly wiped her forehead with a small towel as she worked, but she didn't seem to be sweating. She was a stunning woman, maybe thirty years old, and didn't even notice us when we came into the kitchen.

There were two other chefs taking orders from her and they looked high-strung and harassed… not because Renata was screaming or looking upset about anything. I think they were just nervous and eager to please her and the customers.

Nathan smiled in admiration as he stared at her and I wondered if he really liked her more than he admitted.

"Look at her work, my heroine." Renata heard him and looked up with a smile.

"Ah, Nathan," she said in a foreign accent. "It's only 11 o'clock and you're in the kitchen already. Didn't you like the pasta tonight?"

"It was delicioso. I came in to introduce a new friend. Renata, this is Nicky… Dr. Nicky. She's a medical student." Renata wiped her hands in a towel and held one out to shake hands.

"My, my. Nathan never brought in a doctor to introduce me to. He must think I need one. Are you a psychiatrist?" She giggled. "Nathan often tells me I need one. He does too. Ah, I guess we all do sometimes." We all laughed.

"I've heard a lot about you, Renata, from Nathan, that is. I really think you deserve a medal. Your story is very impressive and your cooking is remarkable." Renata bowed her head to me.

"Thank you. Nathan has good taste in friends." Nathan put his arm around my waist.

"And if the two of you agree, I'll drive you both home after we close."

Closing was 2 o'clock in the morning, so I bowed out of that offer. I suddenly felt very tired and knew I should be going home soon, even though I was having such a good time. I liked Nathan and Renata a lot, even though I had just met them.

Nathan walked me to the street after I said good-night to Renata and wished her luck. He hailed me a cab and as I was about to get in, he grabbed me by the shoulders and turned me to face him.

"Nicky, can I see you again?" My wish had come true and I nodded yes. "What's your number? I'll memorize it now."

"You'll really remember it?"

"Go ahead and try me." I told it to him and he recited it back. "And now I have to run back inside so I can write it on a napkin. Then I'll really remember it." He gave me a kiss on the cheek and walked quickly into the club again as I got into the cab. He was charming and I was happy that the evening had turned out so well after all.

136

As I lay in bed that night, thinking about what a wonderful evening I had had, I began to think about Mrs. Suma's funeral. Should I go? After the last Suma funeral, I didn't feel like going to any other funerals for the rest of my life. What if I saw or was seen by the guy who tried to shoot at me? I admired the woman greatly and was truly sorry that she had passed, but there was no way that I was going to hazard another chance at being spotted by someone dangerous. She would just have to be buried without my being there. Nathan hadn't even invited me – not that he had to – and I wasn't close to the family... at least not yet. I would have to see what would happen with Nathan. Maybe he would call me tomorrow. I sighed, rolled over and closed my eyes, hoping he'd call soon.

The police precinct was in a nice section of town on a street with beautiful old townhouses. I called Jack and made an appointment to see him so I could return the transmitter. I had had enough of him and enough of the whole case. It was apparent that everything had cooled off and that no one was after me anymore. It was uncanny that I kept meeting and getting to know people from the Suma family, but no one could have orchestrated those events even with the smoothest touch.

If I had my way, I would have just gone to the East River and thrown the transmitter into the murky water, but I knew that good tax dollars – mine included – were going into the cost of that contraption. And maybe it was against the law to throw away police property. For all I knew they might have turned off the transmission by now anyway.

So, Jack was expecting me at six o'clock after work and I was to meet him in his office on the third floor. It would be a pleasure to throw this thing in his face and tell him to never call me again. I wasn't sure why I was so angry at him except that I knew I cared for him. Well, not for long. Nathan had called me at the nursing home that day and had asked me out for dinner over the weekend. There was a man who didn't waste any time and knew to go after something if he wanted it. Jack seemed like such a wimp now.

He was sitting at his desk, waiting for me, when I was ushered in by another police officer. His feet were propped up on a pile of papers at the corner of the desk and he was studying something in his lap. The office was a real mess: the file cabinet in the corner had drawers open with files popping out and the windowsill was piled with loose papers. His raincoat hung on a coat rack near the door and only one chair across from his desk was empty. The other chair had piles of files on it.

I sat in the empty chair and smiled at him as I fingered the transmitter.

"Hi, Nicky. You look wonderful as usual." I held up the transmitter and placed it on his desk.

"I came to return this. Is it turned off yet?"

"Why should it be turned off? It's been on since the moment I gave it to you. We have everything on tape too… even our dinner date. I listened to that earlier today."

"That wasn't a dinner date."

"What would you call it, then?"

"An excuse for me to meet more of the Suma family." Jack chuckled.

"I happened to enjoy that part of the evening… I mean when you and I were together."

"Jack, let's cut out the bologna." He laughed again. "I came here for one purpose and only one purpose. I am giving you back your transmitter, asking you to take me off this case – if there still is a case – and to leave me alone."

"You're not interested anymore?"

"No. I don't mean to sound ungrateful. Thank you for saving my life and taking an interest in everything. But I'm through with being a semi-police officer, with helping you and with thinking about you." I put the transmitter on his desk with finality.

"And what exactly is making you so hostile?" I paused. I was becoming too angry. I wanted this meeting to end pleasantly and to leave him on good terms.

"I'm sorry I'm getting too riled up. Let's just say I want to go back to being a medical student, in my own world, and to leave you in your own world."

"I thought we were friends." His tone was too even. He was almost playing with me.

"O.K. we're friends. Just don't ask me out."

"Was I planning to?" I stood up, feeling more and more exasperated. I wanted the upper hand in this conversation. I leaned towards him.

"Jack, I have better things to lavish my attention on than you and your interest. I have my career to devote myself to and I have a social life that I have to spark up again. So, I'm going back to do those things and asking you to leave me alone."

"And who is going to take up you social life now?" His tone was quiet and calm.

"A wonderful man named Nathan Suma. We're going out and we may even become a hot item." He watched me silently as I began to walk out of his office.

"Oh, and by the way, Jack. Thank you for introducing us." I closed his door behind me, feeling as though I had made the exit I had hoped for. I wanted to leave an effect on him and I hoped I had hurt him. There was nothing like a little jealousy to produce a small wound.

I was sort of hoping that he would come after me, grab me in his arms and kiss me hard, begging me not to leave him and to have dinner with him that evening. I walked down the hall slowly, but his door didn't open. Well, I certainly was a romantic. I laughed to myself as I stepped into the elevator, knowing I would never be back to the precinct again.

For the first time in my life, I was going to be picked up in a limousine right from my apartment. It would whisk me off to one of the hottest clubs in town – Nathan's – where he would be waiting for me and we would have dinner and dance. I was expecting to have a wonderful time. Nathan was so handsome and debonair and insisted that he send his limousine for me, even though I offered to take a cab.

"A real lady needs a real car and fine treatment," he had said. That was the right answer as far as I was concerned.

My buzzer sounded promptly at 9:00 p.m. and there it was, a white stretch limousine waiting by the curb downstairs. The chauffeur opened the door for me and I sank into the leather cushion of the seat. There was a television, a bar and even a refrigerator. As the car started to go, I opened the refrigerator and peeked in happily… not that I was hungry: I was only exploring. There was a small chocolate cake inside with a note next to it saying, "I know you love chocolate. We'll have this later. N.S." What a guy… he really thought of everything! Maybe I'd marry him someday. Well, on second thought, I wasn't so sure that a nightclub owner and a doctor would make a good combination. I sat back in the seat and gazed up at the sky through the sunroof. If Nathan Suma wanted to show me a good time and pamper me, I wasn't going to stop him. I needed these things right now. The future was another thing entirely.

When I arrived at the club, there was a line of people standing outside waiting to get in. I felt so important as the chauffeur opened the door for me and whisked me right inside.

The manager greeted me by my name and showed me to a table on the dance floor. "Mr. Suma will join you shortly, Madame," he said with a bow and walked away. I felt so important. A waiter brought me a drink and I sipped it slowly, watching the people dance and humming to the music... it was old-fashioned dancing music from the 1940's, but I liked it.

A half hour went by and still no Nathan. Where was he? The waiter said he was finishing some business in the office in back. Impatient, I got up and wandered to the back of the club. There was a dimly-lit hallway which I followed to a wooden door. I heard Nathan's voice on the other side, talking into a telephone.

"I'm not interested," he was saying. "You can't make me do these things. I'm happy in my own world. I know – I know you're short, but I can't help you. You know me... I'm not cut out for those things I'm not tough and I vomit at the sight of even the thought of blood or foul play."

I walked back to my table. Who was he talking to? Was he tied into the underworld like his father, or was he on the up and up? More things to wonder about.

Nathan joined me within a few minutes and kissed me on the cheek as he sat down.

"Nicky, you look smashing, as usual. You're the most beautiful woman in the club tonight." He was all smiles, with no trace of the nasty conversation he had just had with whomever. He spoke as though he had a big crush on me, which I loved, but I was still disturbed over what I had just heard through his door. However, I didn't know him well enough to confront him about it. When would life start being more easy for me? Everything was an obstacle these days.

"So, let's talk about your day, Nicky. What did you do today?" What more could a woman ask for than Nathan, his looks and his charm?

"Well, I was at the home today. Mrs. Travinelli had a stroke and was transferred. She's that nice lady who once gave me a bouquet of flowers. Then I went to visit Jack Jeffries." I paused, waiting to see the expression on Nathan's face. It was blank. "Jack Jeffries, the detective."

"Oh, the one you were with the night I met you? The one who deserted you on your date?"

"How did you know he was the one?" Nathan shrugged.

"Just a guess. Why'd you go to see him? To make up?"

"No, to tell him to leave me alone and never to call me again." Nathan smiled and nodded.

"Men can be real heart-breakers… I know. I always try to treat women extra well to make up for some of my 'brethren.'" We laughed.

"Well, you do a great job." I took his hand but felt it stiffen, so I let go. He motioned to a waiter without missing a beat and told him we would order now

142

"What's Renata's special tonight?" Nathan asked. "Did she stick to the sautéed chicken breast? Good. We'll have two orders of that. You'll love it, Nicky… is that O.K. with you? She sautees it in lemon and oil and puts some kind of herbs on it that are out of this world." I nodded yes enthusiastically.

The dinner was delicious and as we ate, Nathan stroked my arm here and there and gave me a peck on the cheek now and then. He was so attentive and acted as though I were the only person in the room. We danced and he rubbed my back as he held me… I was feeling so happy and appreciated. I could definitely fall in love with someone like this.

When we had finished our deserts, Nathan asked if I wanted to take a ride in the limousine. "If we open the sun roof, we can look at the stars as we go. I'll get some champagne and we'll turn on some fun music."

In no time we were relaxing against the cushioned back of the seat, looking at the sky, sipping champagne, as the limousine drove around the city. Sitting side by side, I put my head on his shoulder and hoped he would kiss me. He didn't move. I turned and kissed his ear lightly, thinking that would be a stimulus, but he still didn't move. He kept gazing up through the sunroof and talking about the club.

"Nathan," I said teasingly, "now would be an excellent time to kiss me." He stopped talking and looked at me very seriously. Then he smiled.

"O.K." He gave me another peck on the cheek.

"Not like that." I grabbed his chin and kissed him gently on the lips. "Like that." Nathan held my head in his hands and stared at me, as though he wanted to say something. Then he kissed me on the forehead and sat back.

"I can't kiss you, Nicky… not the way you want."

"Why?" You're not attracted to me? We were having such a nice time."

"We were. We are. I just can't kiss you. Driver, drop us off here near the water." He was acting so strangely. What was going on? "Come, lets get out and take a little walk so we can talk. It's beautiful here near the river."

"Are you married?" He laughed and nodded no.

We got out of the car after it parked and walked to the East River's edge. Ther were street lamps, a walkway and benches along the river. A few people were taking walks, mostly young couples, and Nathan walked ahead of me to a railing overlooking the water. It was a beautiful night and we watched a boat pass in silence.

"So what's going on, Nathan? Are you all right?" He sighed and looked down into the water.

"Nicky, you know a lot about my family. You met my father in the hospital before he died. You met my grandmother in the home and learned about us all from her, I'm sure. She always loved to tell people about how she made it to this country, lived a secluded life in a big house and how she helped to raise me. She taught me a lot when I was growing up and I modeled myself after her quite a bit. My grandfather basically raised my father and stole him away, pushing him into the business and making him tough but smart."

"It was my father's greatest dream to see me go into the business, but I never wanted to. I was different from him. I had a heart, I felt more for people and I couldn't be a cut-throat. When my father was ten, he was already shooting squirrels and birds. I remember the first

144

time he put a gun in my hand and told me to aim at a rabbit he had put in a cage. The rabbit was in the cage, so he couldn't move and would be an easy target for me. I must have been ten too. I held the gun up to the rabbit as it stared back at me gnawing its teeth together. It was so helpless. I dropped the gun, ran to the cage and opened it to let the rabbit go."

'"What are you, some kind of nut?!"'" my father yelled. He grabbed the gun and shot the rabbit dead with one shot. I cried and ran into the house."

"These kinds of episodes made my father and I grow apart from the very beginning. Why am I telling you all this? Because I want you to see where I come from and why I can't kiss you and hold you the way you want."

"My mother and grandmother saw that I wasn't cut out to run the business. I was a soft boy with feelings who couldn't see hurting others. The kind of work my father did involved wheeling and dealing with criminal-types. But my father kept trying to toughen me up. He sent me on errands in all kinds of bad neighborhoods and I was beaten up a few times by gangs whose territories I had trespassed on. He tried to teach me to fight, but I finally refused to run errands, refused to even touch a gun and tried to do my own thing, so to speak. He gave up on me for awhile... Until I was seventeen. That seemed to be the magic number for him to try again in a heroic way."

"I know you don't understand why I'm telling you all this, but there's a reason, Nicky. Bear with me a minute."

"Anyway, until I turned seventeen, my father didn't have much to do with me. There were times he didn't come home for weeks and we didn't see him much in general. My mother and grandmother became used to these habits and told me he was traveling for the business and making sure we were all well-taken care of. I accepted it like they did."

"When my seventeenth birthday came, my mother and grandmother planned a small dinner party for my closest friends. There were maybe five guys who came and we sere sitting around the dining room table eating a quiet meal, having a very nice time. My grandmother even hired a violinist to play in a corner and I think it would have been the perfect dinner party if my father hadn't decided to join us."

"He came in slamming the front door behind him, dead drunk. He was dressed in his finest, as usual, but smelled like a combination of liquor, sweat, and blood. There was fire in his eyes and everyone stopped talking as soon as he showed up."

"He looked around the room in silence until his eyes landed on me and then he laughed. 'How come there aren't any women at this party? You all fairies like my son?'"

"My mother got up in protest and quicker than you could blink, my father pulled out a gun and aimed it at her. 'Sit down or you'll be real sorry, honey.' She sat down… the anger in her eyes turned to fear. 'Now, son, I want you to get up and come with me…this is not the kind of birthday party I have in mind for you. Get up… now.'"

"You're ruining my party, Dad."

"Oh no I'm not. This isn't a party. it's a senior citizen's club or a fag club. Not sure which, but I'll let you know in a little while. You're coming with me, Nathan. Now get up or I swear I'll shoot your head off."

"I began to apologize to my guests, when he fired a shot into the ceiling."

146

"That's enough blubbering… I've had seventeen years of blubbering from you. It's time you learned a little something from me. Now get going!' He motioned to the door and I left with him in silence. I wasn't afraid of him: I knew he wouldn't shoot me, but I was concerned for my guests and my mother."

"His limousine was waiting outside and we got in quietly. He leaned his head back and told the driver to move on. I didn't ask where we were going. I sat back and stared at him as he closed his eyes and sighed. He was pulling himself together."

"Son, I'm not kidnapping you.' His voice was controlled now. 'I'm taking you to a celebration of my own. I'll show you what I do on birthdays and you can be sure you're going to like it. If you don't like it, then you're not my son and I won't have anything to do with you for the rest of your life.'"

"I didn't answer him and just stared out the window away from him the whole ride. I knew this would be some sort of a test."

"The car took us to the rich section, uptown, and finally stopped in front of a large townhouse that had all its lights on. My father stepped out without looking back at me and I followed him up the flight of cement steps leading to the front door. There wasn't a party going on inside… it was quiet: no music, no people talking. He opened the door with a key, as though he was coming home, and we walked into a big foyer. There was marble on the floors and walls and a red-carpeted staircase leading upstairs."

"She walked into the foyer as if from nowhere, smiling shyly at us. She was beautiful. Her long blonde hair reached to her waist, she wore a red sequence dress with a neckline that plunged to her stomach and a large round diamond dangled between her breasts."

'You must be Nathan,' she said quietly, ignoring my father. My father snickered.

'Tell me this isn't the most beautiful woman you've ever seen, Nathan. Actually, she'd a kid... only twenty one, but acts like she's thirty and has the brain of someone who's seen everything. I should know. Nathan, this is Jacqueline.' She walked up close to me and held out her hand.'"

"'Nice to meet you, Nathan.' She took my hand and stroked it and then put it to her lips. Her eyes were so blue they looked aqua. What a knockout she was. My father smiled at my obvious entrancement with her.'

""Well, I gotta' go now,' he said as he walked out and closed the front door behind him."

"Was she a high-class hooker? It seemed that way, though I still wasn't sure."

"She led me into the living room and sat next to me on the sofa. The room was gorgeous like her. There was a grand piano in one corner and a large armoir that served as a bar... its doors were open and ready to serve. The carpet was so thick your feet sank into it and the curtains were lace but trimmed with gold fabric. What a room. Some decorator had had a field day here."

"Jacqueline offered me a drink, which I took, and then sat down next to me again. She watched me sip my drink as if it were the most fascinating thing that she could be doing at the moment. The drink gave me courage to speak."

"What's this all about, Jacqueline?' She smiled shyly again and put her chin down as she looked up at me. Then she took my hand in hers and put it under her dress on her breast. No underwear. She leaned over and kissed me gently on the lips… her breath smelled sweet. Well, if there ever was a woman who could make a gay man straight, it was her. Wait, Nicky, let me finish. I want to tell you everything, just as it happened."

"I kissed her back and with one quick movement she pulled her whole dress over her head and was completely naked in from of me. She leaned back against some cushions and pulled me on top of her, one hand holding my hand on her breast, the other hand adeptly fingering my groin. She spread her legs and put my hand between them and began to groan with closed eyes.

"It was quite a moment, let me tell you, but it did nothing for me. She was gorgeous, all right, with a body out of a fairytale, but it just didn't affect me."

"I pulled away from her and got up to face the fireplace."

"What's the matter?" she asked softly. 'Don't I attract you?'"

"Of course you do… or you would, but I'm just not in the mood."

"That's what I told her, anyway, so I wouldn't hurt her feelings. You see, Nicky, I don't know exactly when it happened or when I realized it, but I'm gay. That was the biggest disappointment my father ever had."

I stood away from the railing and stared at Nathan. This couldn't be happening. Of all the unluckiest things that could happen to me… no hope for us, that's for sure.

"Jacqueline became very nervous but wouldn't put her dress back on, even after I handed it to her. She began to shake and sat down on the sofa, seemingly unaware of her nudity. I thought she was shaking from the shock of my confession that I didn't want her, but it was more than that."

"Nathan," she said. "Your father is going to be very angry when he hears you didn't want me. It will be my fault.' I told her it wasn't her fault but mine because of something inate inside of me. I just wasn't attracted to women."

"She just couldn't believe it and stared at me the way you are looking at me now."

"You are your father's son and you don't like women?!"

"I guess I started to realize it when I was in high school. I was very popular with the girls and I must have gotten ten invitations to the prom. I took out the most beautiful in the class, but making out with her, dancing with her, gave me no pleasure. I found myself staring at the football stars in our school and wondering what it would be like to kiss them. I knew these feelings were strange and unusual, especially with someone of my background. My father always blamed my mother and grandmother for smothering me too much. Who knows?"

"I'm sorry, Nicky. I want to be your good friend, but I can't be your lover." He tried to put an arm around me, but I pulled back.

"What happened with Jacqueline?" I asked quietly.

"Well, she was very scared of my father and what his reaction would be. You see, he had told her that he suspected I was gay and wanted to know for sure. He said that if she couldn't seduce me, no one could. It was sort of a test. She took it as a challenge and told him she could convert anyone. Well, not me."

"She put her dress back on and pleaded me to tell my father that we had made love. If I didn't, she was afraid he would kill her. But I couldn't do that and I also couldn't believe that my father would kill anyone, especially her. I told her this, but she shook her head."

"Don't you know how you father plays the game? If you don't accomplish what he wants, your life becomes immaterial. You are a pawn to his wishes and desires and that's all you are. He will have me killed.' She started to cry, but I wasn't going to fall for her tears. I left without a word and hailed a cab."

"The next day I sent Jacqueline a note of apology and told her she was the most beautiful woman I had ever seen. When the note was returned to me with the words, "forwarding address unknown,' I made a trip to the city and stopped by her townhouse. No one answered the door and when I looked in the window, the place was completely empty... no furniture, no curtains, no rug. She had left or someone had made sure she had."

"It was another month before I saw my father come home again. When he did, he completely ignored me, walking past me without a word as he came in the door. He wouldn't look at me at the dinner table and just spoke to my mother and grandmother. I hadn't expected him to be so angry at me all this time, just because I didn't take his bait."

"Each time I would walk into a room he was sitting in, he would promptly get up to leave. He couldn't bear to be anywhere I was."

"I asked my grandmother and mother what was going on, but they didn't know. I had never told them about Jacqueline and strangely enough, neither of them had ever asked me about that night. They both noticed the cold air my father was throwing my way and suggested I approach him. Of course, I knew what it was all about, but figured it was a good idea to clear the air."

"Nicky, do you want to talk about us?"

"No… I want to hear your story first."

"Are you feeling pretty lousy?"

"Yes. It's O.K… I can't really do anything about what you're telling me." I don't thing the shock of what Nathan had told me had fully hit. "Go on with your account."

"He was sitting in his study when I walked in to talk to him. He looked up when I opened the door, but looked away as I came in. I told him I needed to speak with him. He shrugged in silence."

"Dad," I began, 'I think we should be on good terms. After all, I am your son.'"

"My son.' He echoed. 'You are nothing like what my son should be. My son should be a man, not a fruitfly. My son should be able to take over the reigns of my businesses… I should have been able to teach you most of what you need to know by now. If you were my son, we'd be talking business now, not about how you pushed Jacqueline away. You don't know what you're missing. I had my suspicions, but somehow I couldn't believe that anyone with by blood could—could—" he stopped. He was very upset. 'I had such hopes for you.' We sat in silence for a few moments and then he stood up to walk around the room. 'What do you do, dream about men? You run around in your underwear in front of other men, thinking you're sexy? Oh, it kills me to talk to you. Get out of here, Nathan. You can stay in this house, but you are not a son of mine. I'll set you up in some small business that will make an income for you. But we will never be together in anything as a father and son should be. You are my son in name only.'"

"I was very hurt. I didn't want to be in business with him anyway, but I was still very hurt. I had never had a relationship with anyone, man or woman, at that age of seventeen, but I knew what I was. And unlike my father, I treated everyone I knew with kindness, man or woman. That made some women and some men come on to me, but I never reciprocated their advances. Women didn't attract me physically and the men who did I'd stay away from. I was feeling too confused and maybe scared at that point in my life."

"So, I'm definitely not the first woman who has developed a crush on you, Nathan. You've told this speech to others."

"Yes. Both men and women. But I care for you, Nicky, and want to be good friends." I nodded. That wasn't the first time I had heard that line either. Boy, my luck with men wasn't skyrocketing lately.

"And what about your father? I guess he gave you the nightclub to run?" Nathan nodded yes. "And did you ever speak to him again?"

"Cordially, at weddings, the few times he came home to stay and now and then on the phone. We were never close, but he kept a protective eye on me from a distance. He made sure I had bodyguards and a large savings account to play with."

"And how did you feel when he didn't survive his heart surgery?"

"I know you and the police have been very concerned about that whole string of events."

"I haven't dealt much with the police."

"What does that mean? When I met you, you were on a date with a cop."

"He was pursuing me, not me him. I think I may even be a suspect to somebody's murder."

"Oh, Ralph's?" I stared at Nathan. How did he know so much? "Nicky, I may not have been very close to my father, but I still loved him and know a lot about the circumstances of his death."

"How did you know about Ralph?"

"I didn't know him. I heard all about what happened and even heard about you before I met you. My father's contacts stay in touch with me still. I knew you were once a suspect to Ralph's murder but I don't think you are anymore."

"And what about your father? Did you know that I am still not convinced that that was his body in the morgue? I'm sorry to be so blunt. I'm not being too hurtful, am I?"

Nathan laughed. "To tell you the truth, I wouldn't put it past him." I looked at him puzzled. "My father had many tricks up his sleeve. I wouldn't be surprised if he wasn't dead. Maybe he made the vanishing act of a lifetime. If he did, I'll bet I know where he is."

"Where?"

"Ah, I'm talking nonsense. There's no reason for him to want to disappear anyway. He had a great life and a great career. Let's get back to you. Can we be good friends, Nicky?" I nodded yes. "I'm glad, because I care for you. Come to the club often and I'll make sure you get the royal treatment. Now can I drive you home?"

"Nathan, don't you want to find your father if he's alive?"

"I see I put crazy ideas into your head. Let's drop it and let's drop my family. Let me drive you home."

"No, I want to stay here for awhile. You put enough into my head tonight that I need to sit and mull everything over. I'm not far from home. I'll walk back and it will do me good." Nathan hesitated, but I gave him a kiss on the cheek and pushed him toward the limousine. "Go. I'll talk to you soon."

"I didn't hurt you too badly, did I?" I nodded no and watched him walk away. He kept turning around to look at me and asked again if I would change my mind and take a lift home, but I really needed to think. The limousine started and drove away slowly.

I collapsed onto a bench and spread my legs in front of me. What a night. What an avalanche. What bad luck with me. Imagine, charming, genteel Nathan being gay. And what plans I had for us... some big romance and maybe even marriage. Well, a doctor and a nightclub owner didn't exactly make a good pair. As my grandmother would say: a fish and a bird.

I watched a boat slowly pass by, its cabin looking cheerful with all the lights on. Why couldn't I find someone stable to develop a crush on? Well, another "good friend" was just added to the list of men I knew.

Nathan was a bit odd about his father too... so non-chalant about his death. Maybe it was an act so he wouldn't appear so vulnerable... men were that way. Well, it just wasn't meant to be. Boy, two men in one month down the drain... first Jack, then Nathan.

I got up and sighed, thinking about what I could do to cheer myself up. Maybe buy myself those fake pearls I saw in the gift shop at the nursing home.

The walkway was deserted, but I didn't feel afraid. I guess my head was too full of all that Nathan had told me. It was also a beautiful night.

As I crossed the street towards the city and away from the water, I didn't notice the car with its headlights turned off inching up towards me. At first I thought it was parked in the street, until I began to walk faster and noticed the car pick up its pace in response. If this were Jack, I would be furious. I made a sharp right turn onto a side street, which was one way the wrong way for the car, but the car didn't seem to care. It made a right turn too. This was getting serious. It was either the police or someone was after me again. Oh, why had I thrown that transmitter back at Jack? Well maybe this was Jack. I turned around and tried to look into the car. There were two men in the front seat and another in the back seat... none of them were built like Jack either. They were much bigger and more muscular: all shoulders. Now I was in trouble.

I ducked into a small deserted park which the car couldn't follow me into because the front gate was narrow. It was a back entrance to the park. I ran across the walkway and out the front entrance to a main avenue. Thank goodness for cars and people. I looked behind me: no car and no men chasing after me. I still didn't feel safe. I hailed a taxi and jumped in.

Where should I go? I couldn't go home...maybe they knew where I lived and were waiting for me there. The taxi driver turned around and glared at me because I wasn't saying anything.

"You gotta' know where you wanna' go, lady," He said.

"Just keep driving. I have to think of an address." He shrugged and sped off, turning the meter on with a quick wave of his hand.

I looked out the back windshield but didn't see the car.

"Driver, take me to the Fairway Hotel." Maybe I would take a room there or at least sit in the lobby till I calmed down. There were always lots of people there. Could that have been my police tail? No... they were always more subtle than that and those men definitely didn't look like police officers. But if they were, I wouldn't be able to tell. Maybe

I was making a big deal out of nothing. I should have let Nathan drive me home. Why was I always by myself when these things happened? Where was Jack right now?

The cab pulled up by the hotel and I looked around before I got out. No sign of the black car. I walked quickly into the lobby and felt relieved as I melted into the people walking around. Everyone seemed wide awake and festive, though it was close to midnight. A violin and piano duo were playing classical music in a corner.

I sat down in a big leather chair against the wall. Just calm down, I told myself. I had lost whoever it was. However, I didn't feel comfortable going home now. Maybe they were waiting for me there. Who could I call now for help? Jack? Nathan? Maybe these men were somehow tied to Nathan. Maybe he even sent them after me... maybe he was really a part of his father's business but didn't want me to know.

My mind was racing and I didn't know what to do. I used to know Jack's cellular number by heart but couldn't think of it now... only the first three numbers. He would be the only one I could trust now. I didn't even know where he lived.

I felt helpless sitting there, not knowing which direction to turn to. Maybe I should just take a cab to the precinct and talk to someone there. They could also tell me if the men in the car were police officers. Yes, that made sense.

I got up and peeked out of the main entrance of the hotel. No sign of the car or the men. I walked out, hailed a cab and headed for the precinct.

On the way, I kept kicking myself for being so nasty to Jack in his office the other day. He was really the only person I could trust. Well, I would apologize the next time I saw him. He would understand. I was just fed up with everything at the time.

The street in front of the precinct was lined by police cars, but deserted. I paid the taxi driver and looked around again before I got out. I only had to make it up the flight of stairs to the front entrance. Why was the street so deserted? Weren't they bringing in any criminals tonight?

I closed the car door gently behind me... for some reason, I didn't want to break the silence of the street. A car honked from very far away. I reached the flight of stairs and began to feel relieved, when suddenly a man appeared from the shadows by the side of the stairs. I was already halfway up the stairs when he said, "Doc, I wouldn't go any further if I was you." I turned around to face him. He had a gun leveled at me.

"What do you want?" I asked.

"You ain't goin' to see your cop friend no more. Get down those stairs and come with me. Now." I was so close, yet so far. Why couldn't anyone come out those doors? Where were all the police?

"How do you know who I am?" I was stalling for time. I heard his gun click.

"The next bullet's going into you, doc. Get down the stairs now." He wasn't fooling around. I descended the stairs with trembling legs. "Now walk with me to the corner." He grabbed my arm forcefully. He was very tall and muscular and had pockmarks all over his face. I thought of screaming, but I didn't think anyone would hear me from inside the station.

There was the black car waiting on the corner, its engine idling, its headlights off. As soon as we approached, one man got out of the car, opened a back door and jumped in. I was pushed into the car, even though I put up a struggle, and before I knew it, I was sandwiched between two men in the back seat. They were mean-looking and ugly. The car zoomed off with a lurch and I noticed that the headlights were finally turned on.

I looked at the men on either side of me and felt tears of fright come to my eyes."

"You're going to kill me, aren't you?" I asked quietly to no one in particular. The man with the pock-marked face laughed.

"Nah, not if you cooperate."

"I guess you're not police officers?" I asked half hopefully. Everyone in the car burst out laughing.

"Do you work for Nathan?" More laughing.

"Please, Doc, stop, you're cracking us up too much… my ribs are hurting," the one driving said.

I sat back, feeling helpless and scared, my heart beating in my stomach. Who were these guys? Were they going to kill me after all? Why was I so stupid as to give back the transmitter? If I were wearing it now, I'd be home-free and a police car would be following us now. Well, at least no one was holding a gun out… they weren't going to kill me yet… not in the car, anyway.

The car sped uptown, racing through a few red lights, as though it were in a big hurry. The men sat silently and the ones on each side of me just gazed out the windows calmly. There was no way I could jump out of the car. First, it was going too fast and second, I couldn't climb over the huge thighs on each side of me. Even their hands were so big on their laps. Someone had hired real strongmen to do this dirty work. The tears came to my eyes again and I wiped them away.

"Aw, come on, Doc," The pock-marked guy began. "Don't be scared. My boss just wants to talk to you."

"Who's your boss? Does he want to kill me too?"

"You'll see. And I don't think he'll decide to do away with you. What you did wasn't so bad."

"What did I do? I'm just a medical student who's been trying to mind my own business."

"Aw, you haven't been doing much of that, you know."

"What's that supposed to mean?"

The man driving waved his hand in the rearview mirror. "Shut up, you two. Manny, just shut up or I'll throw you out of the car." So, we were quiet the rest of the way.

# Chapter 11

The car was headed to the worst part of town, where the slums and deserted buildings were located. Things didn't seem to be getting any better with time. I felt as though I was being dragged deeper and deeper into a pit. All my studying, all my hard work in the past could be ended in one split second by a bullet. Life was definitely not worth much to these people, I was sure, and they didn't care if you were a medical student or a thug… your life was worth the same bullet. Would my body be found in an alley tomorrow? The tears were coming again, but I blinked them away.

We stopped in front of a blown-out apartment building and the driver turned off the engine. He had turned off his headlights a block before we stopped, which I found unusual, but I didn't say anything. Manny jumped out and grabbed me by the collar to pull me out of the car in one rough movement. Then he held me firmly under the arm and pulled me towards an alley by the side of the building. This is where they were going to shoot me. I pulled back and began to scream. A hand cupped over my mouth and I heard Manny's voice in my ear saying, "if you don't shut up, I'm going to have to hit you over the head and drag you the rest of the way on your back." He held me from behind and I felt something hard digging into my side… it was a gun. We stood there for moments and he slowly removed his hand from my mouth.

"I say we just knock her out." One of the men suggested.

"Nah, Rocco wouldn't like that. He said gentle unless she causes trouble. You gonna 'cause trouble?" Manny turned me around and put his face up to mine. His breath smelled like strong garlic.

"Are you going to kill me?" Manny shrugged in response.

"I told you… not if you behave. So far, you ain't doin' so well in that department. You gotta' be quiet and just have a meeting with Rocco. O.K.?"

"Why you being so good to her? Let's get going." Someone gave me a push from behind and we continued into the alley. The smell of decay and dirt permeated the alley. These buildings probably hadn't been occupied for some time.

We came to a basement window and Manny bent down to raise the glass. He jumped through the window and called for me. Another rough push from behind. I bent down and looked into the window. It was very dark in there and I didn't even see Manny.

"Come on, Doc." I heard Manny's voice saying. I put my legs through and felt him grab them and lift me down onto a concrete floor. The other men jumped down behind me.

For a moment we stood in absolute darkness until a flashlight flicked on and I saw we were in a dusty, grimy basement. There were squeals from rats fleeing the beam of light from the flashlight.

I shivered uncontrollably. Nothing good could come of this. I pictured my body in a pool of blood on this floor. How long would it take someone to find me? Again I yearned for that transmitter. What a mess. I was in over my head.

Manny grabbed me by the shoulder and guided me through a doorway and up a flight of stairs. Each stair creaked with our weight. I started to ask where we were going, but they shushed me up immediately and Manny tightened his grip on my shoulder. He was hurting me, but I kept quiet. Talking at this point, I felt, would only make things worse.

Suddenly, I heard distant music. We kept climbing flight after flight of stairs and the music was getting louder and louder at each landing. Manny's flashlight showed the way up the old tiled stairways. Each doorway gaped open, leading to long abandoned apartments. I could make out scraps of wood and metal in some of the entranceways and mice and rats scattered at the sounds of our footsteps.

Maybe they weren't going to kill me. Maybe someone really did just want to meet with me over something. But who? I didn't know anyone who would bring me to a place like this. Could it be a trick so I would walk to the "perfect" place to kill me, far away from anyone's ears?

Manny kept pushing me up the stairs till we got to the top floor and I was breathing heavily from the climb. They all stopped, everyone also panting from their exertion. There was a large hole in the wall, connecting to the building next door and Manny motioned everyone to go through. "You first, Doc."

I walked through the opening and found myself on the top landing of the neighboring building. This was a lot of trouble to go through.

"Where are we going?" I asked. Manny pointed down the stairs.

"Down, Doc. Down to the basement of this building."

So we went down flight after flight of stairs and finally reached the basement. Manny opened a big wooden door and pushed me into a lit room. I was so used to the darkness, that the light blinded me and my eyes adjusted in seconds. I heard two men talking and finally could make out a table where two men where sitting. It was a bridge table and the room was the old boiler room, with old pipes covering one of the walls.

"Doc, I'm glad you could join us." He was sitting at the table puffing on a large cigar. "I'm Rocco." He held out a plump hand and I shook it instinctively. "Stevey, get up." The other man jumped up and offered me his chair. I sat down quietly across from Rocco, thinking that the less I said in this situation the better. I could only get into more trouble if someone misunderstood anything I said. Even though my heart was pounding in my ears, my common sense was starting to command me.

"Doc, I'm sorry for the atmosphere of this meeting, but I'm in hiding, so to speak, so I couldn't make this in a club or a bar. Likewise, I'm sorry to say, I can't offer you a drink." I heard Manny chuckle behind me. The others were all behind me... probably to prevent me from getting up and running out. I definitely didn't have a chance here. I never felt so helpless in my life.

"Doc, I went through a lot of trouble to bring you here and I've got something important to say to you. It's just two simple words: 'butt out.' " Manny and the others laughed wickedly.

I was silent. I was not going to say a thing for fear of getting Rocco upset. He seemed upset enough already.

"Don't you got nothing to say there, Doc?" Rocco continued. I nodded no. "Aaah, I can't believe that." He sat back and puffed on his cigar, smiling at me. "Manny, this medical student has been everywhere, talking to everybody, asking a million questions, and suddenly she's got nothing to say." He puffed again, not taking his eyes off of me.

Suddenly my heart sank into my stomach. They could rape me first. They could rape me and then kill me. That would be more their style… and what a perfect place to do it. I started to breathe heavily at the thought and felt very weak from fear. I couldn't answer him even if I wanted to at this point.

"She's seeing the boss' son… hey, how'd you feel when you found out he was a fairy? A loony tune? She's talking to everyone… detectives, loonies in nursing homes, maybe she's talking to the walls in her spare time. Hey, Manny, that reminds me… frisk her."

"Frisk her?!" I heard Manny's incredulous voice. "She—"

"Not for a rod, stupid. A microphone." I felt Manny's big hands under my arms as he stood me up in one swoop and then frisked me expertly. I sat down again without a word and was thankful at that moment that I wasn't wearing the transmitter.

"O.K., Dr. Steinway. I brought you here for a reason. I tried to warn you to stay away from this whole situation, but you didn't listen. You kept pushing and pushing and probing and so I had to take you here and put some common sense into you. Don't look at me like I'm going to kill you. I'm not. I know I come from a world where one minute I'm telling you I'm not going to kill you and then I get you – pow! – in the back of the head. But I'm not gonna' do nothing to you this time. This is a warning, Doc, and a strict one."

"I know everything you do and I know even what goes through your mind, Doc, so you really have to be more careful. And you have to be content to stay out of certain things."

"I've got a lot of respect for people like you, but people like you have to keep their big noses out sometimes. You're probably used to poking at bodies and sniffing out what's making patients sick, but this here, Doc, is a different situation. Sometimes when there's a cancer brewing, you have to let it alone and let the patient die. Got me?" I nodded silently. My throat was closed by fear, so even if I wanted to say something, I couldn't.

"So, this is what I wanted to say. I'm not gonna' kill you, so get that wild look out of your eyes. Just a warning, Doc. My strict warnings only come once. Another warning and I'm warning you at your funeral." I heard Manny chuckle behind me. "And I don't wanna' go to any funerals, Doc. I want you to stay in your world of saving lives by day and dancing with Nathan by night." More chuckling. "Stay out of my world. There won't be any more warnings now. No more street shootings, no more scaring you by following you in a big car… this is it. Got it, Doc?" I nodded again and he held out his hand. We shook hands.

"Now, if we got that out of the way, you got any questions?" I nodded no. I was still too frightened to talk. "Really, I'm not such a bad guy. I grew up in the streets and I killed someone for the first time when I was nineteen. I was tough, I was mean. Some people think I am still mean, but I'm not at least not in situations like this. See how nice I'm being to you? I give you a few warnings, you don't catch on, so I sit you down in a nice quiet place and talk some sense into you. Right?" I nodded. "Right. Don't be scared anymore… we're done." Rocco got up and shook my hand again. "O.K., Manny. Take her away." Manny tapped me on the shoulder as a signal for me to get up. "And Doc, by the way, I wanna' wish you luck. I still think you'll make a great doctor. You do a lot of people a great thing when you save them or help them. What a life, doing good deeds all day. And me, I do bad things all day." He laughed with the others. My lower lip trembled and I had to do everything I could to keep from crying. It was probably a mixture of fright and relief that was making me quiver.

Manny and his "friends" led me out of the room with Rocco saying good-bye from behind. I guess he was staying there, at least for now. We went all the way upstairs again, crossed over to the neighboring building, and went down again to the street. My heart finally stopped pounding in my ears as I realized that I was not going to be harmed. It really was just a warning.

So, nobody had been trying to kill me... they were just trying to scare me. All of that because I was mixed up with Ralph's murder. Was Rocco the murderer? Rocco seemed to know a lot about my whereabouts and who I was talking to. He was probably having someone follow me while the police were following me... what a mess.

Manny held the car door open for me as I got in. His demeanor had changed considerably: he was more relaxed and joking around more.

But where was Mr. Suma? I had better stop asking questions... even thoughts in my head were probably second-guessed by Rocco.

When the car stopped in front of my building, I jumped out and ran into my lobby without a word, happy to be free again. I didn't even say hello to the doorman... I ran into the elevator, pressed the button and couldn't wait for the doors to close.

When I entered the apartment I collapsed on my bed and stared at the ceiling with relief. I was very lucky to be alive. I had seen bullying at its worst... well, if I had been beaten up it would have been much worse. Thank goodness.

I glanced at the clock. It was two o'clock in the morning. I should be completely wiped out, but I felt wide awake, with my heart pounding in my chest. Too much adrenaline for one evening, I thought.

I collapsed into my bed and stared up at the ceiling. It took a long time for me to unwind, but I finally closed my eyes and fell asleep.

The phone rang. I almost fell out of bed at the noise. It was eleven o'clock in the morning.

"Hello Nicky?" It was Nathan. "How are you?"

"I'm O.K."

"What's the matter?" Could he know about what had just happened? No… he couldn't be in with Rocco. I felt so confused.

"Nothing. I'll tell you when I see you. Nathan, why are you calling?"

"I'm calling to offer you an offer you can't refuse. I have, in my hands, two round-trip tickets to Bermuda. Yes, I said Bermuda – and I want to treat you. You could use it I think, and we could have a real party vacation. Three weeks. How does that sound? You're off from school now anyway, right?"

"With three weeks left till school. Did you plan this? Why do you want to take me? Don't you have someone…" I stopped. I wanted to say a boyfriend, but I couldn't.

"Because you're my friend and I think we'd have a lot of fun. You and I can go man-hunting together." I couldn't help laughing.

"When are you leaving?"

"Later today."

"You couldn't give me more notice?"

"Actually, a friend of mine was going to use them and he broke up with his boyfriend and doesn't feel like going now. He's very depressed and just gave me these tickets an hour ago." I paused, thinking. "Nicky, just say yes. Your summer job is over, you have three weeks to relax on the beach, and what better company than me? Besides, I want to make things up to you."

I didn't have to think long. Getting out of the country with someone who would be fun to be with – all right, he wouldn't make any passes at me – would carry me away from the world of horror I had been in. It would do me good and by the time I returned, all the events that had just happened would be a faded memory. It would be the best vacation I had ever had and Nathan would make it fun.

# Chapter 12

The airport was crowded and people kept bumping into me. Each time someone knocked into me, I jumped or ducked, thinking it might be someone from Rocco's crowd. I kept looking behind me to see if I was being followed. Once on the airplane, I would feel much more secure and safe.

There was Nathan, just as he said he would be, standing by the baggage check. He looked so calm and happy, and he smiled as soon as he saw me. "Too bad he's gay," I thought again. He looked so handsome in his linen pants and polo shirt. His life was so simple, running a successful business, taking off when he wanted to, not worrying about people following him or threatening him.

He gave me a big hug and a kiss and began talking lightly about Bermuda, going biking and eating fish at a restaurant overlooking the ocean. I let his talk lighten my mood as we checked our baggage and then walked to the gate. The airport was a cheerful place. People were dressed casually, lugging their bags, talking happily and with anticipation. There was nothing like traveling to escape life for awhile. This trip would make life seem normal again. Thank goodness for Nathan and his ideas.

I put my carry-on on the conveyor belt to be checked and walked through the metal detector, starting to feel much better. Nathan was still talking from behind me about all the things we would do together.

"Did you ever go water-skiing, Nicky?" I heard him say. "Wait till you see the boat a friend of mine has. We'll use it and if you're feeling brave, we'll water ski."

I couldn't picture being brave enough to water ski… I was never athletic or inclined to take risks. I turned around to tell this to Nathan, when I noticed a man standing by a window looking at us with a piercing stare. Oh no… was this more trouble, or was I being paranoid?

I grabbed Nathan's hand as soon as we had our carry-on's again and pulled him to walk faster.

"Hey, take it easy, Nicky. What's the rush? The plane's not leaving for a half hour."

"Turn around and look at the man in the brown jacket. Is he suspicious-looking or what?" I asked in a whisper. "Does he look like he has a gun, or am I being paranoid?" Nathan chuckled.

"Paranoid? You're as paranoid as a fly in a spider's web." He turned around and his smile vanished when his eyes met the man's. He was still staring at us and straightened up when he saw Nathan turn around. "Nicky, I don't know who that guy is, but he sure is staring at us. Let's walk more quickly."

We quickened our pace and the man began to walk behind us. Couldn't I ever get away from these horrible people? All I was doing was going on vacation. Why was it so hard to do anything without someone following me or threatening me? Well, we were so close to the gate… I had to get onto that airplane and be safe again.

Suddenly I felt a strong hand on my arm which stopped me from walking. I swirled around to see another tall man looking down at me. There was someone else holding Nathan's arm as well, so the four of us halted and stared at each other. The two men seemed to come from nowhere. My heart was beating in my throat. Well, they couldn't shoot us in the middle of an airport. They must be Rocco's men. But why? I had just finished with them. There was also no way that I was going back to a deserted building again.

"Are you Nicky Steinway?" The man who was holding me asked. I nodded yes, too terrified to talk. Nathan squirmed in the other man's grasp, saying, "hey, what's going on here anyway? Do you know who we are?"

"Yeah, we know exactly who you are. That's why we're here."

They pulled and pushed us through a nearby doorway and shoved us into a pair of chairs. The room was some sort of lounge, with soft chairs, sofas and tables scattered around the room. Outside I could see the planes standing by their gates. They could shoot us in here if they wanted to… it was private enough and with gun silencers, no one would know a thing. I closed my eyes for a few moments. This was not how I had intended on leaving this world. After escaping a gun shooting, a car trying to run me over and Rocco in that filthy basement, this was how my life would end?

Nathan stared at me as if to say, "what is going on?" and I shrugged. I really had no clue as to who these men were or why they were here.

"We'll be right back," one of them said. They left through the door and I heard it lock. Nathan jumped up behind them and tried to prevent them from closing the door, but he wasn't strong enough to prevent it from closing.

Nathan looked around the room and then turned to me. "What the hell is going on?"

"I don't know, Nathan. These must be Rocco's men. Maybe they don't want us to leave the country."

"There's no way out of this room, unless we take a chair and break the window there. Even then, it's a big drop to the ground." He collapsed into a sofa and stared at the ceiling. "Who's Rocco?"

I moved closer to him and told him quickly what had happened that night. Nathan sat quietly as I spoke, soaking up every word I said.

"So you think these might be Rocco's people?" He asked after I finished. I nodded yes.

"Who else could they be?" Nathan nodded no.

"If it was Rocco and we were doing something he didn't want us to do, we'd be dead by now."

"How do you know?"

"Because I know Rocco. He used to be good friends with my father. We even had him over for dinner a few times. He can be really nice and he can be really mean." Nathan sat back. "No, he wouldn't leave us locked up in a room like this. He'd just kill us. And he would never treat me like this."

I felt a little surge of relief that we weren't dealing with Rocco, but then we were still locked up in an airport lounge and still going to miss our flight if this lasted much longer.

Suddenly the door to the lounge opened and non other than Jack Jeffries walked in. He left the door open behind him and smiled at us as he said, "hello, folks." He sat down on one of the chairs in a relaxed manner, as though he were at a social gathering. As he crossed his legs, he spoke to Nathan.

"Mr. Suma, I'm Detective Jeffries… New York Police Department. You are free to leave. I'm sorry if we caused you any trouble. You can still make your flight."

"What about Nicky?" Nathan asked. Jack nodded no.

"I have to speak to her for a few moments. I'll send her right out to you, Mr. Suma."

"Is she in trouble with the law?" Nathan persisted. Jack re-crossed his legs and sighed. "Not really. You'd make things a lot easier if you'd leave now." Nathan got up and looked at me.

"Go ahead, Nathan," I said quietly. "I didn't do anything and I don't know why I'm being detained." I said the last few words in a particularly irritated tone and gave Jack a dirty look.

"O.K., Nicky. I'll wait for you right outside." Nathan picked up his carry-on, nodded to Jack and left the room. "Don't keep her too long, Detective… we only have fifteen minutes to departure."

"What the hell is going on, Jack? What right do you have –"

Jack interrupted me with a loud whistle.

"Hold it, Nicky… you don't have any right to pounce on me."

"What do you mean I don't have any right?!" I stood up. "You don't give me protection when I need it, you play around with my feelings and now you are ruining my vacation! Who do you think you are?"

"I'm Detective Jeffries and I can do anything the hell I want to. I could arrest you right now for fleeing the country."

"I didn't know that going to the Bahamas was a crime."

"It is when you're a murder suspect." I sat down quietly, feeling a combination of fear and anger.

"You know I didn't kill Ralph." I said softly.

"Maybe, maybe not."

"Now you're being ridiculous." My courage was surging up as I became more angry. "You're dangling me at the end of a string again but I'm not taking it anymore. You have to let me go, Jack. You know I have another semester of medical school coming up in three weeks. You think I would give that up to flee the country because I might be a murder suspect? You have other people to chase besides me."

"Like Rocco? I know about your jaunt with him yesterday." I jumped up and walked to him, standing in front of him.

"If you knew about that, why didn't you save me? I could have been killed in there. What kind of a detective are you?"

"I'm a detective who's been keeping an eye on you. It would have been a lot easier if you didn't throw the wire away."

"Oh, that stupid microphone? You're too much Jack. You didn't protect me at all with that thing. Now can I go?" He nodded no.

"Fine. I'm leaving." I began to walk to the door when he grabbed me by the shoulders and pushed me into a chair. He held me hard as I resisted him and put his face close to mine.

"I don't know who you think you are," He said quietly, "but I am a detective with the New York City police who's trying to solve a murder. As far as I'm concerned, you're nothing but a murder suspect who waves around the fact that she's a medical student. And you think that gets you off the hook. You're nothing but a suspect to me, Nicky Steinway. And you're not leaving till I'm done with you." Yes, he could be tough when he wanted to be, and it worked because I was frightened. I didn't even care about my flight anymore.

"So, what do you want?" I conceded. Jack let go of me and stood up in silence. I looked up at him and waited. He pulled over a chair and sat across from me.

Jack put his head in his hands and was silent. I waited, watching him. What did he want from me? I wasn't a murder suspect... at one point I was helping him get into the minds of people like Rocco. Why was he causing me so much trouble? Now I started to think about my flight and I looked at my watch. Fifteen minutes to take-off.

Jack looked up at me. "I'm sorry, Nicky. I didn't mean to lose my temper. You're not a criminal. You're a good kid."

"Thanks." It was an expressionless "thanks." I just looked at him silently and he stared back at me. I saw that he was formulating something in his mind and was just trying to figure out how to say it.

"Nicky." His tone was soft now and he took my hand and held it. "I don't want to see you getting into any deep trouble. You know, if you leave the country, I can't protect you."

"Have you been protecting me so well lately?" I couldn't hide the sarcasm in my voice. "Do you know who dragged me into the basement of a deserted building the other day? I could have been killed. Where were you that time?"

"I knew about Rocco. We suspect—"

"You knew? How could you know? And if you knew, where were you?"

"Nicky, I'm not your guardian angel. You're the one who threw that transmitter in my face. You made it pretty hard to protect you." I stood up and gasped loudly.

"Jack Jeffries, will you please get off my back and leave me alone?" I turned away from him and walked to the window, my back facing him. "What do you want from me?" There was silence and then I felt his hands on my shoulders. The held me gently and I could hear him breathing.

"Nicky." His tone was soft and almost a whisper. "I don't want anything to happen to you."

"I'm going on vacation with a friend. Is that so dangerous?" My tone matched his. I turned to him and our faces were very close. "I think I'm safer outside of this country than inside it." I began to smile when suddenly his lips were on mine and he kissed me gently. I pulled away and stared at him incredulously. "Are you retaining me for questioning, Jack Jeffries, or for kissing?" He let me go.

"I'm sorry, Nicky. That was inappropriate… very inappropriate. You can go now." He turned away from me and looked out the window. "Just be very careful." I paused, then grabbed my bag and walked quickly out of the lounge. There were no guards outside the door and I began to run to my gate.

I made it to the plane on time and sat down next to Nathan.

"What was that all about?" Nathan asked, as he took my bag and put it under his seat.

"I think a certain detective has a crush on me."

"Oh, I knew that a long time ago." I stared at him bewildered. "Nicky, that night you came into my club with him, his eyes were devouring you."

"He just kissed me."

"What?! Just now?" I nodded yes. "You could sue for harassment or something." I leaned my head against the headrest and closed my eyes. "Do you like him? You think he stopped you just to see if we're having an affair?"

"No, I think he just wanted to make sure I was O.K. I'm not sure. He didn't really say too much to me… just 'be careful.'"

"After he kissed you, or before? Nicky, that's very bizarre."

As the plane took off, I kept my eyes closed and thought about the kiss. It felt too good. Why had Jack detained me? Was it to give me a warning, or just to see me again? I smiled to myself. Was I flattering myself too much by wondering if he just wanted to see me and kiss me? No, he was out of control when we kissed… that couldn't have been the plan. He could be fired for something like that. I wondered if there was a hidden camera in the lounge and other police officers saw it on tape. Then he'd really be in trouble. Still, I liked his kiss and liked the feeling of being in his arms.

No, a detective and a doctor wouldn't work. Too different. Well, maybe when I got back I would give him a call under the pretext of checking on the progress of the case. Maybe he'd ask me out to dinner… or, he'd just bounce me on the end of a string again. He was too mixed up. If he really liked me, he would have asked me out by now.

I opened my eyes and saw the steward coming with the drink cart. Yes, I'd have a cola… that would make me feel better. And this vacation I wouldn't worry about anything. Not about Jack, or school or my safety. I deserved a real break now and Nathan and I were going to have the time of our lives… or try to anyway.

# Chapter 13

Getting off of the plane, we went down a metal staircase right onto the cement runway and the warm air blew into my hair and felt great. There wasn't a cloud in the sky and I squeezed Nathan's hand excitedly. Deep down inside I knew I was going to have a great time. Nathan smiled , obviously echoing my thoughts and then gave me a hug. It was too bad that I wasn't with a real boyfriend… well, maybe I would meet someone on this island. Relaxation was the main goal now, with all I had been through recently. Here there was no Rocco, no cars trying to run me down, no guns and no Jack Jeffries, thank goodness.

Standing by the baggage claim, I still looked around the room, trying to see if anyone was staring at me or had a familiar face. The paranoid part of my brain told me that someone could still have followed us here. But each face looked fresh and new. Each person was in his/her own world, only concerned with finding their bags and rushing out to start the vacation or business trip or whatever. I sighed a small sigh and chided myself for looking for one of Rocco's men or a detective. We were safe here and no one cared what we did.

The cab to the hotel had worn out its shock absorbers and must have been twenty years old. The engine heaved itself up the hills and the cab driver looked as though he was working very hard to steer the car.

But we made it to the hotel intact. Nathan had picked it and made all the arrangements and he certainly had done a good job. He looked at me expectedly as we drove up the semi-circular drive in front.

The Prince Hotel was at the edge of town but was built on the water, so the views were either of the town or the bay. Boats passed back and forth in a slow pace, as though on vacation themselves. The pool was large and the room we had was a suite booked under the name of Mr. and Mrs. Suma. I looked at Nathan questionably when we were at the front desk and this was announced.

"I thought it would be easier this way," Nathan said quietly in the elevator. "No questions, no weird looks... though I'm sure lots of unmarried people book under separate names."

"So, you're a little old-fashioned?" I asked.

"I guess so. Well, in certain ways."

We had a terrace overlooking the pool and bay and after collapsing on one of the double beds for a few moments, I walked out on the terrace to breathe in the fresh sea air. What a great idea this had been.

Nathan patted me on the back.

"Nicky, do you know what everyone does here as soon as they arrive? Mopeds. Want to rent one? I'll show you around." Nathan had been to Bermuda many times, even as a child, he had told me on the plane. It was an escape for his mother, who rented a house here each year for months at a time. Nathan was free to explore the town, the forts on the water and all the hotels. He knew short-cuts to everywhere and also knew the areas to stay away from.

We rented two mopeds and Nathan led the way on the winding roads of the island. The weather was perfect, the ocean licked the shore and the wind caressed my body as we drove. This was what life was all about.

We stopped to sit on some rocks overlooking the ocean. Nathan turned to me and stared.

"What?" I asked.

"Nicky, have you resolved in your mind about the whole thing in the hospital?"

"Have you?" I asked back. He shrugged. "Do you think that your father is still alive?"

"Do you?"

"What is this, Nathan, a game of cat and mouse?" We sat in silence. "Where would your father be if he were alive? Would he be in the United States or somewhere else? Maybe Italy?"

"I don't know for sure. And to answer your other question about whether he's alive, I also don't know for sure."

"Boy, this is the first frank conversation I'm having with you, Nathan."
"Well, the whole thing has been on my mind, especially lately, for some reason. Now that you probably feel safe, it's a good time to air dirty laundry. Maybe it's better that I don't know for sure. If he were alive, he wouldn't want to be with me or see me anyway. I was always a wimp to him." I put my arm around him, but was silent because I had nothing to offer to comfort him.

"You know, Nathan, I am sort of in the same boat as you. I am not really close to my parents either. They're in their own world and seem to always be traveling. Yes, we talk on the phone, but I don't feel close to them. When I see a mother and daughter eating lunch in a restaurant or going shopping together, I envy them."

"I know how you feel, Nicky. I wish I had been able to be closer to my father too."

"So doesn't it bother you terribly that your father may even be alive and you don't know where he is?"

"No, because deep in my heart I know he's dead."

"And what about your mother? You know, I met her at the funeral. She was- uh- is beautiful."

"Yeah. We talk a lot over the phone and we're pretty close."

"You never talk about her."

"Maybe not. I think about her a lot though. She's probably working on her next husband already."

"That's a weird thing to say."

"You don't know my mother. She's a very dependent person. She's stunning, sophisticated and intelligent, but she's one of those women who always needs a man in her life. My father took good care of her money-wise, but she needs someone to lean on... Someone to slip her arm around at dinner parties."

"You make her seem so shallow."

"No, I don't mean to. Well, let's change the subject. In fact, let's ride and explore some more."

"One more question, Nathan. Does your mother know you're here in Bermuda?"

"Probably."

"What do you mean 'probably?'" Nathan shrugged.

"We keep tabs on each other's whereabouts."

"And does she know you're here with me?" He shrugged again and didn't answer. Instead he got up quietly and held out his hand to help me up. "Sometimes you're really hard to talk to, Nathan."

How close to his mother could he be if she might not even know that he was in Bermuda? What kind of a family was this? Well, I couldn't figure everything out all at once. I wanted more information, but Nathan was sending out signals to leave him alone.

So, we got onto our mopeds in silence and I began to follow Nathan again. Well, maybe I was taking everything too seriously. We came here to have a good time and that was what I was going to do. I knew that if I tried to dig more into Nathan's family and his relationships, I would only get frustrated and maybe even get into trouble. I would leave it alone for now. I began to concentrate on the wind hitting my face and on the ocean on our left.

As we followed the road parallel to the ocean, we went up and down hills, sometimes leaving the ocean below us, sometimes riding on the level of the sea. We were high on a hill when I saw the man. When he saw us, he began to wave his hands in the air to catch our attention. As we got closer, I saw that he looked frantic. He yelled to us, "please stop! I need help!" Nathan turned to me and nodded, signaling that we should stop.

"Please help me," he said as we pulled up to him. "My sister – my sister is down there." He pointed down to the ocean. "We were on our mopeds and she was going too fast… I guess she lost control. She went over this cliff and is down there. Please, she's unconscious. Can you help me get her up here and to the medical center? I think she's bad."

I got off my moped and walked to the edge of the cliff. There she was, lying on the sand, about a hundred feet  below. She was on her side and wasn't moving. I also saw her moped not far from her, the ocean's waves licking its wheels.

"As the tide comes in, she'll be taken into the ocean. I can't take her up by myself," he said urgently. The cliff was steep. It wouldn't be easy. I looked at Nathan.

"O.K.," Nathan said calmly. "Let's go get her."

It was difficult climbing down the rocks to get to the beach below. I scraped my hands and knees repeatedly, though Nathan kept giving me a hand. I was sweating, though there was a good sea breeze running in with the waves.

"It's a good thing we have a doctor here," Nathan said with a half smile.

"Really?" the man asked. He looked at me expectedly, as though waiting for me to confirm the fact. My heart sank. Any time someone pointed out that I was a doctor, everyone's expectations rose, whether it was at a cocktail party or in a situation like this. Now this man will think I know everything, including how to save this lady's life. And I had no medical equipment.

"Yes, I'm a medical student," I said quietly. I saw him shrug in disappointment.

"Oh, a medical student," he echoed solemnly.

Nathan reached the lady first and turned her over on her back.

"Don't move her!" I cried. "She might have a broken back and then you might do more damage to her spine."

"Oh great," the man said. "How are we going to get her out of here if we can't move her? By helicopter? By the way, there are no helicopters on the island, oh medical student." I narrowed my eyes as I looked at him.

"I'm only trying to help you. I could just leave now if you want."

"No, no, I'm sorry. I'm just upset."

"Why don't we see if she's breathing and has a pulse?" I said to dismiss him.

She was breathing on her own and her pulse was strong.

"I guess it's just a concussion and a few broken bones," Nathan commented matter-of-factly.

"That's easy for you to say." The man answered. "How could you be so callous? Who are you two anyway?"

"I'm Nicky Steinway and this is Nathan Suma. I'm sorry if we've offended you. We're only trying to help." The man sighed.
"I'm Lucien and this is my sister Amy. We were traveling pretty fast on our mopeds and I just saw Amy go over the cliff and – and –" he shuddered. "You've go to help us. She's got to be all right."

In one swift gesture, Nathan picked Amy up and put her over his shoulder.

"I didn't know you were so strong. Are you all right, Nathan?" I asked. He nodded.

"Sorry, Nicky, we have to move her or we'll all drown as the tide comes in. Let's get out of here before she becomes too heavy for me."

I could barely climb up the rocks without carrying someone, so I don't know how Nathan managed. Now and then Lucien would help him by fixing an arm or moving her torso more onto his shoulder. We did it and as soon as we reached the road again, Nathan gently lied her down. She was very limp, but her heartbeat was strong and regular. I checked her breathing and it was regular too.

"We have to get her to the hospital," Lucien said staring down the road. "I hope someone comes soon."

Sure enough, a truck whirred towards us and Lucien jumped into the road to stop it. The truck had no choice but to stop, or it would have run Lucien over. The road was only a single lane.

"What the hell you doing'?" The driver yelled. "Get outta' my way, man." He was a native and the back of his truck was filled with cement blocks.

Lucien walked up close to the man, pointed to Amy and told him in two sentences that we had to get to the hospital quickly. When the driver saw the body, he nodded and told us to get in the back with the cement blocks. I didn't relish the thought of taking a bumpy truck ride on hard cement.

"Can you handle this alone?" I asked Lucien. "We'll help you put Amy in."

"Oh no, please come with me. What if she stops breathing on the way? I won't even know what to do. Please don't do this to me." He lifted Amy into the truck and turned to us.

Nathan put our mopeds into the truck without a word, as if knowing I wouldn't turn Lucien down. He jumped in the back, pulled me up and Lucien followed. The truck started up again and, just as I had predicted, I felt every bump in my back. They apparently didn't make trucks with shock absorbers in Bermuda and sitting on cement wasn't helping a bit. I hoped Lucien knew what we were doing for him.

I held Amy's wrist in my hand, keeping track of her pulse, and every few minutes I checked her breathing. She could have no broken bones or she could have a broken back, for all I knew. Unfortunately, I hadn't rotated through orthopedics yet, so I knew very little about bones and joints at the moment.

The medical center – if you could call it that – looked like a block of concrete. It was a squared-off building with the paint fraying on the outside to reveal the concrete blocks beneath. I sighed. Well, I wasn't coming here to work… just to drop a patient off and get back to having fun.

The truck screeched to a halt – well, at least the brakes worked – and I almost fell out the back for lacking something to hold on to. Nathan grabbed me by the arm and saved me from the fall.

We promptly jumped down and I looked around for someone with a stretcher. No luck. There was a small sign reading "Emergency" by the door nearby but no sign of any people. What happened on this island when there was a real crisis or emergency? I shook my head and turned to Lucien and Nathan.

"Looks like I'll have to go get some help." Nathan jumped off the truck.

"No, Nicky, let me go." He ran into the building as I checked Amy's breathing and pulse again.

What kind of a hospital was this? Here we had a dire emergency and no one was around to help us or even see that we had arrived. I sighed. I was too used to the hospitals in New York City where as soon as anyone sat down by the emergency room entrance, they were whisked right in. Well, any doctor who worked out here had to be a little crazy anyway. This was too far from civilization. Bermuda was nice for a vacation, but there were no medical meetings and no professional stimulation. A journal coming in the mail was probably all the medical education a doctor could receive on this island.

"Hello, I'm Dr. Allen." I was checking Amy's breathing, so I did not turn around to face him. I was feeling so irate and frustrated at not getting immediate help, I began to let him have it immediately.

"What kind of a place is this anyway?" I asked. "No attention, no help, no one here to see that we came with a very bad emergency…" I turned around as he hopped up on the truck and I stopped talking as soon as our eyes met. He was gorgeous.

I watched him do a preliminary examination on Amy as two men waited nearby with a stretcher. He felt her neck and her back, pulled out a stethoscope to listen to her chest and asked me for a history. Lucien jumped in with that and I just stared at Dr. Allen as they moved her onto the stretcher. She was still very limp.

Dr. Allen was tall, tan and had wavy black hair. His eyes were light green and darted around as he gave orders to the men wheeling Amy inside. He turned around and held his arms open to me in order to help me to jump down from the truck. What strong, confident arms.

We faced each other as he held me by my shoulders. Dr. Allen smiled. "What's your name?" he asked.

"Nicky."

"Dr. Nicky, your friend tells me." I nodded. "Well, Nicky, this is not New York City. Usually we are telephoned about emergencies coming to the hospital and in that case we are here waiting for them… especially a case like this. What's the matter, you don't have a cellular phone?" He smiled good-naturedly. "Come in while I attend to her and then we'll talk." He shook my hand. "Nice meeting you."

He ran to follow the stretcher and Nathan came up to me.

"What a looker he is." Nathan said into my ear. "Too bad he's not—"

"Please, Nathan. Don't even say the word."

"What? What word?" He teased. "Gay?"

Lucien was thanking the truck driver and giving him some money. He then walked up to us and thanked us profusely. We shook hands.

"Listen, you two don't have to stay here. You've done a lot. I can call you a cab, if you'd like."

"Oh no," Nathan answered and glanced at me. "We want to make sure Amy will be all right. Right, Nicky?" I nodded.

"That's very nice of you," Lucien said quietly. He turned around and walked ahead of us into the emergency room.

"Besides," Nathan whispered in my ear. "We both want to get another look at that gorgeous doctor." He snickered and I poked him playfully. "Let's see who gets him first."

The Emergency Room was nothing like any in New York City. It was a small room with one window near the ceiling. There was a circular fan hanging form the ceiling and a few cabinets lining the walls. There were two beds standing parallel to each other and a simple nurse's station… that was it. Well, this was the Caribbean.

Amy already had an intravenous line and was hooked up to a nasal cannula of oxygen. Dr. Allen was listening to her chest with a stethoscope when we walked in. I looked around for a waiting room and didn't even see one. We sat down in a corner where there were a few chairs.

He really was very nice looking and very well-built. I wondered if he was married. I turned to Nathan and he was staring at him too. This was a pretty comical situation. Here this girl could by dying and we both were drooling over the doctor caring for her.

He was oblivious to us as he checked all the monitors and calmly stated orders to the nurse next to him.

When he was done, Dr. Allen walked over to us and smiled.

"It was very nice of you to care for this lady. Most of the natives would have run away from a situation like this."

"I don't know if the ride on the cement truck helped her any," I said quietly. "Do you think she has any broken bones?"

"She may. We're sending X-ray over right now and a CT-scan is going to be done too."

"You have a CT scanner here?" I said impressed. Dr. Allen chuckled.

"Nicky, this may not be New York, but a CT scanner is a bare necessity in any medical center." He spoke so well and was so sophisticated. He must have been raised in an upper class setting... he was also just stunning... and his lips were so kissable.

"And how does a doctor exactly end up in a hospital like this? I assume you're American." Nathan said quietly. He was hypnotized by Dr. Allen's looks too.

"Why don't we all discuss that over coffee? Our patient is stable and the cafeteria is just down the hallway." Nathan and I looked at each other and nodded. I was actually pretty hungry.

So, we followed him to a small cafeteria and I ordered a paper-thin hamburger and French fries while Nathan had an orange juice. He was on a diet. But Dr. Allen joined in with a plain cup of coffee. Maybe he was on a diet too.

"Nothing like a beautiful woman with an appetite." Dr. Allen smiled at me. There was an admiring sparkle in his eyes and I began to think he was interested in me. Nathan coughed and said he wanted to go back to the emergency room.

"I've had a tough day. After you finish your lunch Nicky, let's head back. I'm going to rest on one of the sofas in the lobby." With that, Nathan got up, nursing his orange juice, and left.

Dr. Allen's eyes didn't leave my face as Nathan left. "How did you come to be on the island, Nicky?"

"Vacation. How about you?"

"I got an offer I couldn't refuse. I was also fleeing a nasty divorce settlement and had it with Boston. I wanted to start over in a new place very far away and with a complete change to it. I happen to be very happy here, despite the incredulous look on your face. Believe it or not, people can be content in a place like this. Life is more simple but more rewarding."

"You couldn't get me to stay here for good. You're so far away from modern civilization."

"Just what I want. You see, Nicky, I was born into a very wealthy family. I had everything anyone could want… the best cars, a big house, servants… and I thought I needed all of that to be happy. I found a very lovely lady to marry who came from a very rich family as well. It was supposed to be the match made in heaven, but it wasn't. She was very spoiled and besides having me for a husband, she had many other men to suit her fancies. I couldn't stand for that and that was the end of it all. I disappointed my parents by leaving her… they were enthralled with the fact that Josefina came from the wealthiest banking family in the country. I was not impressed with her or her family."

"So why did you marry her?"

"She was beautiful, enchanting and captured me in her spell. She could do that, you know. And she could get anything or anyone she wanted to. Well, enough about me and my sordid past. Why hasn't anyone snatched you up yet?" I shrugged.

"Right now my only concern is getting through medical school. I couldn't be married right now. I can barely take care of myself these days, let alone worry about a husband."

"You're smart." Suddenly the overhead pager paged Dr. Allen to the emergency room. He looked hard at me. "How about dinner tomorrow night?" My heart jumped.

"I'd love to."

"Where are you staying?"

"The Prince Hotel downtown."

"Can I pick you up at eight?"

"Sure." He got up and smiled.

"I'll look forward to it immensely." He shook my hand and vanished too quickly.

"So he really asked you out?" Nathan asked on the ride back to the hotel. We were driving our mopeds a little too fast, but my head was spinning a little from Dr. Allen… I didn't even know his first name. "Gee, and I thought he might be interested in me." We chuckled.

"So, what should we do tonight besides go shopping for a new dress for you? After all, you want to impress this doctor, since I didn't." Nathan turned his cheek to me. "You know, there's a fancy dress shop in the hotel."

"Nathan I brought a dress. Do you buy a new outfit every time you go out with someone new?"

"If I'm trying to make an impression. Wearing something new that makes you look especially nice makes you feel special."

"Let's call the hospital later and see how Amy made out," I thought out aloud.

Amy woke up about an hour after we left the hospital and had suffered a bad concussion. They were keeping her for observation. When I called the emergency room and spoke to the head nurse, Lucien got on the phone and thanked me over and over.

"If it hadn't been for you and your friend, Amy might not have made it. I will always be grateful to you for saving my sister."

"Lucien, I only did what anyone would do in the same circumstance. If you need anything else, just let us know. We'll come visit her sometime soon. Maybe tomorrow."

Nathan and I ate in a seafood restaurant with a terrace overlooking the main street in Bermuda. It was a warm night and eating as we watched the people walk below us was very enjoyable. At the same time, we could hear the sounds of the ocean not too far away.

This vacation had really been the best thing for me. All day I hadn't thought of Ralph, or guns or the police. It was probably the first full day I was free from those thoughts since the whole thing had happened.

"You know, Nicky, if you want to, after lunch tomorrow we can take a boat or the mopeds across to another part of the island and I can show you where my mother and I used to stay when we came here. It's a beautiful house that's always rented. The owner lives in Tokyo but rents the house all year round by the week, the month or the year. We could walk by it, if you want. There are beautiful gardens." I nodded yes... it sounded wonderful.

# Chapter 14

Are you sure it's all right that we're coming here, Nathan? This is private property."

"It's fine." Nathan said as he swung himself off of his moped. "The owner knows me and it's not like we're here to rob the place. Maybe no one is renting the house this week anyway."

I followed him to the front door. It was open. Nathan pushed it open and we walked inside.

"Nathan... I don't know if this is right."

"Come on, Nicky. It's O.K. I don't think anyone is here."

We walked into a grand living room. There were floor-to-ceiling windows covered with sheer white curtains. They opened onto a wrap-around terrace that overlooked the ocean from the top of a cliff. The view was breath-taking.

"Now I see why you came here, Nathan." We walked back to the living room and Nathan walked behind the bar. "What are you doing?!" I asked with a warning in my voice.

"Nicky, take it easy. Mr. Takayama always keeps the bar stocked, whether the house is being rented or not."

"So that gives you the right to steal a drink? What's wrong with you? I think we should leave. There might even be people upstairs. They'll think we're robbing the place. Someone might come down the stairs with a shotgun."

"Boy, someone's imagination is running wild." Nathan calmly drank from a glass. "Want some scotch?"

"No, and I'll meet you outside." I walked out to the mopeds and gazed up at the house again. It was gorgeous, with terraces gracing every window and a Spanish tiled roof finishing off its beauty. What a house.

Nathan came out within minutes, we got on the mopeds and zoomed off… not quickly enough for me, but quickly enough so that no one saw us.

Dr. Allen came to the hotel in a two-door Mercedes sportscar. I had never been picked up in such a nice car and it made a great immediate impression on me.

"So, you like the car?" He asked. He must have seen the way I was studying the dashboard. I loved cars and I especially liked nice, expensive cars… probably because I was a long way from being able to afford one of my own.

It was a beautiful night with a warm breeze and I wore a simple red dress with spaghetti straps. I didn't talk to Nathan as I got dressed. I was mad at him for dragging me into that house earlier that day. How could he be so unthinking?

So, I put on my perfume and my shoes with my back to him and when the front desk rang to say that my date had arrived, I left without saying good-bye. I was probably being too hard on him. It was just Nathan's nature to be a bit carefree. I would talk to him later if he was still up.

"You look beautiful, Nicky," Dr. Allen pushed me out of my thoughts.

"Thank you- you know, I don't even know your first name."

"Seth."

"Seth? You don't look like a Seth."

"So, what are Seth's supposed to look like?"

"I don't know."

"The name 'Seth' was given to me because of my grandfather. His name was Stanley. Now, don't you want to know where we're going? I picked a great place that's right on the water. You'll love it. Do you like seafood?"

"Oh, yes."

"Then hang on… I'm going to step on the gas so I can treat you to the best tuna you'll ever wrap your tongue around." With that, he shifted the car and we sped off. I tightened my grip on the door's armrest and swallowed my stomach.

The restaurant was wonderful. The tables were outside, right on the water, and the stars were brilliant. The ocean lapped against the shore nearby and Seth was charming. He joked, told me stories and held my hand.

"So tell me, Nicky, what are your dreams?"

"Well, first I want to be an ophthalmologist. I'd like to write some kind of a book that makes a difference in our society and be a little famous too."

"Famous for what?"

"I don't know… either something medical or non-medical. Maybe I'll write the great American novel."

"You write?"

"As a hobby."

Seth held up his glass in a toast. "To Nicky: the most beautiful doctor and writer I've ever met." Oh, he certainly could be charming… and his breeding was showing.

Well, over dinner he swept me off of my feet. I was a little giddy from the wine, but the tuna steak was definitely the best I had ever had.

Seth guided me out of the restaurant and we got into his car.

"Where to now?" I asked.

"Would you like to see my house? There are no dishonorable intentions, Nicky. I have a beautiful deck overlooking the ocean and we can sit and talk and get to know each other better. Then I'll take you back to the hotel." It sounded wonderful.

As he started the car, I turned to look at his profile. He was so handsome… probably one of the most handsome men I had ever gone out with.

"So how does a guy like you end up on an island like this?" I asked.

"I told you… I was escaping."

"Escaping from the evil wife?" He nodded yes. "And what would the wife say?"

"The ex-wife would say the same thing and that I was out of my mind."

"You left money, position, status, to practice medicine on a small island full of tourists."

"That makes me happy. I didn't need the money or the status of being a lap dog to a rich lady."

"Are you ever going to get married again?" Seth shrugged in silence.

The drive was gorgeous. A warm breeze tickled my face and I rested my head against the headrest to enjoy the ride. I closed my eyes as we talked, but I caught Seth glancing at me a few times. Maybe he was as taken with me as I was with him.

When the car stopped gently, I opened my eyes and caught my breath. We were in front of the house that Nathan had taken me to.

"This is your house?" I asked with surprise in my voice. I think Seth mistook my shock for being impressed.

"Yeah. Quite a place, right?" He jumped out of the car and opened my car door.

"You own this place?" I tested again. Maybe I was misunderstanding him.

"I have for five years now. I fell in love with it the minute I saw it. You should see it in the day time."

"Who owned it before you?" Would he say a Japanese guy?

"Boy, you sure ask a lot of questions. One of the islanders." So he was a liar.

"Where was the islander from?" Seth stopped and looked down at me thoughtfully.

"Is this an interrogation?" I laughed falsely.

"Oh, I was just curious. What kind of an islander would own a house like this? He would have had to be doing well."

"Not that well. The guy was bankrupt. He had a business in town that wasn't doing well. He still lives on the island... just in a smaller house." He was a very good liar. I sighed. Why was life always so complicated? I finally met a guy I really liked and he was already lying to me for some reason. Unless Nathan had his story wrong. But a Japanese owner just didn't fit into Seth's story.

Seth opened his front door and turned on the lights as we walked in. The sound of the ocean pounded from outside. There was the same living room before me. I looked at the bar, wondering if Nathan's Scotch glass would still be there. No, it was gone.

Seth looked so proud of his place. His place indeed.

"Want to see the deck? The ocean is beautiful at this time of night. Come out with me."

I followed him onto the deck and he turned on the lights outside. The sound of the ocean was so tranquilizing and I sighed again. This could have been the perfect evening… why was he lying about something so stupid? Something was going on.

I leaned on the railing and looked down at the ocean. All I could see was the white sea foam near the shore because it was dark. I felt Seth's arm come around my shoulders.

"Would you like a drink?" He asked softly.

"All I want is the truth from you."

"What do you mean?"

I turned to him and his face was very close to mine.

"You don't own this house, Seth. Why would you lie about that?" He laughed.

"Of course I own this house. I bought it when I moved here. How are you so sure, Nicky?"

"Let's say I have some inside information."

"Well, your inside information is wrong. Can I kiss you? I wasn't planning on it, but now that you're so close, I really want to." Our lips were very close. He leaned forward slowly and kissed me gently. His arms wrapped around my shoulders and he pulled me closer so that our chests were touching and he kissed me harder and harder. I liked his kisses and my head began to spin. He pulled away and looked at me intensely.

"Your kisses are marvelous, Nicky." He bent forward to kiss me again, but I pushed back and out of his embrace. "What is it, Nicky?" I was silent and leaned against the railing again. "The house is still bugging you?"

"How could you lie to me on a first date? Please take me home."

I turned the key in the lock of the hotel room, purposely making more noise than usual, hoping I would wake Nathan up if he were sleeping. I let the door slam a little loudly and was happy to see that the light was on. Nathan was sitting up in bed reading a book.

"Oh, I'm so happy you're up, Nathan."

"Yes, here I am, always the bridesmaid, never the bride. How did it go? Did you score?" I sighed and collapsed on the bed, sitting by his knees.

"Nathan, I think he totally lied to me."

"About what?"

"About the house." I told Nathan what had happened, how we had had a delightful dinner, how he had charmed me to death and then had brought me to what he called "his" house. "And you told me that you always rented that house."

"Yes."

"When was the last time you rented it?"

"Last year. But I spoke to Mr. Takashama just last month to reserve the house for a few weeks this spring. He is definitely the owner... not your Prince Charming."

"So why would he lie about something like that? Why not tell me he rents it?"

"Could be something as simple as his wanting to impress you. Maybe he really lives in a shack."

"But he's a doctor. He's doing well. He's head of the emergency room for goodness sake."

"I'm sorry, Nicky. I can tell you're very disappointed. I would marry you if I were straight." We both smiled and hugged. "Men can be real rogues… take it from me. I am one."

"A man or a rogue?" I laughed softly.

"Both, of course." Leave it to Nathan to make me feel better.

"So did he ask you out again?"

"Yes, for tomorrow night, but I won't do it."

"Why not go out again to find out the truth and why he lied?"

"Because when I told him he was lying to me, he denied it so strongly and told me to go call Mr. Takashama myself and find out the truth. Then I should call him in the hospital and accept another date." We sat in silence for a few moments. "You know what? Why don't you and I have dinner tomorrow night at some swanky place?"

"I can't, Nicky. I have plans. Someone I met at the bar tonight. So, don't wait up for me tomorrow night… I won't be home till morning."

"You are a wild animal, Nathan Suma."

"Thank you."

The next morning I was lounging by the pool listening to soft music that a small band was playing. I had my eyes closed and was enjoying the soothing sounds of people laughing and jumping into the pool. Nathan was eating a late breakfast in the coffee shop and was going to meet me when he was done.

I started to doze off, when I felt the weight of someone sitting on my lounge chair. I opened my eyes and blinked in disbelief when I saw Seth.

"Hi, beautiful." He said quietly.

"Why aren't you at work?" I asked coolly.

"What a thing to ask me. Here I make the trip to your hotel, search you out, call you beautiful and you want to know why I'm not at work."

"You're a flirt." I was not going to show him that I was impressed that he had come to find me."

"And you are a hard lady to get through to."

"I am when you lie to me."

"Oh, that again?" We sat in silence. "Listen, Nicky, I want to make up with you and ask you if you'll have dinner with me tonight. I'm pretty crazy about you." He really was so charming. My willpower was melting. "I came all the way over here just to ask you out and to straighten any misunderstanding we have between us."

"Who owns the house we were in last night?" I asked quietly.

"I do, and I can prove it to you. Just let me take you to dinner tonight and I'll show you the facts. O.K.?"

"O.K."

"Good!" He slapped me on the thigh gently. "Now, can I have a kiss, so I can get back to work? I'm going in a little later today, but I have to get going now." Without waiting for an answer from me, he leaned forward, grabbed me by my shoulders and gave me a long, hard kiss. His lips made my mouth yearned for more and I kissed him back. I wrapped an arm around his neck and pulled him to me so he was practically lying on top of me. He gave me another kiss and then pulled back.

"I'm afraid the guests around this pool wouldn't appreciate a hot and steamy scene right now. Save it for later." He kissed me on the forehead and got up. "I'll pick you up at eight, O.K.?" I nodded yes. "And we're going to have a roaring wonderful time… I'll make some plans for us. See you later, Sweetheart." He blew me a kiss and was off.

I really was quite taken with him. Seth was charming and very smooth. There were so many questions I had about him, though. Why had he gotten divorced? Would he ever come back to the United States to visit me or marry me? I couldn't believe I was even thinking in terms of marrying him already. He had swept me off my feet, all right, and his kisses were wonderful. I would look forward to tonight.

I leaned back into my chaise lounge and closed my eyes again.

"Well, well, well," I heard a voice exclaim. "What do we have here? A love scene perhaps?" It was Nathan. "You took him back pretty quickly." He sat down on the lounge beside me. "Here I am, coming to the pool to take a nice dip and I see two people making out. Then I realize – why yes! – it's none other than my good friend Nicky and the man she threw away last night." I laughed.

"Well, he told me that tonight he will prove to me that he owns that house. Maybe I'm being stupid about the whole thing and jumped to conclusions too quickly."

"Sounds to me like love talking." Nathan sighed. "It's a good thing we're only here for a short time... otherwise you might not want to go back to New York and finish your training. Barefoot and pregnant in Bermuda in Seth's rented house." I echoed his sigh. Who knew what the right thing to do was? Well, I would have a good time tonight and enjoy the rest of the vacation. After that, no man or beast was going to alter my plans of returning to New York. How could Nathan say such a thing?

"Nathan, you're too much."

"All I can say is that I see trouble coming, Nicky Steinway. You'd better be careful with your heart."

Nathan threw a towel at me and ran off to jump into the pool.

Was I playing with fire, seeing Seth Allen? Well, it was a vacation. What was wrong with a little romance? Just because I liked someone didn't mean it was a dangerous situation. Nathan was just being over-protective.

There was an area next to the pool with tables and chairs where food and drinks were served. After sitting for awhile and then taking a dip in the pool, I decided to get a drink. I got up, walked to the bar, which was made of bamboo, and ordered a Daiquiri.

I looked around the pool and bar area and sighed happily. What a good idea this had been. All the "adventures" that had happened in New York before I had come here seemed very far away. In Bermuda I felt safe and secure and very distant from any troubles I had had before. No speeding cars, no guns, no Rocco, no one following me… it was a good feeling. Then I would return to my training with a fresh mind, forgetting any danger I had felt in the past. Whoever was after me before obviously had forgotten about me too because otherwise, I'd be having more trouble even here.

No, no one had followed me, no one was out to get me and life was back to normal.

Suddenly, my eyes rested on a face and I gasped. No, it couldn't be him. He was sitting at a table eating a salad, not aware of my gaze. Maybe I was mistaken. I walked a little closer and looked at the side of his face. It was him.

He turned abruptly and stared at me. Oh no… it was definitely Jack Jeffries.

"Hi, Nicky. What a nice surprise." He wore an ugly green shirt with palm trees all over it. Typical of a detective who didn't know how to dress.

"What are you doing here?" I asked quietly. I didn't quite know if I was happy or angry to see him. Had he followed me here?

"Well, that's a warm welcome. Sit down and keep me company."

"Did you follow me here?" Jack's smile vanished.

"You know, detectives go on vacation too sometimes. You are so self-centered Nicky. You think the whole world is in love with you."

"What a mean thing to say."

"I'm sorry. That was uncalled for. Please, sit down next to me and we'll start over again. Hello, Nicky, fancy meeting you here." I still stood above him.

"You really didn't follow me here? Is this a business trip? Am I still a suspect for anything?"

"No, no and no. I hope I got that straight. Come sit down, Nicky. I want to be your friend. Why don't we have a drink together?" I couldn't figure out why I had such antagonistic feelings towards Jack. After all, he had saved my life in New York and was just doing his job when he stopped me in the airport. He was basically a nice guy.

I sat down at his table as the waiter brought me the drink I had ordered. "I don't know why I get so angry with you sometimes, or so suspicious. I'm sorry, Jack. It is a total coincidence that we are on vacation on the same island, right?"

"Well, not a total coincidence. I knew you were here and when my vacation time came this week, I hadn't made any plans, so I came to Bermuda. I didn't come to check on you or to reprimand you or to follow you. Just came to say hello, in a certain respect." I smiled. It was quite a compliment to be followed to the Carribean.

"And what about that kiss in the airport? Did your following me here have anything to do with that?" I was flirting.

Jack looked down at his salad. "I'm sorry about that. Again, I was out of line. I got carried away with something. You bring out the best and the worst in me."

"And why is that?"

"Nicky, stop trying to wrap me around your little finger. So, you're a pretty medical student with a sharp wit. I like that in a woman and I just kissed you. It was a harmless quick kiss."

"That was a kiss you could get fired or sued for."

"Ah, you wouldn't sue me. I saved your life back in New York."

"Well, if you ever rub me the wrong way again, I'll sue you and the New York City Police Department." I said it playfully, but it was meant as a warning.

Jack looked at me hard as if trying to figure out whether I was kidding or not.

I broke the silence. "what's new with the case? Are you still working on it?"

"Yes, I'm still on it, though I'm not getting anywhere. I don't know why someone was trying to kill you at one point. Someone thought you knew too much. They obviously backed off, because otherwise you'd be dead now. They would have followed you to Bermuda as easily and as quickly as I did." He was being coarse and perhaps was trying to scare me, getting back at me. 'Oh well," he sighed, "let's not spar, Nicky. We are both here to have a good time, so let's do it. What are you doing for dinner tonight?"

"Are you asking me out? Can't anyway. I have plans." I was happy to turn him down and I hoped I had hurt him a little. I still couldn't understand why I wanted to hurt him. He was nice, handsome, a good kisser… maybe my feelings were stronger for him than I thought.

"Maybe tomorrow night?" I nodded automatically.

"I'll pick you up at your room at eight. Is that all right?" Yes, I said. "Room 510." I did a double-take.

"How did you know what my room number was?"

"I looked it up in the hotel lobby."

"And how did you know I was even at this hotel?" Jack shifted in his seat. There was silence. "Are you sure you're here on vacation, or are you casing the area?" Jack laughed nervously.

"Nicky, it's just as I said. I had some vacation time coming to me and I decided to follow you here. It's a long way to go for a dinner date."

Someone was calling my name. It was Nathan. I turned around and waved to him.

"I'm going now, Jack. See you tomorrow night." Jack smiled and muttered, "sooner than that." I turned to him and stared at him.
"What does that mean?"

"Well, you never know... we might bump into each other before tomorrow night." I nodded and said good-bye.

"What – oh – what is going on with you, Nicky?" Nathan and I were sitting in our lounges again. "What is that cop doing here?"

"He says he followed me here to ask me out to dinner."

"You are one popular lady." I smiled. "And if you believe that, I have The Brooklyn Bridge for sale." I turned to him with a puzzled look on my face. "Nicky, cops don't just show up in places like Bermuda. They never 'happen' to be on vacation. They're always tracking someone down or casing an area for something."

"So, why do you think Jack Jeffries is here?"

"Not because he's madly in love with you, the way you want to believe. He's on a mission and I smell a skunk."

We sat in silence. Could it be that I was still a suspect in Ralph's murder? Is Jack following me? He did ask me out. Maybe that was just his way of getting more information from me. But I didn't know anything. I had no idea who killed Ralph and why someone had tried to kill me. And Rocco… he had come out of nowhere.

Suddenly, life was getting complicated again.

"Nathan, do you think I'm safe here? Maybe I'm a suspect in a murder case, or maybe Jack came out to protect me from something."

"Cops don't protect people. They just try to be near an unfolding situation so they can make the necessary arrests. That's all they care about… arresting people. And the people they arrest are not always guilty."

"Boy, you certainly don't think very highly of detectives. How do you know so much about them?"

"Let's just say that I've had run-ins with people like Jack Jeffries. Remember: I am my father's son." I was quiet. I had never seen Nathan so serious and angry. He was always so happy-go-lucky. This conversation certainly rubbed him the wrong way.

All day, as I was by the pool or playing tennis or just taking a walk, I kept looking around to see if anyone was following me. I knew I was not the expert on being able to tell if I was being "tailed" or not, but I couldn't help looking at bushes or just behind me. I never saw the same person twice during the day, but I still had a feeling of foreboding… like something bad was about to happen. My gut was usually good about bad predictions, but I kept pushing the bad feelings away. I was probably being ridiculous… no one was following me, I had a date with a gorgeous doctor tonight and another date with Jack tomorrow. Nathan was just being foolish with his views of the police and detectives. Just because he had some bad experiences in the past didn't mean they were all out to get me. I was innocent and Jack knew that. Otherwise, he wouldn't want to go out with me.

I was carefully getting dressed that evening when Nathan came into the hotel room. He looked me up and down and whistled. "Boy, you sure look good tonight. That doctor must be a really hot date." I had bought a new dress in town and was slowly and meticulously putting on my make-up. I didn't answer him. Over the course of the day I had become a little disillusioned with Nathan. There must be a lot of things in his past that he would never want to talk about. He must have had run-ins with the police and must have had to tackle some dangerous situations with his father's people.

"Nathan, do you ever think about your father?"

"What brings that question on?"

"I don't know. To me, your father's death is still very puzzling and if my father disappeared under weird circumstances and there was this medical student who saw his body, but it wasn't his body, I'd be very confused."

"Yeah, but you forget that I didn't get along with my father and that he hated me."

"So his death doesn't disturb you?"

"I didn't say that." Nathan sat on his bed and stared at the carpet. "I guess I don't really like to think about it. What happened was beyond my control. I didn't play a part in it and I can't fix it and bring him back. So, I try to block it all from my mind."

I was silent and decided not to pursue the subject. It would only hurt Nathan.

"Anyway," Nathan said in a lighter tone, "tonight you and I are going to have a great time. We'll re-group later and tell each other about the other's evening. What are you and doctor doing?"

"Going out to dinner. It sounds like a great idea, Nathan. Let's forget all about our troubles or anything that would make us sad and just enjoy Bermuda. After all, we are leaving soon."

So we each got ready and before a half hour was over, Seth was calling me from the lobby.

We toured the island in his sportscar, Seth being as charming as ever. He told jokes, told me how beautiful I looked and was very attentive. There were many times I had to tell him to keep his eyes on the road instead of staring at me so we wouldn't crash. It was all very flattering.

He chose a very romantic restaurant for dinner with candles on the table and lit torches on the walls. There was a man playing a guitar softly in a corner and the wine was adding to the happiness I felt. Yet, during the whole dinner, I kept wondering when he was going to bring up the subject of the house and his so-called ownership of it. He didn't say anything and I was hoping that I wouldn't have to bring it up first.

When we were done eating, Seth suggested that we go to a picturesque cliff to watch the ocean.

"It's still light out and we could talk there. The scenery will take your breath away… even more than my kisses." Good… maybe that's where he would tell me about the house. Why was it so important? I wanted to trust this man and I couldn't trust him or let my feelings get any stronger until I knew the truth in every sense of the word.

He drove us to a cliff where an old fort overlooked the ocean. We got out of the car and walked through the fort. There was even an old cannon in a corner of a stone-walled room. We sat down on the sand and gazed quietly at the sea. The sounds of the waves below us were soothing and Seth put his arm around me. I put my head on his shoulder in response and we sat in silence. I was waiting for him to say something and he was probably formulating his words.

He sighed deeply. "Nicky, you know I am starting to care for you a lot." I sat quietly, waiting for him to continue. "And I know you are awaiting my explanation about the house. But there's more you should know about me than just relating to the house. I want to tell you a little about myself and the real reason why I am here on this island."

"Is there so much to tell?" I asked quietly.

"Yes." He was silent for a few moments and his face was troubled. "I can never to back to the United States again." There was more silence and he turned my head so he could kiss my lips. He kissed me deeply and held me tightly while the ocean spoke to itself below us. Now I was trembling a little from his kisses, but at the same time couldn't wait to hear what he was about to say. It was true that all the pieces didn't fit together when it came to Seth. He was too sophisticated to be on an island like Bermuda full-time. Not that there was anything wrong with Bermuda... it was just that he was very cultured and didn't seem like someone who would be satisfied being so isolated from the rest of the world.

"You see, Nicky, I murdered someone in New York and they're still looking for me." I stiffened and stared at him. Seth? A murderer?

He stared right back at me and waited for me to say something.

"You're joking, right?" Was all I could come up with. He smiled, but nodded no. "Who did you kill?"

"I want to take you to the house and show you."

"And why are you telling me all of this?"

"Believe me, I have my reasons, Nicky, and I will explain all of them to you at the house." He pointed to a house on a cliff not far away from where we were sitting. "That's the house over there. Come, let's go… it's getting cool outside anyway." He helped me up and I found it too much of a coincidence that we had ended up near his house… but I guess that's what he had wanted or anticipated. However, it wasn't cool outside. If anything, the warm breeze felt good. Something was up, but I would go along with him because he seemed so intent. Maybe I was hot because I was so upset. If I thought we had a future together, all of my hopes were dashed right now… I could never have a future with a murderer. However, I felt safe enough to follow him to his house.

As we walked up a hill to the house, with Seth being very attentive, watching each step I took and helping me up, I wondered if I was, indeed, safe with him. If he killed someone in the United States, what would stop him from killing me?

I followed him anyway, thinking that I was probably being foolish for having such dark thoughts.

The house was dark and Seth climbed over a railing on the back porch to get in. I waited at the front door as the lights on the first floor were turned on, giving the house a warm glow, and then the front door opened. Seth wrapped his arms around my waist and kissed me hard on the mouth.

216

I wasn't feeling sure of myself at all. On one end, I liked the guy very much and his kisses made me dizzy. On the other end, the word "murderer" kept running through my mind and I didn't feel quite safe. Nothing he could explain to me could excuse himself in my mind. Why was he telling me all these things? It was better if I didn't know. Who could guess that my simple vacation would get so complicated?

Seth took both my hands in his and led me into the house, walking backwards. His eyes didn't leave mine for a second and he seemed to know where the furniture was as he walked. He led me into the living room. When we were standing in the middle of the room, I pulled my hands out of his and folded them in front of me. We stood staring at each other in silence as the wind from the ocean blew the curtains into the room.

Seth broke our staring competition by going to the bar and pouring himself a drink.

"Do you want one?" He asked.

"You just told me that you care for me, then you tell me you're a murderer… yes, I think I could use one. Just make it a soda, though… I'm dizzy enough right now without any alcohol." I answered. If we hadn't been so far from town and civilization, I would have just walked out the front door and made an escape. My tolerance of this man was receding by the minute… now I was having second thoughts about being with him, no matter how handsome he was or how delicious his kisses were. But then another voice inside me told me to listen to what he had to say. Maybe there was a logical explanation that would fix everything. I sighed. A logical explanation for murder? There couldn't be one.

We sat down on a sofa together, I tucked my legs under me and turned to him, ready to listen to his story. He sighed.

"I told you that I married a very beautiful, very rich woman. I felt very lucky to have her as my wife. She had a gorgeous body, long, straight blonde hair and deep aqua eyes. She had been an only child, so she was spoiled and used to being pampered. I could handle that and in fact, was looking forward to spoiling her. Even when we met at a party, after talking for a few minutes, she handed me her empty glass and said, 'rum and vodka,' as though I were her servant. She was presumptuous, thought everyone in the world existed to fawn on her, but I didn't mind. I fell in love with her almost immediately. Me, I was the emergency room physician at a major teaching hospital and she was an heiress."

"I think all she did all day was go shopping and have facials and body massages. That was her life. She didn't even want to get married. Her dad gave her money, put her up in an apartment on Park Avenue in New York City and told her to play. Her father was a real estate tycoon. She wasn't looking for a man, except as a toy or a plaything. She would have one-night stands and be happy to throw a man's heart out the window. I don't even think she could have any feelings for anyone but herself."

"So, you murdered her?" I interrupted.

"No, not her. Let me finish. Anyway, when I met her, I was very taken with her and followed her around the room at the party. This amused her and she started paying attention to me and holding my hand. She would throw these sharp looks at me as though she were studying me up and down. I ran across the room to get her a drink, a napkin or an hor-d'oevre… I was like her slave for the evening. I didn't care. She was the most beautiful woman in the room and I was happy to be with her. So, I was tickled when I offered to take her home and she accepted."

"To show you how spoiled she was, she asked me, as I hailed a taxicab, why I didn't have a limousine or at least a driver to take me home. I did a double-take and told her because I was a doctor and doctors don't drive around in limousines."

"It amused her that I was a doctor. She had always gone out with rich businessmen or sons of her father's friends. These men fawned on her and bought her expensive presents, but they were boring to her. She enjoyed hearing about the emergency room, the patients, the life and death drama. It was something new to her and refreshing, so we had a great time when we went out."

"What was her name?" I asked. "would I know of her?"

"Josephina DeCarlo. You may have heard of the DeCarlo real estate management company. That's the father. He owns a big chunk of Manhattan... some major buildings."

"Anyway, before I knew it, Josephina was asking me to marry her. It happened one night after we made love. We had known each other for three months and she just told me she wanted to be married to me. 'I want to be a doctor's wife,' she said calmly.'"

"I knew we weren't meant for each other. We were so different. If she shopped all day and spent ten thousand dollars, that made her happy. I told her I couldn't support her the way her father had, but she didn't care. She said her father would always give her a generous allowance and that I wouldn't even have to work if I didn't want to. Of course, that was out of the question... my work is my therapy. She was so open and giving and compromised on every issue that bothered me, that I saw no problem with marrying her."

"And you should have seen her parents when we went to their house and told them we wanted to be married. You would think I was a Roosevelt or a Vanderbilt. I couldn't figure out why they were so happy. I finally concluded that they had that doctor syndrome... you know: Parents fall in love with doctors. Oh yes, he'll take care of our baby, he'll add respectability to the family and if the family business goes under, he'll always bring home enough money to live on... well, if $200,000 is enough for a year's wages."

"Anyway, the mother hugged me, the father gave me his favorite cufflinks right there and Josephina glowed. She took one of her mother's diamond rings and said that that would be her engagement ring for now, until the real one came. Very bizarre, right? But that was Josephina and that was her family... very rich and not to be figured out."

"Well, apparently, her parents thought that I would take the tiger out of Josephina."

"What do you mean by 'tiger?'" I asked, very engrossed in his story.

"Josephina was used to having everything at her fingertips and getting her way all of the time. Whatever Josephina wanted, she got and if she couldn't get it, her father would buy it for her. Whether it was a fur coat, a diamond tiara, a designer dress or a man. She had never been married before, but she didn't need to be. She bedded any man she decided to and she could have any man she wanted. Josephina had everything: the gorgeous face, the perfect body, the brains and the money. But one thing she didn't have was a heart." Seth took my hands in his. "She didn't know about hearts or sympathy for others. She wasn't anything like you. You, you know about people and how to handle them... and your kisses are like chocolate." He leaned over and kissed me lightly on the lips. "I wish I had met you before Josephina. Then you could have your wish of us being together in New York City. I'd follow you anywhere." He stared at me for a few moments and I couldn't help wondering if this whole thing was a put-on leading to something else. For some reason, he wanted to bear his soul to me. Maybe it was because he was falling in love with me, or maybe because he had an ulterior motive. Yes, I was becoming cynical about the whole situation, but it wasn't like me to trust a murderer. I still wasn't sure if I was even safe at the moment… all my senses were heightened as a result.

"Anyway, Nicky, we got married in a lavish affair at the Plaza Hotel. I think her parents must have spent a million dollars on that wedding. We had everything: a ten-piece orchestra, three singers, all the food you could imagine and flowers galore. That's the wedding Josephina wanted and that's the one she got. She had to outdo her friends. As for me, I couldn't have cared less if we had gotten married on a desert island. I was just happy that I had Josephina for my wife and could have her and be with her whenever I wanted. Well, that's what I thought, though I was quickly proven wrong. Josephina didn't have a tiger within her… she had a monster." Seth let go of my hands and ran his fingers through his hair as he sighed.

"The honeymoon was glorious. We went to Tahiti and made love every morning, every night and every afternoon. She was incredible and had quite an appetite for me. But when we got back to New York, it was as though a switch had turned off. She smiled at me from across the breakfast table, but that's about it. Most nights when I came home she wasn't there and had been out all day. I would stay up and wait for her to come home, but when she did come home, she always avoided my questions and would start a fight. I became too persistent."

"So, I concluded that she was having an affair, though we had been married for all of three months. I hired a private investigator and had her followed. Sure enough, she was meeting someone in a hotel every afternoon. He was an old boyfriend that she had wanted to marry at one time. But her parents had disapproved because he had had a questionable family background… mafia and nothing but pure mafia. He was a hit man or something of the sort."

"I have to admit he was very handsome. I just don't know why she didn't love me. She never did and married me only because her parents wanted her to. They held the purse strings and could cut her off – and would have cut her off – if she didn't do as they wished. So, I guess she figured she could marry me and have him on the side, thus making everyone happy. Everyone but me, that is."

"So, you killed her."

"No I didn't. Let me finish. One night I came home and the house was completely dark. It was about 11 o'clock at night and I walked to the kitchen to get some juice. I didn't think that Josephina was home, so I didn't even bother to call out or look upstairs. If she was home, she was fast asleep anyway. So, there I was, drinking some juice in a dark kitchen, when I heard some noise in the living room. Then a lamp knocked over and I thought there was a burglar in the house. I saw that the alarm was not on, so I grabbed a gun we kept in the kitchen drawer and walked slowly into the living room. I had never used a gun in my life, but my father-in-law gave me one when I got married. He said it was good to have a gun in the house, as long as there were no children around, in case we were robbed. It was hideous to me, but at that moment I thought it would save my life."

"I called out, in case it was Josephina, but there was no answer. And then I saw the silhouette of a man by the screen door that led to the deck outside. He was fiddling with the lock on the door, obviously trying to get out. I told him to put his arms up, but he turned around and reached for something on his hip… I thought his gun. So, I fired and he fell to the ground with a groan. I shot him and killed him."

"I heard a scream upstairs… it was Josephina. She ran down the stairs and turned on the lights as she went. You would think she would be worried about me, but she wasn't."

"Where are you? Where are you?" she creamed over and over again. I didn't know who she was talking to, me or him, but I answered, 'in the living room.'"

"The lights turned on in the room and I saw him. He was face-up, with the blank stare of death on his face. His eyes were open and there was a huge bloodstain on his chest with blood dripping onto the carpet form his chest wound. She screamed again and ran to him. She lied on top of him, his blood getting all over her nightgown, crying hysterically, saying his name over and over and over. It was her mafia boyfriend. He was trying to leave the house without my knowing. They had heard me come home and he was escaping."

Seth had told the whole story without emotion, but his eyes stared at the ground with a tinge of horror in them.

"Josephina looked up at me with tears dripping down her cheeks. 'Murderer,' she said quietly. "murderer... murderer... murderer...' She must have said it a hundred times, each on louder than the other, until she was screaming at me at the top of her lungs."

Seth paused and we sat in silence. Something was replaying in his mind and I saw his eyes piercing a hole in the coffee table. I listened to the sounds of the ocean as I waited for him to go on. I was horrified at the story he was telling, yet at the same time I wanted to hear the whole thing and find out what had happened. How did he escape the United State and how did he end up here? Why were they still looking for him? Had he had a trial?

These questions whizzed through my mind as I looked at him. He suddenly looked like a broken man who sat hunched on the couch.

"Then I knew I couldn't stay with Josephina. She hated me at that moment and I responded to that realization by running out of the house. I ran and ran, though the park, down every road in the neighborhood, not knowing where I was going exactly. Then I decided to go back to the house and work something out with Josephina. Maybe we could hide the body... maybe we could start over again... I wasn't thinking rationally."

"When I got back to the house, I saw five police cars in the driveway and I didn't think twice before I turned around and ran away again. No one saw me as I went into a nearby forest that I knew very well. I had often walked the dog there. I slept on the ground that night and was a real fugitive. For the first time in my life I lied on the grass with the bugs, the rodents and sounds of the forest. It was a spooky night and I felt very alone."

"I lived in the forest for a few days, eating grass, berries and whatever I could find in people's garbage at night. I knew I wouldn't last long like that, so I decided to sneak into my house one night, grab some cash I had hidden away and make an escape somewhere... perhaps out of the country. The problem was that I knew how the police worked. They probably had an eye on every airport, every bus station and every outlet from town. I felt afraid, lost, deserted by my wife and very, very alone. I wasn't sure what to do exactly, but I knew I couldn't get anywhere without some money."

"It was two o'clock in the morning when I approached my house. There were no cars in the garage – I figured Josephina had moved to her parents' apartment in the city – and all the windows were dark. I went inside through a window we always kept unlocked. We did that in case one of us locked ourselves out of the house. It's funny how strange a house looks to you if you haven't lived there for a few days and when you know you won't be back to live in it again."

"I couldn't help but walk into the living room and look at the spot where the body had been. There was still a large bloodstain in the carpet. I collapsed into the sofa... it felt so good to sit on pillows again and to sink into something so soft. I had been sitting and living on the hard ground."

"It's amazing how one instant can change your whole life, Nicky. One moment I had a beautiful house, a good job and a beautiful wife, and the next moment the police were after me and I was nothing better than a common criminal." Seth looked as though he were going to cry and I felt like hugging him, but something stopped me and I just stared at him, waiting for more.

"Seth, if you had told the police that you killed the guy, thinking he was an intruder in your house, how could they prosecute you?"

"Because he had very important connections and murder was always murder, in my mind. I was also a frightened, desperate man who was probably not thinking so clearly. In hindsight, I would have been just as frightened and fled the same way because of his connections."

"Anyway, let me tell you what happened next." I sat back, mesmerized.

"As I sat in the living room," Seth went on, "thinking what to do next, the lights suddenly turned on and two men were standing in front of me. Oh no, the police, I thought."

"As if reading my mind, one of the men stepped forward and said, 'no, we are not the police.' They were both wearing dark suits and I figured they were friends of my wife's boyfriend. Oh no... now I was going to get killed by them."

"Let me introduce myself," the man went on. "I am Maurice and I work for a very influential man named Mr. Suma. It turns out that you are a very lucky man because Mr. Suma and the guy you killed were mortal enemies. Your wife's boyfriend was out to murder Mr. Suma and you were kind enough and gracious enough to get to him first.'"

"I sat very still, waiting to see what he would say next. I had no choice anyway. They both had guns in their hands."

"'Anyway,'" Maurice went on, "'Mr. Suma wants to get you out of the jam you're in. You see, we've been waiting for you to come back here. I'm surprised the police didn't have the same thought.'" Maurice pulled out an envelope from his suit pocket and dropped it into my lap. "'In there you will find a passport with an alias name, airline tickets and ten thousand dollars in cash. There is also a bogus medical license in your alias' name and a job waiting for you in Bermuda. If we drive you right now, you'll make your flight, so think fast.'" I didn't move. My mind was racing. I could face the police, the courts, the attorneys, or take the coward's way out."

"Mr. Suma is very grateful for what you've done, Doc, but you have to think very quickly. If you take his offer, we will get you out of the country and you can start all over again in Bermuda. If you decline this offer, we will not be back to see you again and you will be on your own. So, take it or leave it. Again, we need to know in about two minutes.'"

"So let me get this straight… you've been sitting here waiting for me to show up, not knowing if I even would show up. I happen to come tonight and you happen to have airline tickets for a plane that leaves, what, a half hour from now? What if I had shown up tomorrow, or yesterday?"

"Let's just say we have connections at the airport. Don't ask too many questions, Doc. I would also advise that we leave as soon as possible because one never knows when and if the police might show up.'"

"I felt so frantic. Could I run upstairs and get my cash? No, Maurice didn't advise it… we were in a hurry and it wasn't wise to let anyone find out that I had come back to the house."

"In my mind, there was nothing much to think about. I was a wanted murderer and my wife would be more than happy to testify against me in any court."

"I'll take your offer." Maurice and his assistant snapped into action without another word. They turned off the lights and Maurice grabbed me by the arm and led me to a car parked on the grass in the backyard. We jumped in, the assistant started the car and we zoomed out of the neighborhood. I looked out the back windshieild. No one was behind us and there was no sign of any police cars."

"It felt good to be in the backseat of a speeding car. I closed my eyes and rested my head back. What a mess this all was. Maybe I wasn't doing the right thing, but it definitely was the easy way out and that's what appealed to me at the moment."

"Maurice began to speak. 'When you get to Bermuda, there will be a man waiting for you at the airport. He will be holding up a sign saying, 'Dr. Allen.' He won't talk to you. He will drive you to your new house and will give you papers with the address of the new hospital you'll be working in. You're going to be an emergency room physician in Bermuda, Doc, and we don't ever want to see you in this country again. Understand?' I nodded."

"Can you imagine being given a new identity, a new job and a new life all in one day, Nicky?"

"I looked out the window, staring at old familiar landmarks and buildings I had taken for granted in the past. I would never see America again and I was memorizing the scenery. I didn't want to forget what a gas station or a diner looked like... I didn't even know if they had these things in Bermuda, but suspected that nothing would be on the grand scale that everything was in The United States. I was giving up my citizenship, my identity and my whole life because I had killed a man and didn't want to spend time in prison."

"When we reached the airport, Maurice jumped out of the car, opened the door for me and grabbed my arm again."

'Come on, Doc, we don't have much time' Suddenly I realized that I didn't have any luggage. Wouldn't that look suspicious? Maurice shrugged. "Well, we couldn't think of everything." It was almost comical, looking back, but at the time I was scared and desperate."

"Maurice kept pulling me forward as we walked quickly through the airport. He looked at one of the screens which listed the departures and immediately seemed to know where he was going."

"I kept looking around us, wondering if there were any police in the airport keeping a lookout for me, but so far no one was bothering us."

"All at once, Maurice pulled me aside and pushed me into the men's room. It was deserted."

'You idiot,' he said to me in a hiss, 'Stop looking around with those wild eyes of yours. We have to be like two tiny bugs in this airport... no one should notice us. You're inviting trouble with those big eyes of yours.' I nodded at him quietly. I was scared stiff. 'Now, just follow me and keep your eyes on the ground... understand? I'll get you on that plane safely if you listen to my instructions. Otherwise, I can't guarantee anything. You got it?' He was snarling by now.'

"I got it," I said quietly. He grunted and walked out of the room without looking back, obviously knowing that I would follow with my eyes to the ground. And I did.

"Sure enough, I boarded the plane without incident and sighed in relief as the plane took off. Were there police on the plane? I decided not to look around. If there were, they would come to me sure enough.

But from take-off to landing, no one disturbed me, except the steward as he served the snack."

"The plane landed smoothly and the sight of palm trees cheered me up and calmed my fears slightly. Would someone arrest me as I got off the plane? I pursed my lips in thought. If I were going to be arrested, I thought, it would have happened by now. Maybe Mr. Suma paid off people to ensure my safety. Nothing would surprise me at this point. He had really come to my rescue."

"Coming off the plane, there was a man holding a sign up with my new name. I walked up to him cautiously, wondering if it might be a trick of the police. I stood in front of him without a word.

"Dr. Allen," he said quietly. "I recognize you from your picture. Welcome to Bermuda. I will take you to your house. Then I will show you the hospital where you will start working tomorrow. Come, I'll escort you through customs."

"And that is the whole story. This is the house I live in, you saw my hospital and no one has bothered me or chased me or accused me of anything for ten years."

"And was it the right thing for you? Do you have any regrets not facing a jury? I asked quietly.

"I might be serving a life sentence in prison right now, sharing a cell with a pervert."

"Do you think there's a chance you may have been judged innocent? You did think the guy was an intruder."

"I don't know. This is the fate I have chosen and I feel that Mr. Suma is watching over me from afar. I saved his life and he saved mine."

We sat in silence for a few moments as I absorbed everything he had just said. What a story that had been. Who would know that so much had happened to this man? I thought.

"And anyone who fell in love with me and wanted to share her life with me would have to stay here with me... or come back to me after her training."

"That's a lot to ask," I responded quickly.

Seth leaned close to me and kissed me gently on the lips.

"Too much to ask?" He asked softly.

I stared at him in silence. "Of course, you don't have to give me an answer on that now."

"Seth, we hardly know each other and it sounds like you're offering a marriage proposal."

"It's to let you know that I am very serious about you. I am very attracted to you." He wrapped his arms around me and began to kiss me strongly, leaning me backwards gently so he could lie on top of me. Then his hands reached under my skirt and began to pull down my underwear. Something wasn't right and I turned my mouth away from his. He began to kiss my cheek as though nothing was wrong.

"Seth, I can't." He still pushed on, trying to undo the buttons on my skirt. Finally, I grabbed his hands and tried to pull them away, but he was strong and seemed to be incensed.

"What's the matter, I'm not good enough for you?" he asked softly.

"I'll scream," I warned. He smiled.

"Go ahead… there's no one within a mile of here."

Then he lost patience with my clothing and tried to tear it off. I struggled and slid to the floor, with him still on top of me. Somehow I managed to roll onto my stomach. He was still trying to pull at my clothing when a deep voice from across the room shouted, "stop it!"

I looked up and saw a man holding a gun. He wore a beige suit and a white hat and his eyes bored into the two of us.

Seth's grip loosened and he sat up to put his head in his hands, as though he were a defeated man.

I stood up and pulled my clothes together, buttoning my skirt and blouse. This strange man didn't even scare me, for some reason. Perhaps because I was still recovering from the past few minutes. Between that horrific story and then almost being raped, I felt overwhelmed. This man had saved me.

"Doesn't look like she's going to marry you, huh, Doc?" The man in the corner of the room chuckled sarcastically. "You made a good try, though." He laughed and his eyes didn't leave Seth.

I turned to Seth. "You know this man?" I asked.

"Cut it out," another voice echoed from a doorway. I turned and saw another man. He was large too and wore a black suit, a black shirt and black tie.

I suddenly felt weak. Who were these men and why did Seth seem to know them? He wasn't alarmed to see them and just kept running his hands through his hair as he looked away from them.

"Seth, what's going on here?" I asked quietly, being careful not to move, now that my clothes were buttoned again.

"What's going on is that you've cooked Dr. Allen's goose." The voice was familiar and I looked up at the staircase where it was coming from. I gasped when I recognized his face. Was it possible? Could it be? I did a double-take. It was Mr. Suma.

# Chapter 15

He seemed very relaxed as he walked slowly down the staircase, obviously enjoying his grand entrance. I felt weak as I stared at him. He was grinning at everyone, seeming to be very happy where he was at the moment. Maybe he was even savoring my surprise and shock.

Mr. Suma sat down on a sofa across from me and didn't take his eyes off of me as I caught my breath and tried to recover from my astonishment. The other two men put their guns away as soon as Mr. Suma motioned them to do so and there was absolute silence in the room. Seth still hadn't looked up to even glance at Mr. Suma. He was still looking down at the floor with his head in his hands, his elbows on his knees.

"Dr. Steinway, you look like you've seen a ghost." Mr. Suma chuckled. "But you knew I wasn't dead all along, right?" He crossed his legs and looked at me thoughtfully. "You know, you put me to a lot of trouble, Doctor." I was silent and was beginning to feel frightened again and trapped. I was certainly outnumbered in this room and if I wanted to flee, there was no hope for survival. I'd have to make a dash for the terrace and jump over the railing onto the rocks below. I would definitely break some bones doing that.

Mr. Suma seemed very calm and was smiling at me.

"I don't want you to be afraid of me, Dr. Steinway. I mean you no harm right now. I just want to ask you a few questions."

I turned to Seth and studied him again.

"I'm very confused right now." I wasn't addressing anyone in particular, but certainly felt overwhelmed and perhaps even in danger. Were they going to kill me? Were they about to kill Seth? He seemed to know them and obviously wasn't threatened by them, or he'd be running out of the room right now.

"Of course you are confused. You are facing a man you thought was dead, you're wondering what lover boy over here is all about and you are worried about the two men with the guns who are standing behind me." Mr. Suma smiled. "But as I said, I mean you no harm right now."

"And later?" I asked bravely.

Mr. Suma flashed his smile at me again. "I really have nothing against you, Doc. But you have caused me a lot of grief and aggravation lately. And the one thing I can't figure out is whether you are working with the police or not. That's what I would like to know."

"Working with the police in what way?" I was confused.

"Do you know how many tails I've had on you? Do you know how many nights you've kept me up? All because you were in the wrong place at the wrong time, putting your nose in the wrong places." His voice was getting serious now and his smile vanished.

"Were you the one behind all of my close calls? You know, someone tried to shoot me on the street in New York City." Mr. Suma held his hand up, motioning me to stop talking.

"I am the most powerful man you will ever meet, Doctor. I control many things and many people. If I had wanted you dead, you would have been dead a long time ago. You know why you're not dead yet? Because I was playing with you, trying to find out what you were all about. Also, you helped me. I had a bad eye infection, if you remember, when I was in the hospital, and you cured it. Anyone who helps me in any way doesn't get killed unless they show harm to me after. And I wasn't convinced that you meant to harm me."

"I didn't – I wasn't trying to harm you. I just couldn't figure out what happened to you. You disappeared into thin air. And then I found Ralph –" Mr. Suma held up his hand to silence me.

"I at least owe you an explanation. You have been through a lot over the last few weeks and perhaps it is all my fault. Perhaps I shouldn't have gotten you involved in the mess I am in, but it just happened. A lot of it was out of my control. I am not really a mean person… I am just tough and I have to protect myself."

"You and I come from very different backgrounds, Doctor Nicky. I don't have to tell you that, I'm sure. Is it all right if I call you Dr. Nicky?" The two men by the doorway put their guns into their belts, as if sensing that the acute episode was over. "As soon as I was born I was expected to fill a certain role and I did. I had to take over from my father and that was that. I was hoping that Nathan would fill my shoes someday, but he just wasn't cut out for it in any way. Sometimes I still hope that he might turn around and become more like me." Mr. Suma waved his hand at me and sighed. "Not gonna' happen." We sat in silence for a few moments and I decided not to say anything or interrupt him. Number one, what he was saying was very interesting and I felt that I was going to find out the whole story now. Number two, if I said anything, I felt I could only get into trouble by rubbing Mr. Suma the wrong way.

"When I found out that you and Nathan were going to this island together, I really became very excited. Not only because I wouldn't mind having you for a daughter-in-law – you know, a doctor in the family is very respectable – but also because I hoped that you and he were – were – you know… doing something physical together." He sighed again. "Nathan is too soft. He doesn't have a lion's heart like me. Not tough like me. You know, Doc, you're tougher than he is. You would have made a good son. Ah, I'm talking nonsense."

"The fact is, you deserve an explanation for all that you've gone through the last few weeks. It was all because of me. You are an innocent, I think, but I've had to keep an eye on you to make sure. And I've had to give you a few warnings."

"Dr. Allen, where do you keep my cigars?" Seth motioned with his chin to a cabinet near the bar. Mr. Suma signaled to one of his men to go to the cabinet. Then he turned to me again. "Some doctors are useful, and some, like Dr. Allen, are totally useless. I wouldn't have minded if you two had become a couple. He would have kept you out of trouble, Dr. Steinway. And now, here you are, in my lair and I have to figure out what to do with you." I sensed danger by the tone of his voice.

"What do you mean?" I asked quietly.

"Should I start from the beginning? Then you will see what this has been all about. Dr. Nicky, I am a simple man. I have simple needs, but I will defend myself and my family in any way I know how if I need to."

"I come from a simple background but my life has become very complicated lately. I have a lot of people coming after me. There is more than one person who would like to see me dead. You met one of them... Rocco."

"Rocco?!" I asked.

"We are old friends. But nothing lasts forever. He deceived me." Mr. Suma looked very sad as he stared at his hands. "He sold me out to the Feds. You know, he took a big risk in seeing you the night he kidnapped you temporarily."

"How do you know about that night? " I asked in surprise.

"Doctor, I know a lot about you and I have followed your every move since we met. Rocco, you know, is in the witness protection program. Did you know that he used to be my right hand man? We were close and knew each other's secrets. Then he turned on me to save his own skin. He surfaced for a brief moment to speak to you and warn you to get out of the situation you are now in."

"What situation is that?"

"Come on, Suma, have a little mercy on the kid... she's only –" Seth tried to interject.

"Shut up!" Mr. Suma raised his voice and turned red. "She should know the whole story before we leave here." Seth put his head back in his hands and looked down at the floor. I was beginning to feel more scared because I could tell by Seth's face that something was up. Mr. Suma was baring his soul for a reason.

"Doc, I'll be frank with you. I think you've been collaborating with the police to try to capture me. I've been sending you warnings to stay out of my hair and not pursue what happened to my body or who killed Ralph. You just wouldn't listen. Then you even had the audacity to follow me to this island."

"What?!" I cried. "I didn't know you were here. I wasn't even sure that you were alive. I was beginning to think that the body I saw in the morgue really was yours."

"No, that's a good try, Doctor, but no cigar. You've been with that cop a lot… more than I feel comfortable with. Maybe you've got a wire on now. Check her, Mac."

Suddenly I felt two hands frisking me roughly. I didn't move or resist because I sensed I was in real danger now. Mr. Suma's tone was becoming more and more harsh.

"You know that clown Rocco? Yeah, I know you met with him at his request, you might say. Well that was a very brave move on his part, because I'm out trying to find that son of a bitch." Mr. Suma took a puff of his cigar. "He's testifying against me in court and is in the witness protection program, as I said before. He knows that if I ever find him or even sniff him, I'm going to blow his brains out. It so happens that after you met with him that night, there was kind of a showdown between my men who followed you and his men. All of my men were killed except one, who somehow got back to me and told me what happened before he died. It took a lot of guts to show himself to you and give you a warning to stop snooping around. I guess he's still looking after me in a way… or trying to."

"Rocco at one time saw and knew about everything I did. We grew up together in the streets and always trusted each other. Now we're talking fifty-five years of knowing each other. And after all that time and all that we've been through, he got caught by the Feds and decided to squeal on me instead of taking his punishment on the chin like a man. So, he's been in court saying all kinds of rotten things about me. Then he disappears into the witness protection program. Do I care? Besides losing my best friend, do I care? No. Do you know why? Because I'm dead, Dr. Steinway. I'm in some morgue somewhere lying in a freezer and you can't prosecute a dead man, Doc. Unless some smart aleck medical student comes around, poking her nose in places she doesn't belong and tries to put two and two together. Then she brings the mortician in on it who starts to make all kinds of phone calls. Get me, Doc?" I was silent and starting to become very scared. I was seeing that my existence was no longer necessary to Mr. Suma and, in fact, I was probably in the way now.

But Seth surprised me and jumped up suddenly.

"Mr. Suma, you are being unfair. She's harmless and I won't let you-" In a swift motion, Seth had a small handgun in his hand. I didn't know where he had gotten it from, but he aimed it at Mr. Suma.

My next action could be explained by an inate goodness within me, or my teachings from medical school about the preservation of life or just by a reflex. Whatever the reason, some instinct guided me to also jump up and push Seth sideways as the gun went off. It discharged into the ceiling, but at the same time, one of the bodyguards shot at Seth to stop him. Mr. Suma ducked and within seconds two men had tackled Seth and were holding him down. "Cut it out, Suma! Let Nicky go and leave us alone!"

"Those are big words coming from someone like you," Mr. Suma said quietly as he stood up, glaring at Seth. "Why should I listen to anything you say after you've just tried to kill me?"

I felt a pain in my left shoulder and looked down. The whole left side of my blouse was soaked with blood. Was it my blood? I touched my shoulder and almost passed out from the pain. I was horrified, but didn't say a word. I felt that my very existence was tenuous at the moment and I didn't want to draw attention to myself. Mr. Suma was glaring at Seth.

"You are a failed doctor, a murderer and I've done nothing but help you," Mr. Suma continued. "Then you try to pay me back by trying to kill me?! What kind of a person are you?" He turned to one of the men who was holding Seth down. "Take him out and take him down," he said quietly.

"No!" I cried instinctively. "You can't do that!" Mr. Suma turned to me and looked at my shoulder.

"My man hit you, Dr. Steinway, and you saved my life." He shook his head and muttered something in Italian. Then he began to give orders to his men very quickly and as he spoke, they did as he said like clockwork. "Angelo, get Dr. Allen out of here and put him in the basement. Marco, get Dr. Steinway into a bedroom upstairs and let's get out of here. Dr. Steinway, you have just saved your own life by saving mine. I don't overlook things like that. Now all I can do is wish you well. You are officially a made woman."

I began to walk away from Marco as he approached. I was frightened and didn't trust what Mr. Suma was saying. I felt that I was still in his way. But a wave of dizziness took over and I fell into a chair. I suddenly felt very weak. I must have lost a lot of blood. Maybe I was bleeding to death.

Marco stopped coming towards me when I collapsed into the chair, as though he was afraid to go near me.

"Leave her alone," Mr. Suma ordered. "Maybe moving her will make it worse." He came close to me and kneeled by me. "I'm sorry, Doc, real sorry. But I've go to go now."

I thought I heard the distant sound of a helicopter. It was getting louder and louder. Was it possible, or was I delirious?

I watched with blurred vision as Seth was lead out of the room, struggling between two of the men. The helicopter sound was getting louder and louder. No, it definitely was not my imagination… it was indeed a helicopter.

As though seeing the look of puzzlement on my face, Mr. Suma came closer to me and said softly, "This is my mode of escape, Doctor. You will never see me again. I have a very good life waiting for me. You could do me one favor. If you would be so kind. Say good –bye to my boy Nathan and tell him not to try to find me. If and when I want to see him, I will know how to track him down. That goes for you too. Oh, and one more thing… try to stay out of trouble." He smiled at me and kissed me on the cheek. "You will not have any more trouble from me."

I was dizzy and didn't even have the strength to look up at him. "Thank you," I said automatically.

"You're welcome. And now, if you will excuse me, I have a ride to catch." I closed my eyes as he ran out to the patio doors.

# Chapter 16

N icky." I heard his voice, but didn't see him. "Nicky, you're awake." Was it Nathan? I turned my head to the left a little and saw Jack. He took my hand and my head began to swim a little again. My heart was beating in my shoulder instead of my chest.

"What happened?" I said in a whisper.

"Don't try to talk. I can't believe you made it."

"Oh yes, Dr. Steinway," another female voice sounded from somewhere. "He's been sitting at your side for forty-eight hours straight." A nurse came into view at the head of my bed. My vision was still waxing and waning. "You two engaged yet?" I couldn't answer. I felt so weak.

The nurse held my hand and took my pulse.

"Looks like you're going to come out of this one," the nurse went on. "You had some incident there, young lady. Your vital signs have been stable, so I knew it was just a matter of time before you woke up. I'll leave you two alone for five minutes, but then you have to leave, detective. She needs her rest." Jack nodded and squeezed my hand as the nurse left the room. I closed my eyes and the blackness returned, covering my vision and my hearing with its cloak.

When I opened my eyes again, he was still there holding my hand. My vision was clearer, though the pain in my shoulder still bore through my body.

"Jack." He looked at me and smiled.

"How's the sleeping beauty?"

"What happened? Am I dead?" Jack chuckled.

"Far from it. You're doing fine, if you'd only stay awake long enough to let me say a few words to you. How do you feel?"

"Like I was run over by a truck. Why do I have so much pain in my shoulder? Why is my head swimming?"

"Can you stay awake long enough to hear the story? I don't know if you're well enough to even understand what happened. It's a miracle that you are alive." I tried to sit up, but the pain in my shoulder prevented me from moving. "Don't try to move. You took a bullet in your lung and lost a lot of blood. They had to remove part of your lung and do a lot of stitching. If I had gotten you to the hospital one minute later, you would have been a corpse. Sorry... police jargon."

"Where's Seth? Where's Nathan? Mr. Suma? Was there a helicopter, or did I dream it?" Jack sighed and stroked my hand.

"We don't know where Mr. Suma is right now... he fled from Bermuda in the helicopter and is probably on the other side of the world right now, for all we know. Nathan is back in New York running his club again, though he calls me everyday for a status report on you. They're not letting any visitors in to see you – except me, or course

– till you're stronger. I get special police privileges because of my status, you know." He smiled. "I tell them I have to interrogate you." My eyebrows raised a little. "No, you're not a murder suspect. I'm just kidding. Don't doctors ever have a sense of humor?" I sat in silence for a moment because I was so weak. Finally I murmured, "Seth."

Jack sat in silence for what seemed like minutes to me, even though it was just seconds.

"Dead?" I asked quietly.

"No. We found him locked up in the basement. Instead of killing him, I guess Mr. Suma decided that Seth should live out his worst nightmare: going on trial. He will be charged with murder and I'm sure he'll get himself a good lawyer. Who knows? He may get off." I sighed.

"What day is it?"

"About one week after your school started. Don't worry… I spoke to your dean and he knows you'll miss about three weeks of school." I sighed. "It's O.K.: you got a police excuse."

"You know, you're not funny." I closed my eyes and the world was black again.

When I opened my eyes again, I felt a presence in the room. The room was dim and only a lamp in the corner was turned on. Wa s it night? I definitely heard breathing.

My head felt as heavy as a stone, but I somehow managed to turn it to face him. I gasped. It was Rocco sitting by my bed staring at me. Was I dreaming? Was this real?

He was playing with a button on his jacket as he looked at me and our eyes held for a moment.

"Are you awake, or are you sleeping with your eyes open?" He asked. What a question. "I'm awake." I was afraid to talk and even breath. Had he come to kill me? Where was the nurse? Could I find the button to call the nurse? I didn't even know where it was. My eyes were locked into his and I couldn't move due to fear.

"You're going to smother me with a pillow, aren't you?" I asked quietly.

Rocco chuckled. "No, that only happens in the movies. I actually came to tell you something very important. Something I thought you would like to know." I waited in silence, not believing him, feeling my heart pounding in my ears. "I heard about what happened in Bermuda and that you saved Mr. Suma's life. You know what that means?" I still didn't move or speak. I was waiting for him to say something like, "that means I'm gonna' kill you."

"It means you're a made woman. That means no one on our side is ever going to harm you and that if you're in trouble you need to contact us."

"Us?" I asked. "I thought you're in hiding, so to speak. Mr. Suma would kill you in a minute if he thought –"

"Excuse me, Doc," Rocco interrupted. "Mr. Suma and I go way back and – yes, - I am testifying against him and I'm on his blacklist, so let me say what I was saying in another way. If you ever need him, you figure out how to contact him and he'll take care of any problem you have. You can also get a hold of me anytime to do the same thing."

"Why did you really come here? I don't know how to contact him and I'll never find you… you're in the witness protection program. I don't even know why you risked coming in here."

"I came here because I wanted to thank you. You see, Mr. Suma and I were real close at one time... like brothers. I still love him, though I had to save my hide before his. I feel very bad about that, but it was the only way to survive and stay out of prison. So, I came to thank you for your heroism. That was a brave thing you did."

"I can't believe you heard about it. I thought only the police knew about it."

"The police and Nathan. Nathan's still got connections and we've still got ours too." I thought for a moment.

"Are you still in touch with Nathan?" I asked. Rocco nodded yes. "Could you ask him to visit me?"

"You know, he's a big man now."

"Why?"

"Well, with his father officially in hiding, someone has to take over the business." My eyes opened wide.

"No." I said quietly. "He told me he had no interest in it."

"He helps out a lot. Anyway, I'll tell him to come by." Rocco took my hand and held it. "Mr. Suma was and is like a brother to me. I don't expect you to understand it. You're great, Doc. You're brave and you've got your head screwed on the right way. Just had to tell you that. You'll make a great doctor too, Dr. Nicky." I couldn't help but smile.

"See, I didn't come to kill you." We laughed together and Rocco squeezed my hand. "You're safe forever, kid. Just remember that. And you'll see Nathan soon." He winked at me and then he was gone.

Had it been a dream? He was so different in the hospital room than he had been in the abandoned building's basement. He was friendly and human. It must have been a dream. Maybe the pain medication was doing it. However, my hand still felt the pressure of his squeeze.

My eyes closed and I was sleeping again.

# Chapter 17

It was a warm September afternoon when I found myself standing in front of Nathan's nightclub. It was only four o'clock in the afternoon and the club was closed, but I knew someone was inside. They would be preparing for the night… after all, it was Saturday.

I was still getting some dizzy spells now and then, when I became excited about something or upset, so I was determined to stay calm today. I had to see Nathan one more time and find out what happened to him. Was he continuing at the club? Was he taking over the business? I had no idea. He hadn't called me or tried to get in touch with me while I was in the hospital or rehabilitating at home. Jack had called and visited almost everyday and was Mr. Attentive. I was even starting to wonder if I should start to go out with him… he was certainly very caring and asking me to dinner regularly. I just hadn't said yes yet. I was still hung up on the doctor-detective relationship. It just didn't fit in my mind. How could two people in such different fields have enough in common to make a relationship work? We never ran out of things to talk about… well, I would think more about that another time. Right now, I was staring at the front entrance of the club, wondering if I would be trespassing if I tried the front door.

It was unlocked. I turned the doorknob and opened the front door. The lights were on inside, but there was no one around. The chairs were up on the tables, the room smelled like ammonia from the freshly-scrubbed floor, and the stage was dark.

"Anyone here?" I called out. "Nathan? Are you here?" No answer. Someone could come in and steal all the glassware and dishes and no one would even know it.

I knew where Nathan's office was, so I walked towards it. Because I knew Nathan I guess I wasn't trespassing and I couldn't really be arrested because we were technically friends. Now I was thinking like Jack. I guess he was rubbing off on me. I found the door to his office and it was closed. I put my hand on the doorknob to open it when I heard a voice inside. It was Nathan's.

"What do you mean the situation isn't working over there?" his voice said. He must have been on the phone, because no one answered. "Oh, I see. Well, you have go get rid of him. Yes, I know, I know. If it's not working, then it's not working and if it's his fault, then you don't do business with him."

I opened the door without knocking and saw Nathan sitting at his desk. He had a cigarette in his mouth and the room was smoky. His eyes popped open when he saw me. "Listen, I have to go now. Do what I said and I'll call you tomorrow. Right. Ciao." He hung up and stared at me in silence. I stared back at him and didn't know what to say first, because I felt a combination of anger, hurt and disappointment all at the same time.

Why hadn't he called or visited me while I was at the hospital to see how I was? I could have been killed. Didn't he care about me? Here he looked like a hotshot at this big desk, giving orders, and I thought we had a special relationship. I thought we would watch over each other at least to a degree.

I watched his eyes as they stared at me and the expression changed from surprise to an intense stare, to a soft look and then a smile. But I wasn't sure that the smile was sincere. I knew that Nathan was a good actor too. At this point, I wondered if it had been a good idea to come unannounced. Perhaps my life was even in danger here.

"Nicky," he said softly.

"Nathan." I was the femme fatale now, the neglected woman, the wronged woman… the one who was almost killed and not even visited at the hospital.

He got up and shook my hand, taking my hand with two hands and kissing me on the cheek. I stamped my foot and cocked my head at him. I ruined the soft mood at once.

"Where have you been, Nathan Suma? I thought you fell off the earth. You knew I almost died." Nathan motioned to a sofa and we sat down next to each other. He suddenly hugged me tightly and was the old Nathan again, looking me with the kind eyes I knew from the old days.

"Oh, Nicky, where can I begin? I'm sorry. I would have died too if you had died." There was a pause. "Well, no, not literally, but yes, figuratively." He laughed awkwardly. "Listen, first of all, I have to thank you for saving my father's life… I mean, in Bermuda. You really did save his life. You will be protected for the rest of yours because of it and my family will do anything for you… I mean, I will do anything for you forever."

"Even visit me in the hospital?" He looked down at the floor sheepishly. "I'm sorry. Cheap shot. But why didn't you visit me? Why did you disappear?"

"I know this sounds like a bad cliché, but I've been busy. I took over a chunk of my father's business. Been in training, so to speak. I was in Bermuda for awhile, and then out of the country, so I couldn't come to see you. I was getting status reports, though, and I knew you were all right. I was planning on coming to see you soon."

"So, you're stepping into your father's shoes?" I couldn't believe what I was hearing. "Nathan, you once told me you weren't cut out for it."

"I don't know if I am, but so far I'm getting the help I need and I have a lot of good assistants, so to speak. I don't deal with every aspect, either. But I don't want to talk about that. I want to talk about you. Tell me what's going on."

"Well, I started another year of school and I like it. On Monday I am going—"

"No, no. I don't mean that. I mean, that's great, but I want to hear about Jack. What's going on there?"

"Are you going to hold what I say against me?"

"Why would I do that?"

"Because he's a detective."

"No. As long as he treats you right."

"Nathan, I'm not working with him and I'm not out to get you or your father or pursue anyone or anything. I just came to visit you and see why you didn't want to be friends anymore. I became attached to you and I missed you. Not in a romantic way, or anything. You know what I mean. I was very scared in Bermuda and I almost got killed. I am not pursuing anything related to what happened there."

"Nicky, I'm asking you if you're having a romance with that Jack guy, not if you're trying to have me arrested. I know you're not working with the police… I want to know if you're dating the guy and if you like him, you silly girl."

"No, I'm not dating him." I sighed and leaned back into the sofa. "Now tell me what's going on with you and why you disappeared and didn't even send me a postcard from wherever you were. We were pretty close, you know. I thought we were friends."

"You know, a lot has changed since I saw you."

"So much that you can't see me anymore and can't visit me in the hospital when I'm dying?" Nathan shook his head.

"You didn't die."

"We sat in silence, each pondering our thoughts, I suppose. Nathan crossed and uncrossed his legs. I wasn't leaving until I got an answer and I definitely wasn't afraid of him, even though I knew somehow that he had changed and that his situation had changed. He was a little tougher now and seemed to have more going on in his head. His eyes shifted more and he looked at me differently now… more intensely.

He had obviously taken over at least a part of his father's business and seemed to have a lot going on, but I didn't want to lose him as a friend. Could we still keep in touch? Could we still have some sort of relationship? Were we too different at this point? Were our worlds too far apart? I watched him for a few moments and then took his hand.

"Nathan, can we still be friends, or are we on two different planets?" He sighed and didn't answer immediately.

"You know, your policeman friend is waiting outside for you." I blinked in surprise. "Oh, you didn't know? I believe you." He sighed. "So, are you going to tell me what's going on with you two?"

"Nothing." He nodded and told me he believed me again. Nathan squeezed my hand again.

"Of course we can always be friends. I love you, kiddo. We had a wild time in the Bahamas, you know, and we made it. You saved my father's life, and –"

"And you didn't visit me in the hospital."

"Are you ever going to forgive me for that?"

"I guess so. Maybe next year." He hugged me with a laugh and I decided then that he would probably never tell me why he didn't visit me and why he dropped out of my life for that month. If I hadn't come to see him that day, he may never have come back to see me, but now I had formed the link again and we started our friendship again. I felt good about that and I wanted to keep him in my life. He was someone I was fond of and wanted to keep an eye on.

"Well," Nathan said as he stood up. "Don't you want to see if your policeman friend wants another date?"

"How do you know he's outside?" I followed his gaze to a closed-circuit camera screen and saw Jack sitting at a table in the club. Someone had let him in, I suppose, or he had snuck in through the opened front door like I had.

"He obviously followed you in. You might as well see what he wants. You'll get more action out of him than out of me... that's for sure." He hugged me again and said he'd call me next week as I left. I was glad I came as I left his office and entered the main dancing area where Jack was sitting.

He looked up at me as I entered the room.

"Hey there," he said quietly as I came over to him.

"What are you doing here?" I responded with half of a smile. I wasn't sure if I was happy to see him. Had he followed me here? Was it a romantic kind of following or a professional kind of following?

He shrugged and asked if my business with Nathan was over with.

"I didn't have any business with Nathan. I just had to see if he was all right. I – wait a minute… are you asking me as a detective, or on a more personal level?"

"Nicky, I think once and for all you should know that I am just trying to look after you. I really came here to follow up on my dinner invitation. You know, you were supposed to have dinner with me in Bermuda, if I remember correctly."

"It would never work between us, Jack."

"Why?" I sat down next to him at the table.

"You know the old expression: a bird and a fish can fall in love, but where would they make a home?' You are a detective, I am going to be an ophthalmologist. What kind of a combination is that?"

"Look how well we worked together on this case. We make a great team and you know we are attracted to each other. In between solving cases together, you can practice ophthalmology, I can do my work and we can have a great life together."

"Now you're jumping the gun."

"So, let's just start out with a simple dinner. There's a great Italian place three blocks from here. And I know you love Italian food."

"And how do you know that?"

"Who doesn't love Italian food?" I looked at him quietly. He was very handsome, and I was attracted to him. He had saved my life and he was a good guy. How could I dismiss all the attention he gave me when I was in the hospital? How could one dinner hurt? He saw my thoughts in my eyes.

"Tonight at eight? I'll pick you up." I nodded. "Meanwhile, let me walk you home."

"Aren't you working now?"

"On my lunch break." We got up and he walked me out of the club, the lights turning off magically behind us as he began to tell me about a new case he was working on.

LaVergne, TN USA
19 November 2010

205591LV00004B/196/P